MW01480827

The

Sentimental

Journey

A Novel

Tammy Sinclair

Tammy Sinclair

DEDICATION

I wish to thank my wonderful husband, Tony and my two amazing daughters, Allyson and Jenna for their encouragement, patience and for always rooting for me.

I also want to thank my Mom, who is now waiting in Heaven. Throughout my life, she constantly encouraged me in my writing. When I first started this story, I would read the beginnings of the first draft aloud and she would always want to hear more. She sadly never got to hear the ending, but it's to her that I especially dedicate this book.

Mom, thank you for always believing the best in me, for always being my cheerleader, loving me unconditionally, and encouraging me—not only in my writing but in my relationship with the Lord.

Lastly, I want to express my heartfelt appreciation for all the many men and women who served and sacrificed for their country during WWII. To all those who risked their lives on the battlefields and even to those who worried, waited and worked on the home front, this story is also dedicated to all of you.

Tammy Sinclair

ACKNOWLEDGEMENTS

A big thank you to my beta-readers, who gave me incredible feedback in the earlier stages of the novel. Also, a thank you to those who did the same in the final stages, leading up to publication. Their help, dedication, and encouragement have been invaluable.

Appreciation goes out to members of the supportive online writing community, who were a great help throughout the entire process.

Tammy Sinclair

AUTHOR'S NOTES

The World War II era has always been my absolute favorite time in history. The music, the movies, the fashion…they have always held a special charm for me. Most of all, I've been captivated by the poignancy of the time. So many parted with their loved ones, never knowing if they'd ever see them again. There was also an intense fight for freedom and resulting patriotism that unified the country during those uncertain years.

You'll find many songs from the war years mentioned throughout this story. Whether you're familiar with them or not, I encourage you to look them up and give them a listen. In fact, to fully capture the ambiance of the scenes, you might even want to pause, find the song title online, and then listen while you continue reading!

I really hope that as you read about Kara's journey, you'll feel a little as if you're stepping back in time along with her.

Tammy Sinclair

TABLE OF CONTENTS

The Sentimental Journey

CHAPTER ONE

If there was one thing Kara wanted more than anything that evening, it was to do nothing—absolutely nothing at all. She relaxed into the soft cushion, taking a luxurious sip of her chamomile tea. It was laden with honey, just the way she liked it. An empty frozen entree container sat on the coffee table while she finished checking over the day's emails. She loved this kind of tired feeling in a strange sort of way. It was the kind of tired that she could really sink into on a Friday night.

Those sweet little three-year-old children—how they could have so much volatile energy bottled inside, Kara would never know. They were adorable, all right, but they had drained every last molecule of energy from her this week. Her co-worker had said it was because of the spring weather. Whatever the reason, Kara was determined to drink in this calm solitude now. The quiet ticking of the clock, mounted behind the kitchen wall, sounded almost therapeutic.

And then she remembered the antique trunk.

That quiet, stately old trunk that seemed so intent on keeping its many secrets locked up all these years…only now that she had it opened, it seemed to be waiting impatiently for her to come and explore all the hidden treasures of the last century.

Should she? She glanced at the time on her laptop. It was still so early—not even six-thirty. It didn't seem to matter, though. She could feel the pull of bedtime already.

She pushed a wayward section of her hair behind her ear for the umpteenth time. In the last few months, Kara had received several compliments on her layered hair, which currently hung slightly past her shoulders. But these chestnut layers had a habit of stubbornly falling in her face a little too often.

She leaned forward again, deleting the two advertisements in her inbox and concentrated on the email from her best friend, Shannon. It wasn't like her to use this way of communicating and she noticed it was written in a kind of journal style. As Kara read the description of her first day of vacation in southern California, she had just the slightest twinge of envy. The crazy rides, the warm, sandy beaches…it all sounded amazing.

Not that she was truly jealous—not *really*. Shannon had slaved over finals this past year and she deserved it. Still, she also knew it would be ages before she could have any kind of vacation on a preschool teacher's salary. And having parents whisking her away to California as a college graduation present? No longer a possibility.

She sighed and glanced around her. Still, she had this house. Only twenty-one years old and she was already a homeowner. She knew not many her age could say that.

Kara scrolled through the rest of the emails. Taking another sip of her tea, she resisted the urge to check out everyone's latest social media statuses and abruptly snapped her laptop closed. She pulled her afghan around her and snuggled down, closing her eyes.

Should I watch an old movie? Or go explore the attic again?

Despite her sleepiness, her mind kept drifting back to the attic. It was only last week when she first laid eyes on the old trunk. She had already been living in the house for a while, but until last week, she had been too preoccupied with teaching and settling in her new home.

Going up the narrow staircase and peeking into the attic had been the extent of her exploration. Until last Friday, that is.

When she finally ventured in there, it had only taken her a minute to find the old weathered trunk, nestled under a layer of dust. It sat hiding in the dark corner, behind a small partition, and covered up with tattered blankets.

Unfortunately, it had been locked with no sign of a key. Kara guessed that's why none of the previous tenants had tampered with it. Or perhaps they hadn't even discovered it, hidden behind the little half wall. Nobody probably wanted to explore up there, anyway. It *was* dark and the floorboards seemed to creak just by looking at them.

She had never been one to let a little dust and darkness stand in her way when it came to exploring, though. As she pulled the blanket up tighter around her shoulders, she let her mind wander. There were so many memories of summers growing up in this town... those kids in the neighborhood...and the ring leader—*what was his name? Justin Weston*! All of them traipsing through the woods and checking out abandoned barns in the fields. She gave a slight shudder, remembering the wild opossum...

Though that was a long time ago, she knew she was still that same girl deep inside, even if her life hadn't exactly been filled with a lot of excitement lately. Kara carefully reached her arm through her blanket and took another swig of tea, thinking about the present little adventure she had waiting.

So, maybe *adventure* might be a bit of a stretch, she thought, smiling to herself. It was just that anything from the past always intrigued her, especially antiques. And the hidden trunk had all the earmarks of being nearly a century old. Maybe it had belonged to the very first owners when the house was built back in the 1920's. Or perhaps it was even older, dating back before the home. It had been so easy for Kara to let her imagination wander as she lay there. Who had placed it there? And most importantly, what was inside?

Kara's phone went off, jarring her from her reverie. She grabbed it clumsily from the coffee table and attempted to clear her throat.

"Hey, Kara!" came the voice on the other end.

"Shannon?"

"Uh-oh, did I wake you up?"

"No, just resting. What's been happening? Isn't this day three or something? I just read your email..."

"Yep, day three. My phone was completely dead earlier and wouldn't let me do anything. So I decided to use my laptop and write out a kind of synopsis of our trip so far."

"It was fun to read. I felt like I was right there with you."

"I wish you were! The first day we were getting settled so we just went to the beach for a while. Checked out Santa Monica pier—you saw the photo I posted, right? So this was day two in the park. Oh, you really should be here with me!"

"I know. Maybe someday. At least you have Travis and Collin to go on the rides with you." Kara leaned back to get comfortable again. "Granted, your younger brothers aren't nearly as fun as I am!"

"Well, you know I'm not much into rides. But I think I rode Splash Mountain maybe four times! We've all seen a couple shows, and Mom and I have done some shopping. One more day here over at California Adventure and then we're off to San Diego. By the way, did I tell you I heard from Parker?"

Kara spent the next ten minutes listening to her best friend talk about the various texts that had gone back and forth between Shannon and "the guy she kind of liked but wasn't sure". An *on-again, off-again, confused-again thing, as they liked to call it.* But at least it was more than anything Kara had going on at the moment.

"And what about Derek?" Shannon asked, predictably. Kara thought she should know by now that this subject was a lost cause.

"Not a thing from him in a couple weeks. But hey, time to move on."

"You deserve better than a player like him, anyway," her friend consoled, and after a few minutes of listing the many advantages of forgetting about him, she mercifully changed the subject to something more positive.

"What about that trunk in the attic you were telling me about? Did you ever get it opened?"

"Oh, remember Mr. Perch?"

"The name's familiar. Isn't he the old, retired friend of your grandfather's?"

"That's right. Anyway, I gave him a call and he came over with some of his tools and had it opened within twenty minutes. I gave him a plate of my famous oatmeal cookies for his trouble, and…"

"But what was inside?"

"Well, that's the thing. I haven't had time to go through everything yet. When Mr. Perch was over this morning, I could only glance inside before having to hurry to work. But from what I could see, there are some old dishes, a quilt, and a bunch of old papers." Kara couldn't disguise her enthusiasm as she remembered the find.

"Hmm…I was hoping it had something a little more exciting," Shannon replied, flatly.

"What—like a body? You just don't understand how cool it is to know someone else had these treasures decades ago. There's a whole story wrapped up within each item, but we'll probably never know them."

"I think you're in the wrong business. You definitely should look into a career with antiques—be a curator or something." This advice was followed by a crunching sound in Kara's ear as Shannon took a bite from a crisp apple.

"You're probably right," Kara admitted.

"Well, I need to go…" *More crunching*. "I'm so tired and we're getting up pretty early again tomorrow."

A few minutes later, they said their good-nights and Kara then set her phone back onto the coffee table, glancing at the clock. Nine-thirty and now she was completely wide awake, thanks to Shannon. And her mind was back on that attic.

She took one last sip of her tea. Okay, so she didn't have a big date tonight and she wasn't in Disneyland. But for now, she did have a little date with that treasure trove of antiques upstairs! Other people might consider this a pathetic way to spend a Friday night, but she didn't care. She promptly set her cup down and headed directly toward the attic.

The access was through a door in the back of the kitchen. She hurried through to open it and from there, she climbed the narrow staircase. She was thankful she didn't have claustrophobia since the walls on either side seemed so close.

Once at the top, she saw that there was still some early evening light pouring in from the small window, but it was fading quickly. Noticing the bulb on the ceiling, she pulled the chain, but the result wasn't much of an improvement. For a brief second, she thought of going back to find her flashlight, but instead, she plunged ahead.

The floorboards seemed to verbally protest as she crossed over them. She peeked around the half-wall and there the old trunk sat in the dimly lit corner. Within minutes, she had lifted the lid, her fingertips first caressing the musty quilt—no doubt, made with loving hands by some grandmother decades ago. She sneezed from the little billows of dust as she rummaged through a loosely wrapped stack of old newspapers. Though it was hard to read the yellowing pages in the current light, she noticed the dates were mostly from the 1930s and '40s. Some appeared to be brittle and she would have to carefully bring them downstairs later for closer examination.

That's when her eye caught sight of something she hadn't noticed before. Sitting on the cold attic floorboards, Kara lifted the small, cedar box out of the trunk for closer inspection. *If only the light was better up here!*

She could tell, though, that the box was intricately carved, with several small hearts and various ornamental designs. She hesitated for just a moment before removing the lid. Kara caught her breath. A watch glittered inside, beset by jewels, and it seemed to defy the darkened attic by sparkling in the shadows.

Kara was never one to be thrilled over fancy jewelry and expensive stones but this watch—it was one of the loveliest she had ever seen. It appeared to be a ladies' watch, the face decidedly feminine and exquisite.

Maybe it was because it contrasted against the dimly lighted room full of dusty boxes and discarded old memories. Whatever the reason, Kara couldn't take her eyes off of it. Several minutes passed before she realized that there was a note attached to the inside of the lid. Her hand instinctively reached for it.

Could it have been a gift from an ardent admirer in days gone by, she wondered? Kara had always been swept away by a good love story; perhaps this held a secret of some past romance of decades ago. She detached the note and unfolded it with anticipation, pushing away the little nagging feeling that she was somehow intruding on strangers.

She squinted in the darkness but it was so hard to make out the words. She could see that the handwriting was in beautifully written cursive. Holding the yellowed paper up towards the window and the hazy stream of light, she finally read the entire note, at last:

Hold this time in your hand; it will bring you back. Time will retreat to glimpse what once was. And what could be again. "

No, not a love letter, exactly. But what could it possibly mean? It didn't make very much sense…like a cryptic message in some mystery novel. Still, it intrigued her. It was obviously written a long time ago. She could tell by the yellowed edges of the note as well as the style of ink on the page. And it had been written for a reason. *But why?*

What was left of the fading light had almost disappeared now. She supposed she should leave— perhaps return up here in the morning. What *was* it about antiques that roused her curiosity so much? The watch in her hands still defied the shadows, the jewels glistening like snowflakes. She slipped it over her wrist to admire it. The band hugged her wrist daintily, almost as if it were made for her. She held out her arm and turned her wrist, gazing at it from various angles.

Then without warning, the room seemed to spin crazily about her. At the same instance, light seemed to spark directly from the jewels, shooting outward into the air. Kara thrust her arm away. She tore off the watch, hurling it away, as the room—and everything—seemed to turn upside down. Kara gasped and shut her eyes tightly against the strangeness.

When she opened them only seconds later, the spinning had abruptly stopped and daylight was streaming through the small attic window. She didn't dare move. Still in a state of shock, she sat motionless.

Soon she became aware of birds singing from nearby branches outside. And then the sound of a woman's voice calling cheerfully from below…the gentle clinking of dishes and cups…and outside, a clatter of what sounded like bottles.

Kara remained frozen but her thoughts frantically raced, even as the sounds around her held a sort of tranquility. She began to wonder if she had just experienced a strange fainting spell, those extreme kinds that she had heard about, complete with spinning and vertigo. After a few moments, Kara slowly stood, all the time bracing herself as if she could topple at any second. Or else the world around her would.

With tentative movements, she made her way over to the staircase. All the while, her thoughts tried to make some sort of sense about what was happening. *How could morning sunlight be streaming in?*

She realized she must have passed out for some reason and what had felt like just seconds, was in reality, hours. Night had come and gone. She hoped there was nothing seriously wrong with her and realized she'd better make an appointment, just in case.

But who had come into her home uninvited?

As she descended the narrow staircase, Kara could hear voices chattering away in the kitchen. At first, she thought it must be from outside but as she approached the door, they became clearer.

Kara stopped at the bottom step. If strangers were actually in her house, would she even be able to do anything about it? Not if the intruders were truly dangerous, she realized. She had no weapon—nothing at all to defend herself with. She did notice they were female voices, but that didn't necessarily mean she wasn't in any danger.

If only she had brought her cell phone with her!

And what about her current physical condition? She paused, considering it for a moment. For someone who might have been lying passed out for hours, she felt amazingly well, she decided. A little wobbly, perhaps, but she suspected that might be more out of confusion and anxiety than anything else.

The voices were definitely coming from her kitchen.

She couldn't stay up in the attic and hide forever; she had to face the intruders, come what may. She took a deep breath while her shaking hand found the door handle.

CHAPTER TWO

"Betty, please give me a hand with the bacon while I start in on these eggs. Did you bring in the milk already?"

"Yes, Mama, the bottles are in the icebox."

"Good girl. What are your plans later today?"

"Janie and I are off to the movies this afternoon. There's a new Bette Davis picture playing…I forget the name of it, but you know me and Bette Davis. Anything with her has to be good!"

"Yes, I…"

The chatter abruptly stopped as two pairs of eyes stared at Kara, who stood on the threshold of the kitchen. *Her* kitchen. All she could do was stare back. No one uttered a word for nearly a minute, although Kara knew she should say something—anything—to these strangers who seemed to suddenly be taking up residence in her home. Before her mouth could form any words, the other woman spoke first.

"Miss? May we help you? What are you doing here…and just why were you in the attic?"

Her voice was stiff but not exactly unkind. To Kara's ears, however, the words barely made any sense.

"Ex...excuse me?" she finally managed to sputter. "What *am I* doing here? What are *you* two doing here? Listen, I don't mean to be rude, but I don't even know you..."

It was then that her confused eyes were able to focus in on the woman and what appeared to be her adolescent daughter. The mother wore a button-down dress almost completely covered by a long, ruffled, white apron while her daughter wore a similar apron over a puffy-sleeved pinafore.

And the kitchen...why did it suddenly look a bit different? What *was* different, anyway? Something about the décor... Oh, nothing was making any sense! Maybe she was still in her unconscious state in the attic and this was all a hallucinated dream brought on from...*something*. What was in that new Asian tea she drank earlier, anyway?

The mother and daughter continued to stare at her with bewildered faces.

"Young lady, we don't know you, either. Since you refuse to tell us why you have been sneaking around our home, I will have to ask you to leave immediately. I wouldn't want to have to telephone the police."

Kara just stood, gaping. *Were they on the level?*

"I should add," the woman continued, as she slowly took a sidestep toward the dining room, "that my husband is at home. Right upstairs. If I need to call for him, he will be down in only a moment. Again, *I must ask you to leave*."

Could that be true? Could this woman's husband be upstairs...here, in her own home? And if so, where did this family come from? Perhaps they actually were a family of incredible swindlers...but then, how could they hope to swindle her out of her home when she owned it legally? And she couldn't have wandered into another house...she had come directly down the attic stairs! Suddenly, she began to feel very queasy and light-headed.

"Excuse me...I don't...I'm not feeling very... " Kara began to say, and then the red and white kitchen faded into darkness and she crumpled to the floor.

***

Kara's eyes opened not with a flutter, but more with a sudden jolt. She gazed quickly around at her surroundings. She was lying on a camelback sofa in someone's living room. Antiques decorated the walls and mantle while a large console radio stood against the wall. Even all the furniture seemed to be of a vintage style. And then it all began to come back to her...the wristwatch, the bolts of strange light...the strangers in her home.

Wait—was this my living room? She sat up with a start, a cool washcloth tumbling from her forehead. She didn't have time to take the questions any further because the woman she had seen before slowly came in, carrying a tea tray.

"There, now, just take it easy. I telephoned for the doctor; he should be here at any moment." Her voice sounded strangely comforting in spite of everything. "Are you feeling up for some tea?"

"N...no. Thank you," Kara answered, repositioning on the sofa as she continued to eye the woman in confused silence.

"Do you remember fainting?"

Kara slowly nodded.

The woman put the tray down onto the coffee table. "My daughter and I helped you in here and onto the sofa and then I telephoned Dr. Barris straight away. My husband is dressing and will be down shortly." She hesitated, and then added, gently, "I am not sure what you were doing in our home, miss, but you are obviously distraught or sick. I thought it best to have the doctor look at you....and forego the call to the police. *For now.*"

She added the last two words for emphasis, but then, warmth passed through her eyes before she turned and poured herself a cup of the steaming, hot liquid.

Kara took a shallow breath. "Please," she began. "I'm wondering if you could help clear some things up for me. I guess…maybe I *did* become ill because I'm feeling very confused at the moment."

"What is it?"

Kara drew in one more breath, this one even shakier than the first, as she tried to form the right words. But a knock sounded at the front door before she could continue.

"That must be Dr. Barris now," and the woman hurried off to answer it. Kara could hear the sound of hushed voices and then a moment later, an older gentleman carrying a black bag appeared. Perhaps he could help her find some answers to what was happening to her.

***

After the short examination was over, he put his stethoscope away.

"There now, young lady. You appear to show no signs of anything serious that I can tell. If the fainting spells continue, be sure to let me know." His voice was reassuring and grandfatherly. "But suppose you tell me what you were doing in these good people's home this morning?" he asked, calmly.

"I…this is my…." Kara clamped her mouth shut. Clearly, he also thought of this house as the family's home.

*Unless he was **in on it** with them!* She remembered seeing a movie where a whole group of innocent-looking people were in some evil plot against a poor, unsuspecting man. Even so, if she claimed that this was, in fact, her home, there's no telling where she might end up— perhaps in a straitjacket. She shivered.

"Did you spend last night in their attic?" In a gentler voice, as if he could detect her growing fear, he asked, "Don't you have a home of your own at present, young lady? Is that it?"

Kara grappled for something to say. "I...guess that's right. Not anymore."

He nodded and patted her shoulder. "I see. Now, don't you worry. We'll figure something out." He turned back to the woman who had been standing at a discreet distance. "How do you and Mr. Jeffers feel about letting her rest for an hour or so here while we figure out a place for her to go? She needs a little rest and liquids before sending her on her way. Don't want her fainting again. Or do you feel uncomfortable with that, Mrs. Jeffers?"

The woman looked over at Kara, thoughtfully. There didn't seem to be much suspicion or concern left in her expression.

"I think that is perfectly fine. Especially since Mr. Jeffers is here." In a quiet voice, she added, "I think the poor girl is just lost and afraid. Who knows, perhaps she's run away from a terrible situation. But...where do you think you might be able to put her up?"

The doctor looked down in concentration; then shook his head. "I'm going to have to think on that a while. Send her to me, after she's had a chance to rest and perhaps I'll have thought of something by then." With that, he said his good-byes and was gone.

Kara lay there, trying to make some sort of sense of what was transpiring. A part of her wanted to panic...yet another part of her wanted to simply understand. She knew she wasn't crazy! Things had gone on completely normally until those moments in the attic. She looked about her...to the walls, the décor, the windows...it *could be* her house. No, *it was* her house! But it was almost as if it was in a different time.

Her eye caught the sparkle of a decorative glass dish on the other side of the living room. She watched almost mindlessly as the sunlight bounced off the nearby ornate wall mirror hanging above it and reflected down onto the dish's iridescent colors. The image reminded her of another: the watch she had placed on her wrist when it all began. She glanced down at her now empty arm.

Time.

What was it that the note she'd found had said? Something about time...and retreating backward...*No, it was too unbelievable!*

"Mama, should I serve breakfast now? I mean...is everything all right?" The daughter had peeked into the room, nervously glancing at Kara before her mother answered.

"Certainly. Oh, and there's your father now. Dear, this is the young lady I was telling you about. She has no place to stay and is just resting up while Dr. Barris tries to find a place for her."

Into the living room strode a somewhat tall man with a pleasant face. He gave Kara a polite but hesitant smile and nodded. Despite the apparent concern that furrowed his brow, he possessed a calm and friendly air. Kara felt herself relax, ever so slightly.

"As I told you upstairs, I think she's harmless enough," his wife said in muted tones to him, though Kara's sharp ears caught every word. "Perhaps, a slight bump on the head or something, though the doctor didn't find any obvious signs of a concussion. I don't know…there's something about her…I think she might be all alone."

He took a step towards Kara. "Won't you join us for breakfast….Miss…?"

"Oh…Kara. Kara Michaels." Her own voice sounded small to her ears.

"Kara?" he asked, looking perplexed. "That's kind of an unusual name, isn't it? But …it's very nice!"

"Miss Michaels, I think the doctor wanted you to rest. Can I bring you an egg and a piece of toast to eat on the divan?" his wife asked.

"Well…I don't want you to go to any trouble. You've already been very kind."

"It's no trouble; I'll be back in a few minutes with a plate for you. Do you like orange juice?"

Kara numbly nodded and the family all headed into the kitchen. She forced herself to relax into the pillow and closed her eyes. A few minutes later, the woman returned and handed her the small plate of food and a glass of juice, disappearing again around the corner. The plate itself was not Kara's. It was a beautifully ornate china plate with tiny painted roses.

Propped up with pillows, she sat listening to the hum of conversation at the breakfast table from the other room. The walls were thin and their voices carried so that she was able to hear their every word. After a while, it made her feel strangely homesick...but for what, she wasn't quite sure.

"Who do you think she is?" It was the girl's voice disguised in a sort of noisy whisper.

"I'm sure I don't know. But let's not worry about that right now. She's only here for a few hours and just needs a place to rest. Dr. Barris will likely find her a place to stay and help her get back on her feet."

"Hmm, I wonder why she ended up here..." It was the husband's voice.

"Why don't we all talk about something else right now," the woman suggested. "By the way, Betty, what time does your movie start?"

"Two o'clock. Janie's stopping by here for me and then we're going to walk over. I don't really know who the co-star is. Paul somebody, I think. But I wish it was Tyrone Power instead. I'd pay a whole dollar to see him—he's so dreamy."

"Well, he couldn't have dreamier eyes than I do, could he?"

"Oh, Daddy," followed by giggles.

"Well, your mother thought so once upon a time."

"Oh, by the way! I thought we should have a party the night after Jerry gets home from training. You know—a real party with some of his friends! What do you think, Mama?"

Her father cleared his throat. "You know, most of Jerry's friends aren't even here anymore. A lot of them have already been sent overseas."

"I know," the girl's subdued voice answered. "I guess I was thinking of Jim—he'll be going over with him. And a few others like Stephen Harold and Ben. And some of the girls, of course."

"Oh, I see. But it just may be possible that Jerry won't be in the mood for a big party when he first comes home. He might just want to relax a bit before he has to leave again."

"Well, sure...of course, I didn't think we would throw a party the very night he comes home. We can wait a whole day...that would be fine."

"We'll see, Betty." This time it was the mother who spoke. "We don't need to decide that right now. But remember, he'll only be here a short time. It will just be good to have him home again for a while."

There was a lapse in conversation and then Kara heard the father's voice say quietly, "Maybe it does call for some sort of send-off, though..."

"Oh, good, then you agree, Daddy?"

The mother's quiet voice followed. "A send-off, Ray? I don't know...I'm just not sure I'm up to celebrating our son shipping off."

After a moment, "Your mother's right. But what about just a little gathering with some friends? After all, it wouldn't just be for Jerry, but for his buddies and their families. What do you think?" It was obvious the question was directed at his wife.

There were a couple minutes that followed when the only sounds were the clinking of utensils hitting plates. If there had been an audible answer, Kara never heard it.

Kara tried to nibble at her toast. If this had been any other circumstance, she would have felt like an eavesdropper but as it was, she strained to hear their conversation. She needed to make some kind of sense of all of this.

Eventually, she heard the daughter's voice again, her tone subdued.

"Where do you think they'll send him?"

"I don't know. Anyway, I don't think your mother wants to talk about that just now."

"Oh... all right."

After another moment, "By the way, Betty, please don't stay too late after the movie, filling yourself up with sodas like you did last time," her mother said. "I don't want you going and spoiling your appetite for supper again! We're having baked chicken."

"I won't, Mama, I promise." Renewed enthusiasm laced her voice as she added, "And don't forget, *Your Hit Parade* is on tonight!"

"Oh, I know…"

"With *Harry...*" The daughter's voice drifted off.

"Harry?" her father asked. His voice had a playful tone. "Harry who?"

"Dad-dy!"

"Oh, you don't mean Harry James, do you?"

"The one and only. I could just sit and listen to him play for hours."

"Well, Betty Grable might have something to say about that."

A giggle followed.

It was a sweet and amusing conversation on the surface, yet more strangeness began to envelop Kara as she absorbed what they were saying.

She probably was one of the few people under the age of thirty—or maybe even sixty—who had been able to identify the who's who of the Swing era. She didn't know them all, but she definitely knew quite a few. Her mind rattled off the information: *Big Band trumpeter, Harry James. Married to pin-up movie star, Betty Grable*...She had even seen them both in movies, watching the old classics with her mom.

As she continued listening to the cheerful banter, the reality of their conversations crept slowly into her flesh and she shivered. *Am I really back in time?*

There was no way she could continue just sitting here any longer. Forcing herself up, she placed her plate carefully onto the coffee table. From there, she slowly moved about the room, examining the furniture...the console radio. A photograph of the family in a silver frame sat on the end table, which included the son they obviously had been discussing just moments before. She was intrigued, but she kept moving. She felt an urge to investigate...to search the house. Yet, she hesitated to forge ahead to the top of the stairs, especially if they already thought of her as an intruder.

Before she could examine anything else, the mother came back into the living room just then. Kara guessed by her expression she was startled to see her up and about.

"Oh, how are you feeling now?"

"A little better, thank you."

"That's good. Oh, and if you're looking for the powder room, it's up the stairs, first door on your left."

"Thank you," Kara murmured and with that, the woman retreated into the kitchen.

Kara stared over at the staircase for a moment and then slowly made her way over. Climbing the steps, she realized she still did feel a little bit woozy, as her grandmother used to say. But she just had to see upstairs. *This is my house, after all...isn't it?*

Reaching the top, she noticed all of the bedroom doors were kept ajar. She drifted down the hallway and carefully glanced into each bedroom. Beautiful, immaculate rooms—one with a canopy bed draped in white, which Kara guessed belonged to Betty. Then she peeked into what was apparently the son's room. There was some kind of triangular pendant on the wall, a couple trophies, a bookshelf, and a small writing desk by the window.

Then Kara stepped a few more feet down the hall to look at what she knew as her bedroom. She stood in the doorway, completely transfixed. The room held a beautiful large, cherry wood four-poster bed with a matching end table beside it. The table was topped with a delicate lace covering and a lovely lamp. There was also a matching vanity table against one wall with a matching cushioned seat. On the other wall hung a small framed print of an impressionist painting.

And there was also a calendar.

Kara stepped over the threshold for a better look. On the top half, a beautiful color photograph of a springtime tree covered in flourishing pink blossoms. Directly underneath, in bold lettering:

"*May 1943*"

CHAPTER THREE

At the sight of the calendar, Kara supposed she should have felt like fainting all over again. But after everything she had just seen and heard in the past hour, a part of her almost expected it.

She backed up into the hallway and took a couple of deep breaths. If the house was a part of some elaborate trick, it would be proven once she left it for the outside world. This thought frightened her, too. Although she didn't want to quite admit it, she was beginning to believe that she truly was no longer in her world—at least, in the world she always knew. If this crazy idea proved true, what would she do?

Her instinct was to call someone she knew to come rescue her. Except…if she had been thrown back into a strange time warp, then there would be no cell phones, she realized with growing panic. What followed on the heels of that thought disturbed her even more. If this was true, then everyone she knew—Shannon, even her father…most everyone in her life—had not even been born yet. This notion sent a jolt through the pit of her stomach; she leaned against the wall until it subsided. *Just breathe*, she told herself.

She could hear voices downstairs. After attempting a few more slow breaths, Kara decided that this was as good a time as any to actually use the facilities. It was, after all, what her 'host' assumed was the reason she was upstairs. As she entered her bathroom, even the decor was completely different. She tried to ignore that for the moment. *Just stay calm...*

By the time she emerged back into the hallway, she could distinctly hear music. It seemed to be floating up from the radio she'd seen downstairs and Kara immediately recognized the distinctive Big Band sound. She shook away a tingle that ricocheted down her spine.

When she reached the bottom of the staircase, she noticed it wasn't the radio playing, but the console record player. Beside it stood the young girl, facing away from her. Her foot was moving to the music so intently that Kara was sure she would break into a jitterbug at any second.

"It's sure nice music," Kara remarked as she cautiously approached. She was determined to try to remain as calm as possible—at least on the outside. And until she got a handle on the situation.

The girl abruptly turned around, startled. Her expression appeared wary, but she gave a tentative smile.

"Yes, it's the best." She had spoken quietly, barely audible over the music. She picked up the album, gazing at it. "I've had this one for months but I'm still not tired of it. Don't you just love his style?" She looked back up at Kara with a sparkle in her eye, apparently forgetting to be uneasy.

"Glenn Miller?"

Kara had heard the song now playing countless times—the song that most likely put Kalamazoo on the map. There wasn't apparently any need for a reply to something so obvious, however. Kara forgot her own fears for just a moment, too, and smiled back. It was obvious that whatever concerns this young girl must have over a stranger in the house seemed to be tempered by good music.

As the teenager became oblivious of her once again, Kara made her way into the seating area of the living room and eased down into a nearby cushioned armchair. She could relate to having the music erase some of the nervousness. Hearing it now, she could almost feel her grandfather with her again.

She remembered when she was about ten or eleven, he would tell her stories of his youth while they listened to all the Big Band hits. He'd point out the names of the songs and the musicians, while they did jigsaw puzzles or she helped him paint one of his furniture projects. It had been years later—when she was in high school and Grandpa George passed away— that she began listening to it again. She'd find a song online of a slow Glen Miller arrangement, or perhaps Tommy

Dorsey, and just sit there listening…and missing him. It had made her feel close to him again, and from then on, she had been hooked, finding more and more music from the era that she loved.

Now, here she was, listening to it in this setting. *What in the world would Grandpa George think about this?*

She glanced back over at the girl, who was now sorting through a small stack of records. Her light brown hair was medium length and pulled back neatly to one side with a barrette. Wearing a short-sleeved pullover sweater and a skirt that fell just about to the knees, she completed her look with bobby socks and saddle shoes.

"May I ask how old you are?" Kara ventured.

"Almost fifteen." She looked over at Kara politely.

"That's about what I thought," she smiled.

"And you? I hope it's okay to ask how old you are…"

"Of course. I'm twenty-one."

The girl sighed, repeating her words.

"Twenty-one." She was looking at Kara with what seemed like true admiration. "It must be so nice. If I were all grown up like that now, I'd probably join the WAACs. Or maybe the WAVES. What about you? Are you …" She hesitated, as if suddenly confused. "What were….I mean, where do you live?"

"I...I used to have a place to live. But not anymore. My family is very far away right now."

"Oh...that must be kind of lonely."

A silence fell, accentuated by the ending of the Glenn Miller record, which now rubbed over and over against the needle before the young owner lifted the arm and retrieved the disk.

"My name's Betty," the girl told her, glancing back, shyly.

"Nice to meet you, Betty. I'm Kara."

"What do you think you're going to do now, Kara?"

"I...I really don't know."

***

The scent of various blossoms permeated the air throughout the neighborhood; it was one of the few things now that hadn't seemed to change. Somehow, the spring fragrances helped to soothe Kara's nerves a bit as she accompanied Betty and her mother toward town.

"I know this is rather after the fact, but I realized we were never properly introduced," the woman was saying. "I'm Margaret Jeffers. I hear you've gotten a chance to talk with Betty a little while ago. We also have a son, Jerry, who's been away at training. He'll be coming home for a short visit before he has to ship off."

"It's nice to meet you, Mrs. Jeffers."

Kara had been used to addressing adults of all ages by their first names for a while now but somehow, in this time and place, it didn't feel quite right to her.

"I thought since we live so close to downtown, the walk would do us all good. It's such a lovely spring day, don't you think?"

Kara simply nodded. Her eyes were now drinking in her surroundings as the three of them followed the sidewalk through the neighborhood. This had been *her* neighborhood but now she barely recognized it. The houses...the people who strolled through the neighborhood...the occasional vintage car driving past...it was all too unbelievable to take hold of. She truly did feel as if she had stepped into an old movie— only not a flickering, black and white movie but one with vivid, living color, complete with scents and textures.

Kara's earlier fears were confirmed—there was just no denying it now. This was her town, all right. Just seventy-some years in the past. Her senses felt so scrambled. *How did this happen—and what am I supposed to do now?*

After a few minutes, they were approaching Main Street. Before Kara could take in any more of the differences in her hometown, they all came to a halt. She looked up to see a door with an overhanging sign that read, "Dr. Charles Barris, MD". Once inside the building, Mrs. Jeffers announced their visit to the young receptionist. They had to wait only a moment before

Dr.Barris stepped out from his back office and greeted them.

"Come back, ladies, and we'll have a chat." The four of them entered the small office, where several chairs faced his desk. "Please…have a seat," he said to all of them.

Kara's fingers fidgeted in her lap as she sat waiting for the doctor to speak.

"How are you feeling now, young lady?" he asked, his voice tinged with kindness.

"Much better, thank you."

"Well, good. I must say, you look much better." He cleared his throat. "Miss Michaels, I have to be frank. I've only had a short time to give your situation any thought, due to a heavier than expected load of patients today. You see, usually, I only work a few hours on Saturdays but not the case today. However, I did telephone a couple of ladies that I thought might be able to help. Unfortunately, they were unable to point me to any solutions." He paused, apparently trying to read her expression. "Please…. don't think I'm giving up on this. I have daughters, myself, and I would hate to have them wandering around with no place to go."

Kara listened but had no idea how to respond. She had never been in this kind of position before and it left her feeling numb.

"Perhaps if you tell me a little more about yourself? Is there family anywhere that you could go to?"

When she didn't reply right away, he continued, "What brought you here to Amberton in the first place?"

She stared at the doctor, her brain scrambling for a reply. Should she just say that her parents moved out of state? No, he'd ask for their contact information—and they couldn't be contacted.

Suddenly, the strangeness of this fact hit her all over again. *They couldn't be contacted because they hadn't been born yet!* It was still so hard to wrap her mind around this idea, and a sense of loneliness surrounded her.

"I....I don't have any family. I wandered here... sort of stumbled upon this town and...." Her words came out in a jumble.

"But, where did you live before? Where did you grow up?"

"Oh...here in Oregon. But my family is all gone now," she added.

"I'm sorry to hear that. When did they pass away?" Dr. Barris asked, gently.

Such specific questions—why did he have to keep asking specific questions?

Ever since Kara had been a child, she always felt incapable of lying. It just went against everything inside her. She supposed that was a good thing, yet sitting here like this, she realized she could never tell the whole truth—unless she wanted to end up in a straitjacket.

"I…they…." Her heart beat faster. Kara took a deep breath. "I've been on my own for some time…but…"

"Have you been out of work?"

"Well…I am very much in need of a job right now, yes."

"I see." The doctor absently took off his glasses and wiped them with his handkerchief, as if waiting for an idea to form.

"Dr. Barris, I was thinking about the need for female workers at the Kaiser shipyards and if Miss Michaels is willing, I'd be happy to take her over there on Monday." Mrs. Jeffers stole a glance at Kara with a slight, expectant smile.

Kara stared back, stunned.

"Well, now, that might just be the ticket!" the doctor replied, leaning back in his chair. "Still…there's the question of where she might stay. There's a boarding house in town but Mrs. Cordell only takes in those who can pay upfront." He leaned forward again and scratched his chin. "I'll tell you what. Let me talk to my wife and see if she has any ideas. Perhaps we may even put you up for a night or two. But let me telephone her. Would you ladies mind waiting out in the other room for a few moments?"

He slowly rose from his chair as they did and then the three of them found their way back to seats in the waiting area. A woman, who had apparently entered while they were speaking to Dr. Barris, now waited, seated on the other side. She glanced up from her magazine briefly as they filed in, but quickly resumed her article. Her feet were elegantly crossed at the ankles and Kara admired her attire, complete with hat and gloves.

For the next few minutes, Kara took in the sights and smells all around her...the receptionist's tap-tapping on the type-writer nearby, the blur of an old-fashioned Buick driving past the window. Even the rosy scent of perfume mingled with the musty walls of the old waiting room.

She glanced over at Mrs. Jeffers now. She, too, wore hat and gloves and looked to Kara to be in her early forties, though she wasn't completely certain. She appeared fairly youthful and attractive in a fresh, natural kind of way. Wearing plum lipstick that complemented her coloring and her hair done up in the casual style of the day, she seemed to be aware of fashion, yet without being overdone.

"I...I really want to thank you for all the help you've been to me. I mean...giving me a meal, taking me over here...and even helping me find work. I'm not sure how I can repay you, but I truly appreciate it, Mrs. Jeffers."

The woman smiled, her blue eyes glowing with warmth. "You're very welcome. It's really no trouble at all. After all, I would want someone to help my daughter if she were alone." She paused, and then added, "I've always believed that God wants us to show kindness to strangers. Oh, I know we have to be careful, of course... but I could tell that you weren't a real criminal. Just a little lost and alone."

Kara returned the woman's warm smile but she knew her conclusion wasn't far from the truth. She *did* feel lost and alone at this moment—and totally confused.

"In fact, I was thinking," Mrs. Jeffers continued. "If Dr. Barris can't find a good place for you, maybe you might consider staying with us. Just for a little while, until you're on your feet, of course. Now, I'll have to talk it over with Mr. Jeffers, but I have a feeling he won't mind and will trust my instinct on the matter. What do you think?"

Kara wondered if she had heard her correctly. *Stay with them?* Although she had been distraught to suddenly be without a home, she realized it wasn't their fault. From their standpoint, they could have had her arrested for unlawful entry, but instead Mrs. Jeffers was sitting here, extending hospitality.

"Miss Michaels?"

"Please...call me Kara."

"All right...Kara, then. Would you like to stay with us for a while?"

"I...I just don't know what to say. Considering the way you met me, I am completely blown away by your offer."

She was immediately met with two distressed expressions.

"Blown...away?"

Kara mirrored their confusion for all of two seconds—until she realized what she had said. "I mean...I am amazed at your generosity."

Kara swallowed involuntarily and waited for the woman's face to relax. Finally, her brows unfurled and she smiled again.

"Well now, it's not all charity. I'll be glad to get more help around the house. And I'm sure Betty would welcome the extra hands, too," she said, sending a glance back at her daughter who sat on her other side.

"Yes, could you stay?" Betty asked, smiling hopefully.

Kara looked at the eager expression of the teenage girl and then back at the kind woman next to her.

"I think you're about the nicest people I have ever met," she told them. She felt compelled to hug them but wasn't sure how well they'd receive her public display of affection. So instead she just smiled warmly at them.

"Does that mean yes?" Betty asked.

"Yes...and thank you. But only if you promise to give me lots of chores around the house, Mrs. Jeffers."

"I will, don't you worry, so get ready to roll up those sleeves!"

Then, ever so subtly, she glanced at Kara's very long, blue top she was wearing—courtesy of a trip to the mall a few months prior—along with her faded jeans. It seemed obvious that Mrs. Jeffers' statement about sleeves had suddenly reminded her of Kara's strange state of attire.

In fact, Kara had vaguely noticed their confused looks earlier. At one point, she had spent a few fleeting moments wondering what they must think of her, dressed as she was. But it could have been worse, she now thought, wryly. She could have been caught in this time warp wearing her neon-colored athletic shoes instead of these simple black flats. If that had been the case, she wasn't sure Mrs. Jeffers would be as trusting. Thankfully, she wasn't the type to sport tattoos or a nose piercing.

Mrs. Jeffers had already looked politely away by now so Kara, in her embarrassment, glanced about the room again. Her gaze fell on the desk and the receptionist who was busy with paperwork at the moment. She looked fairly young, Kara decided, perhaps in her late twenties. She couldn't help but study the fashion she wore. Her outfit consisted of a simple black skirt with a matching padded shoulder jacket, along with a wide-collared blouse. Her stylish bun with the flourished victory rolls set it off, keeping her from appearing boring in her business attire.

Kara's hand automatically went up to touch her own hair that currently fell in dismally flat layers. At least, they suddenly seemed dismal to her now.

Just then, Dr. Barris appeared in the waiting room, his brows knitted into a scowl. He sat down near them and said, quietly,

"Ladies, I was just speaking to my wife and unfortunately, she doesn't know of anyone at the present time that has any room to spare. Several of the families are taking in boarders already. You might be able to stay at our house for a night or two, Miss Michaels...however, she has informed me that we'll be getting company next week and..."

"Dr. Barris," Mrs. Jeffers broke in. "We were just discussing this. I told Miss Michaels that perhaps she could stay at our home just for a little while. I think it just may prove handy to have another helper around the house and I'm sure she can easily find work at the shipyard in Portland."

"Well! Splendid! That is very gracious of you, Mrs. Jeffers." And to Kara, he added, "I really didn't relish the idea of turning you out with no place to go." Relief was written on his face.

"Neither did I," Mrs. Jeffers agreed as they all rose. "But I want to thank you for all your concern and taking the time to try and help."

"Yes, thank you very much, Doctor. I...I really appreciate everything. You've been very kind," Kara echoed.

He smiled warmly at her in return. "I wish you well, young lady. Do keep me informed on how everything goes with you."

As they stepped back out into the sunshine, Kara was flooded with relief and gratitude. Yet, somewhere underneath remained the feeling that she was a stranger in a foreign land. An unusual kind of land where she didn't know how she arrived—or how long she would have to remain.

CHAPTER FOUR

"I'll be back in time for supper, I promise!"

Kara watched as Betty and her young friend hurried down the sidewalk, all whispers and giggles as they made their way downtown. A smile tugged at Kara's lips. Their fresh faces seemed so innocent and eager for life.

Was I this way at that age? Or was it unique to this time, she wondered? Or maybe, *in spite* of it. This was wartime, after all, she realized.

Kara turned away from the window and found her way into the kitchen where Mrs. Jeffers was busy slicing apples.

"What can I do to help?" Kara asked her politely. She was determined to earn her keep from the start.

"Well, since you asked, I'm getting a pie started. You could mix the dough for me. Everything is already on the counter," she told her pleasantly, pointing to the ingredients beside a mixing bowl.

"Sure..." Kara hesitantly moved toward them. *Had she ever baked a pie from scratch?* Maybe once with her grandma, but that was years ago. Her eyes studied the various ingredients, wondering where to start.

"Uh…Mrs. Jeffers?"

"Mmm?"

"I'm afraid I'm not sure how to make the dough. How much of each ingredient do I use?"

The woman turned around, wiping her hands on her apron.

"Oh…Well, here, let me show you…first, let's get you an apron," she said, pulling a half blue gingham one out of a drawer and handing it to Kara. She threw her a bewildered sidelong glance. "Have you never made pie crust before, dear?"

"Well…yes, once. But it's been a long time."

Mrs. Jeffers gave her what appeared to be a sympathetic look. Kara could almost guess what she must be thinking, wondering what kind of pathetic home life she must have come from. Nonetheless, she acted gracious and extremely patient. The next few minutes passed over a baking lesson and soon Kara was adorned with flour in her hair while she rolled out dough with a big, wooden rolling pin.

"Now, then…" Mrs. Jeffers sighed with satisfaction, wiping her hands on her apron. "I believe this is just about ready for the oven. Mr. Jeffers especially loves apple pie. Now, Jerry—his favorite has always been peach cobbler. I'll have just enough rations left to make it for his homecoming on Tuesday, along with a special dinner. I told you our son is returning home for a little while, didn't I?"

"Yes, I'm sure your family will be so happy to see him."

"We are almost counting the minutes. Since you'll be staying here for a little while, you'll get to meet him."

"I won't be taking up too much room here, will I?"

"Nonsense, not at all. But...I hesitated to mention this. I thought that during the time he's here, we could fix you up a nice bed in the attic. We'll try and make it as cozy as possible for you, of course. Do you think you would mind terribly?" she asked, pausing in her tasks and looking straight at Kara.

"No, of course not! It is his room, after all."

Kara assumed it might be some time before he ever got to sleep in comfort again, much less in his own room. Mrs. Jeffers stepped over to show her how to form the pie crust and crimp the edges as they continued to talk.

"How old is your son, Mrs. Jeffers?" Kara asked, pinching the dough around one side.

"He turned twenty last month. His birthday was right about the time he left for training." She paused and then added, "You know, he's just always been one of those caring souls all his life. I know this is his mother talking, but...." She gave a slight laugh. "I think he's turned out to be a pretty decent young man and we're very proud of him. It's just that... well, he's really only known life here—in Amberton." She sighed, wiping her hands on her apron as Kara finished crimping the last of the edge. "I sometimes worry about what he'll have to face...what he'll have to do." She cleared her throat. "But then...we can't sit by and watch our whole world fall around us without fighting back, now can we?" She slipped a mitt over her hand and picked up the finished pie. "Open the oven for me, will you, please?"

Kara quickly obeyed, but all the while, she wanted to tell her how much she understood... how brave she thought she was as his mother. Instead, she simply said,

"I look forward to meeting him. If there's anything I can do to help you get ready before Tuesday, just let me know."

After the timer was set, they busied themselves cleaning up. Mrs. Jeffers was hanging the dishtowel on a rack as she asked, without turning around,

"By the way, dear, I was wondering...you don't have anything with you, do you? Clothes...personal items?"

"Well, no..." She was suddenly now aware of the obvious.

The woman nodded. "I was thinking...you'll need something to wear when you go to see about that job at the shipyard on Monday. Perhaps we could go shopping for a few things this afternoon before the stores close. We might just have enough time once we take the pie out to cool."

"But... I don't have a way to pay." More realizations seemed to hit her with every turn.

"Oh, don't worry about that. We can find you something and you can pay me back with your first paycheck. I do enjoy shopping so it will be fun! Actually, with the war on," she continued. "It's just not as affordable to go out and purchase ready-made dresses anymore. I confess, I miss it. Not that we were ever wealthy or anything, especially during the tough years. But clothing used to be a little easier to buy a couple years ago. Betty and I have been making our own with patterns as much as possible. But I'm not sure either of us are exactly your size and it's always nice for a young woman to have something new of her very own. We're sure to find you something!"

"That is so nice of you, really. But I don't want to take advantage."

Kara had begun to feel almost guilty with all of the kindness being thrown her way. Here she was, a stranger trespassing in their home, at least as far as they were concerned.

"Oh no, you're not taking advantage, dear, I'm offering! It will be fun and you'll pay me back. You'll be working soon and in the meantime, you will be making yourself very useful around here, I'm sure."

"Well...it's just so kind of you, thank you. I suppose I will need to have a few basic necessities for a while," she relented.

"It's all set, then!" Her face came alive with excitement. "We can leave in just a little while. There are a couple shops downtown that sell dresses and hats and things.... not the selection that they have over in Carlton, and definitely not in Portland. But hopefully, we can find you a few basic things. Supper may be a little late tonight but if we hurry..."

***

"I don't suppose you have this in a more pale blue?"

While Mrs. Jeffers was speaking with the sales clerk, Kara took a moment and unabashedly admired herself in the mirror. She was wearing a smart navy colored skirt and blue print blouse and if it wasn't for her lack of hair-do, she would have felt as though she had stepped right into an old movie.

"No, I'm sorry to say we don't. But this is such an elegant color on the young lady," the clerk replied, stepping over for a closer look. "It fits you perfectly, too," she informed Kara. "You just need the right shoes to go with it. They are sold next door, however. I wish we had stockings but all the stores are out for the duration."

"How do you like the outfit, dear?" Mrs. Jeffers asked her, peering closely at the material on the collar and then standing back to give the outfit a final once-over.

"I love it!" Kara declared, pivoting back and forth in front of the full-length mirror. "But…" she felt her smile falter. "Do you think I'll make enough to pay you back for all this soon? I'm not sure of the wages I'll be getting… and do you think these prices are reasonable?"

In actuality, the prices had seemed all too reasonable to Kara but only compared to what she was used to. She hadn't a clue what was considered reasonable in this time and especially in light of what Mrs. Jeffers had told her earlier. She had mentioned that prices of ready-made apparel were going up and fabric was needed for uniforms. Still, she remained adamant that Kara have a new outfit and it was hard to argue with her.

"Please don't keep worrying so much, dear. These prices are not as exorbitant as some of the places in the city. And you really need something to wear on Monday."

"And I assure you, miss, you'll not find a better bargain for this quality anywhere," put in the saleswoman.

Kara nodded. "Well, if you're sure, Mrs. Jeffers. It is so nice of you to do all this for me."

"Wonderful! Now, if you're quite sure you are satisfied with both the skirt and blouse, we'll head next door and look at their shoes. I must admit, this color is lovely on you." She turned toward the saleswoman. "We'll take these. Don't bother boxing them up, she can just wear these now if you don't mind."

"Of course, Mrs. Jeffers."

About an hour later, the two women were hurrying briskly down the sidewalk towards home. Kara carried a parcel containing her old shoes and clothes, along with another of appropriate undergarments, personal items, and sleepwear. It felt so nice, wearing her new outfit and stepping along in her shiny, black dress oxford heels.

She surprised herself with how much she enjoyed shopping for everything. But what amazed her most was the relief she felt, just to be wearing the appropriate clothing. Even though she had never been a slave for the latest fashion, she certainly didn't relish the idea of standing out like a sore thumb, either.

And there was no denying it, Kara mused with a smile. 1943 certainly had great style, even if they didn't have real stockings!

That evening, the family sat gathered in the living room, the sultry sounds of Harry James' trumpet lulling Kara into a dreamlike state. Supper dishes had been washed and put away, and now she sat comfortably on the sofa— or *divan*— as they most often called it. Song after popular song played on as they listened to the radio show, *Your Hit Parade*. And thanks to her grandpa, she was no stranger to most of what she was hearing.

Mr. Jeffers sat in his chair, looking over the evening paper. Mrs. Jeffers worked on a crossword puzzle near the coffee table while Betty was poring over a magazine on the floor nearby.

"Mama, listen to this!"

"I *am* listening. The song is 'I had the craziest dream'…"

"No, Mama! I mean, to *this*!" Then she cleared her voice and began reading aloud.

"'*So sad that Glenn Ford must go off to war feeling like his Hollywood career is ending. As I visited with him and his charming wife, Eleanor Powel, at their home last week, I was simply shocked to hear him say that he was probably all washed up in pictures. He is absolutely convinced that audiences will not care a bit for him by the time he returns from the war.*'

"Isn't this awful? It goes on here to say that he once went to medical school so he might become a doctor after the war if Hollywood no longer wants him." She set her magazine down with a troubled expression. "Oh, I know doctors are important and all that, but imagine—giving up one's movie career to just work in an office or hospital! The article says that William Holden also worries about the same thing! And then there's Jimmy Stewart and Clark Gable who are already off serving…"

"Oh, now don't worry, dear. I'm sure it will all work out. All those actors are doing a noble thing, putting our country before their careers. But they will more than likely get right back to being successful after the war."

Kara opened her mouth to assure them of this fact, remembering the many movies they all went on to star in later on…however, she promptly closed it again.

Betty turned toward Kara. "Which movie stars are your favorites?" she asked, eagerly.

"Well, let's see…all the ones you mentioned."

"But who's your favorite?"

"Well, I'd have to say, Jimmy Stewart," Kara said, remembering all the times she faithfully watched *It's a Wonderful Life* every Christmas. But she realized she couldn't mention that film out loud because if she remembered right, it wouldn't be even made for a few more years.

"Yes, he's so adorable. I saw him in *Mr. Smith Goes to Washington* and *The Philadelphia Story*. And he's a bachelor, too! But as I said, he's off serving right now. Okay, who's your favorite female movie star?

Kara frantically reached into her knowledge of the era…what were some of those names? *Come on, all those movies I watched with Mom—I have to remember!* She knew if she hadn't been put on the spot, she could easily name a dozen. But with the young girl's eyes gazing up at her expectantly and even Mrs. Jeffers looking up from her crossword puzzle, her brain felt completely frozen.

"Uhh…well, it's so hard to pick a favorite…"

Suddenly, to her relief, a name popped into her head. "Debbie Reynolds!"

She had blurted it out before she had time to think. Silence followed, and even Mr. Jeffers looked curiously over his newspaper.

"Debbie…*who?*" Betty finally asked.

Panic again seized her as she realized her mistake. *Wait…no! It would be almost another decade before Debbie became famous!*

"No…I mean…"*Think further back… further back!* "I meant to say… Judy! Judy Garland." There!

And then, as if to make up for her first terrible mistake, a barrage of actress names—hopefully, all belonging in 1943—began flooding her brain. She began listing them fast and furiously.

"…and of course, Ginger Rogers and Katherine Hepburn, and that one in *It Happened One Night*…Claudette Colbert!…and oh, what's her name…? She's such a good actress, too…oh yes, Barbara Stanwyck!"

The Harry James song on the radio was just ending, which now made his musical star wife, the popular pin-up girl, burst into her mind.

"And Betty Grable!" she added, triumphantly. Her voice had escalated to a fevered pitch while they all stared her way. She was slightly out of breath, but feeling jubilant, almost as if she had just won a spelling bee.

"Yes," she added, between breaths. "I really like… Betty Grable."

She sat there, finally falling silent as all eyes continued to stare curiously in her direction. Suddenly, she wanted to crawl under the lovely rug that covered the living room floor.

"Well…" said Mr. Jeffers, at last breaking the awkward silence. "I've heard Harry James kind of likes her, too!"

Laughter followed, and Kara felt the air release from her lungs.

***

She wasn't exactly sure how it all came about, but later that evening she found herself sitting in front of a mirror upstairs while Betty and her mother worked intently on her hair. Perhaps Kara shouldn't have shown so much interest in the fashionable hairstyles displayed throughout Betty's movie magazine. She couldn't help but soak up the attention now, though. Then, as she saw the hairstyle begin to take shape, it was like icing on the cake.

When they finally declared the style was complete, Kara stared at her reflection. Her hair was parted on the side; the top swept up into a beautiful victory roll. There was a daintier type of roll on the other side, secured with bobby pins and a lovely barrette for effect. The ends of her hair billowed forward in large, soft curls over her shoulders. It was an amazing transformation and she couldn't take her eyes off her own image. Between the fashionable outfit and now the gorgeous hairstyle, it was almost as if she truly belonged here.

"I really love it!" Kara told them as they waited for her approval. "I'm just not sure I could ever do this again all by myself."

"It just takes practice," Mrs. Jeffers assured her.

"And I'm still learning, myself," Betty offered. "This style is still a bit mature for me, but my friends and I like to practice doing our hair sometimes when we get together."

"Well, I hope you'll help practice on mine again," Kara told her.

"I'll be glad to!"

A few minutes later, Kara was being shown her temporary sleeping quarters.

"I hope you don't mind the masculine surroundings. But you are welcome to use it until Jerry comes home on Tuesday," Mrs. Jeffers was saying as she glanced about the room.

"Thank you so much." She noticed that the parcels of items from their shopping excursion had already been brought up and were sitting on the dresser.

"Well...I'll leave you now to make yourself comfortable. Oh, and you are welcome to come to church with us in the morning," she added, pausing in the doorway.

"I'd like that," Kara replied.

The door shut softly, and Kara sat down on the bed, suddenly feeling tired. She realized that she didn't like being alone lately. It brought home the fact that she had been thrust into a different world and she didn't know why.

She wondered now, not for the first time, if there was a special reason she had been sent crashing back in time. But the most pressing question still remained— would God send her home?

CHAPTER FIVE

As the weekend went by, Kara was surprised just how relaxed and comfortable she was already feeling with this family she barely knew. It was almost as if she had known them for ages. The weekend felt leisurely, too. On Sunday, she had gone with them to church and afterward, Kara had helped in her own small way to prepare Sunday dinner. Part of the afternoon, she had even perused the Sunday newspaper that was filled with all the latest news of the war.

But Monday had been a little different. She had risen early to get ready for her interview and rode the twenty-five miles with Mrs. Jeffers to the Swan Island shipyard in Portland. When Kara had first stepped out of the car, all the sights, sounds and even distinctive smells had greeted her so heartily that it had felt a bit overwhelming. This was certainly a part of Portland that she had never seen in her lifetime before: a loud, robust wartime shipyard that seemed to go on for miles. But before she could stand there gaping very long, Mrs. Jeffers had quickly ushered her toward the main office.

She had already dreaded the interview. What did she know about shipbuilding, anyway? She was worried she didn't even know enough about the era she suddenly found herself in. It might be true that she was a history buff, but there was a big difference between knowing a little history and actually living it.

As it turned out, some of her fears were put to rest; the interview had been merely a formality. They needed workers—a lot of them—and the majority of those hired had no previous experience in shipyards—or in any workplace, in some cases.

She would be trained as a welder—a completely crazy idea, Kara thought. Working with hot sparks and metal was nothing she had ever come close to doing in her life. Yet, she kept telling herself that if all these other women could leave their homes and learn something so challenging, then, couldn't she?

For now, though, Kara was glad that the interview day was behind her and she wouldn't have to face training for another week. She had just finished washing the last of the supper dishes and evening was settling in. The sounds of Benny Goodman floated over the airwaves and Kara headed into the living room to sit down for a breather. As soon as she began to get comfortable, though, she realized everyone else was still bustling around.

"Is there anything I can do to help?" Kara asked when she caught Mrs. Jeffers passing through the room in front of her for the third time.

"Oh…thank you, no. Not at the moment. I think everything is in order for the time being. But in the morning, you can help me with that peach cobbler, if you like. Betty will be at school and I could use the extra help."

"Sure. What time does he arrive?"

"The train pulls in at one o'clock. Mr. Jeffers is leaving work to help me meet him at the station. Even Betty is getting off school early." She paused in her tasks for a moment. "It's not as though it's been all that long since we've seen him. It's just that… well, we don't know how long it will be until we see him again. We want it all to be special."

Kara swallowed. "I understand."

"Now then… I think I'm going to finally sit down for a few minutes with a cup of tea. Did you want one?"

"No thank you. But why don't you let me make it for you. It's the least I can do."

"Thank you, I think I'll take you up on that!" She settled herself down on the divan with a sigh. "I don't think I've put my feet up all day."

Kara returned a little later, carrying the special tea tray and set it on the small table.

"How lovely, thank you, dear," and Mrs. Jeffers smiled as Kara poured tea into the little china cup.

"With your serving me tea, I feel even more guilty about dislodging you from the room you just started feeling comfortable in," she added, taking the cup.

"I wouldn't want it any other way. It's your son's room, and he deserves a chance to sleep in his own bed before he has to ship off."

"Thank you for understanding." She took a long sip of her tea. "This is delicious, Kara!"

"Really? I'm glad that you like it. I may not be very knowledgeable in the kitchen," she laughed, "but it's good to know I can at least make a pot of tea!"

Mrs. Jeffers smiled. "It just takes practice. You're learning."

"Well, thanks to you."

"You've only been here a few days…just wait a little longer. You'll be an expert in no time!"

Footsteps were heard from the attic stairs and then Mr. Jeffers peeked in from the kitchen, wearing a comical expression.

"Attic is clean as a whistle, lamp put in and mattress is ready and accounted for." He gave a quick salute and disappeared again and the women dissolving into laughter.

***

It was a warm night and the window was open slightly, allowing a soft breeze to ruffle the boyishly striped curtains. Mrs. Jeffers had told her that she might as well sleep one more night in this room before he returned.

Her thoughts drifted to the day's events and the family's excitement. It touched her, thinking about how close their family seemed to be. They were all so thrilled to have him back, even for just a little while. She felt herself completely caught up in their anticipation; yet, she planned to wait here at the house while they went to the station. She wanted to allow the family to have some time alone to greet him.

I hope the cobbler he likes so well turns out in the morning... in spite of me helping with it, she thought, smiling. She also hoped he wouldn't mind having a stranger suddenly living here in his home. They hadn't even had time to write him so he'd only be learning about her today.

All the excitement buzzing in the air had Kara beginning to feel almost as though her own brother was coming home—if she had one. She already had learned so much about him in her short time here. His favorite songs...his best subjects in school... and how he planned to follow in his father's footsteps and work in the insurance business after the war. She even knew about the time he broke his arm falling out of a treehouse when he was eleven.

She yawned and rolled over, making a mental note of some of her tasks tomorrow. *I'll ask if I can do some extra dusting in the morning.* Sleep began closing in. *Maybe I can even borrow a headscarf to wear. Betty and her mother look so cute in theirs when they do housework...*

Through the open window, moonlight made the bright purple azaleas outside nearly glow. She could even catch their fragrance on the breeze as it wafted in. A feeling of contentment washed over her. She was only barely conscious of just how real this life was becoming—more real than what she had known before. Even her way of speech seemed to be adapting quickly to this era. She hadn't had a slip up in some time.

A song she heard earlier in the day replayed in her mind; the curtain waltzed lazily with the breeze to its melody. Her eyelids finally closed and she fell asleep to the imaginary strains of Glenn Miller's "At Last".

At first, Kara was unsure where she was. The room was so dark she couldn't even distinguish many objects. As her eyes began to focus, she glanced at the little clock beside her bed, straining to see where the hands pointed. It seemed to be a little after two-thirty.

In her half-awake state, the life she was immersed in now seemed to intertwine with what she left behind. Lately, she had been feeling so much like a welcome guest that it was hard to remember—this was actually her house.

What was it her Aunt Carol had said when she handed her the card for her twenty-first birthday last fall?

"Something for your future."

Kara had casually opened a birthday card to find a key inside. When she had looked up questioningly, Aunt Carol had announced that she was gifting one of her several rental houses to her. It would be hers, free and clear—even the property taxes would be taken care of for the next four years. Kara wouldn't have to worry about a thing except for utilities and general upkeep.

"And food, of course! You're on your own there," Aunt Carol had laughed. She then sat there beaming while Kara had been at a complete loss for words. This unbelievable gift had arrived on the heels of so much upheaval and grief. Of course, Aunt Carol was her mom's sister...and she knew. Still, it had been such a shockingly generous surprise that Kara had been speechless for the longest time.

One thought led to another now...though some of it Kara didn't want to relive. She turned over on the mattress, pulling the blankets up to her neck. Losing her mom had turned her world upside down only three short years ago. She had just graduated high school, on the cusp of adulthood, but still needing her mom more than ever.

Her dad had seemed grief-stricken, too. Or so Kara thought, by the way he had withdrawn even further away. Strange, then, how just eighteen months later, he was already remarried and moving across the continent to Baltimore—and mostly out of Kara's life.

To be fair, he had half-heartedly invited her to move out there, as well—if she liked. Somehow, the offer had seemed more of an obligation on his part and when she had finally declined, he had simply shrugged. His politely distant wife hadn't seemed the least bit interested in getting to know her new step-daughter, either. Kara knew she would have definitely felt like an intruder on their lives.

Besides, she had been half-way through getting her associate's degree at that time. Though she could have finished her schooling anywhere, her home was here in Amberton. She just couldn't picture living anywhere else.

Of course, she had also just gotten to know Derek. In hind's sight, she knew that whole thing had only been an infatuation, and even more likely, a distraction from all the drastic changes in her life. Her brief time dating Derek had proven to be nothing more than a lightweight balloon. She had held it by a string for a moment before it went floating aimlessly away. No breakup. He probably hadn't thought there was even anything to break up.

Kara turned over, yanking at the blankets again in frustration. Why was sleep eluding her now? She had drifted off so peaceably just hours before.

Maybe because I've been forgetting who I really am.

What if she remained here, she wondered? Would she eventually lose the memory of her prior life? The question should have frightened her but it didn't. Maybe because, if she were honest, a part of her wished this family she now knew was truly hers.

Something for your future. It was so strange and ironic…this house that her aunt had given her for her future had instead sent her plummeting to the past.

Kara wasn't sure how long she lay there, but apparently, sleep found her once more because when she opened her eyes again, sunlight was pouring over her. She glanced at the clock. About ten minutes after eight. As she stretched, her restless night seemed like a fuzzy, unpleasant dream— a dream which had been annoying but didn't seem of any real importance now. The cool breeze drifted in through the window as if to nudge her completely awake. Remembering the importance of the day, she grabbed her robe and hurried down to help however she could.

***

That afternoon, Kara put away the last of the lunch dishes and then wandered out onto the back patio. No one else was at home and she realized it was the first time she had been alone here since coming to this time. Mrs. Jeffers had just left to pick up the rest of the family before heading to the train station.

There was a magazine lying on the patio table so Kara sat down for a moment to thumb through it. It felt so nice to be out in the sunshine for a while. The whole morning had flown by in a flurry and now was the first chance she had gotten to relax all day.

She browsed the extra-large magazine, glancing at full-page advertisements and articles. Before coming here, Kara would have found them quaint, but lately they were beginning to appear commonplace and completely normal.

Her eye caught sight of the how-to section on hairstyling and she settled in to read it. The pages displayed various versions of the latest styles, complete with photographs and step-by-step illustrations. As Kara studied these intently, she felt almost sure she could duplicate one of them now. Between watching her hair being styled on Saturday, along with this how-to article…well, it was "a shoo-in" as Betty sometimes said! With sudden purpose, she ran upstairs with the magazine in hand.

About an hour later, her glowing optimism had faded. Nothing seemed to be working and the muscles in her arms were crying out in protest. She stood glaring at her reflection and blew at a wayward clump of hair dangling by her mouth.

Pointless! What was I thinking? She looked like she had been caught in a hurricane. Pins seemed to stick out everywhere around her head as if they were playing hide and seek and losing.

She stepped across the hall to glance at the clock. Nearly half-past one! She wasn't sure when the family would arrive home, but she couldn't let them see her like this. And she definitely couldn't meet someone for the first time this way! *Especially that handsome soldier from the photographs...*

She dismissed that last thought quickly and, with renewed determination, gazed back down at the magazine sprawled out on the bathroom stool. She began starting over, brushing out her hair and concentrating on the step-by-step instructions one more time. Even if it wouldn't turn out as elegantly as the model in the magazine, she reasoned, maybe—*just maybe*—she could at least get it looking a little less like some kind of natural disaster.

It took nearly twenty more minutes of concentrated work, but Kara managed to pin the last strands in place just as she heard the front door opening downstairs. She stood back, examining herself with a critical eye. *Hmm, it might just pass!* She kept glancing from the pages to her reflection. Actually, it really didn't seem that far off from the magazine models now, she thought proudly.

After wrestling with her hair for so long, though, Kara felt a little like going somewhere to collapse for a while. Unfortunately, there was no time for collapsing. She heard the voices of the family as they entered and she knew she should head downstairs and greet them. For some strange reason, though, she suddenly had butterflies. They seemed to be doing the jitterbug inside her as if Glenn Miller himself were leading their music.

***

Kara wasn't sure what she had been expecting. She had seen all of the photographs and knew what he looked like. She knew he had somewhat handsome brown eyes, with dusty brown hair that fell in waves before he had joined the Army. So why was she so taken aback when she saw him in person now?

She was taking the last of the stairs just as the family had moved into the living room. They all seemed to look her way in slow motion—at least it felt that way to Kara—while instantly her eyes met and locked gazes with the young man in uniform. He paused, standing fairly tall in the center of the room. He was indeed as handsome as his photograph and for some odd reason, she couldn't seem to move for a moment. At last, she pulled her eyes from him but the effort it took surprised her.

"Kara, this is our son, Jerry," Mrs. Jeffers said with obvious pride. "Jerry, Miss Michaels."

She met him halfway as he extended his hand. She was forced once again to meet his eyes—they were dark brown and full of expression. Though he looked slightly older than his years, his face held an innocent appeal. It was his warm expression that Kara noticed most of all...his eyes seemed to pull her in. She had just met him, so it completely unsettled her.

"It's really nice to meet you, Miss Michaels. I've heard a lot about you from my folks," he said, holding her hand gently in his grasp.

"Please—call me Kara."

"Kara," he repeated, smiling.

For just a moment, she forgot that his family was still there. But she once again reluctantly broke his gaze and looked about the room, a bit self-consciously. *This is ridiculous— what's wrong with me?*

"We were just about to have some lemonade out back," Mrs. Jeffers said. "Please join us, Kara!"

"I...I wouldn't want to intrude on your family time. He just got home and..."

"Nonsense!" Mr. Jeffers broke in. "We've had plenty of private family time since the train station and we'll have more to come."

"Yes...please. Join us," his son entreated quietly but intently.

Kara swallowed. "Well....all right, thank you. Mrs. Jeffers, would you like some help with the lemonade?"

"Oh, no need, thank you, dear. It's all made and I'll just bring it out on a tray. All of you feel free to go outside if you like and I'll join you in a few minutes," she replied, disappearing into the kitchen.

Mr. Jeffers led the way toward the patio door. "Well, let's go, then! Son, would you like to change out of your uniform first?"

"I'm fine for now, thanks, Dad." He paused and motioned for Kara to go before him.

Outside, everyone found patio chairs and before real conversation could even begin, Mrs. Jeffers, true to her word, was bringing out a tray with a pitcher of lemonade and glasses. She poured the first one and gave it to her son.

"Thanks, Mom, this really hits the spot," he said, after a long sip.

"Daddy and Mama agreed we could have a little party while you're here, Jerry," Betty announced as she took her glass.

"Oh? A party, huh. What kind of a party?"

"A going away party for you and your friends. You do like the idea, don't you, Jerry?"

"Oh, sure."

"Great! But of course, not right away. Not tonight or anything! You're probably a little tired."

He laughed, and for the next fifteen minutes, the family continued to chat good-naturedly while Kara was content to stay in the background. She mostly listened, not wanting to infringe on their conversations. But occasionally, she would feel the young soldier's eyes on her and then she would glance his way. Sometimes he smiled, and then, as if self-conscience as well, he'd look away, taking another sip of his lemonade.

But just now, he purposely turned toward Kara. "My mother tells me that you will be starting a job at the shipyard next week."

She nodded. "Yes. On Monday."

She had politely looked over at him for a second, not daring to let her gaze linger there. "I just hope I'm up to the task."

"I'm sure you'll do just fine. There's a real need for those ships right now. You'll be doing your share for the war effort, that's for sure."

"I…I hope so." She wanted to add that it wasn't nearly as much as he'd be doing. She made the mistake of meeting his gaze again, and her heart turned to mush before she could stop it. *What was happening here?*

Thankfully, Betty was the next to speak, breaking the spell.

"I almost forgot! I got an A on my algebra test yesterday!"

This was followed by lots of congratulations as Betty seemed to drink in the praise.

"Never knew my little sis was such a genius," Jerry teased her, tussling her hair.

"I tried to tell you ages ago!"

The banter continued for a few more minutes before Jerry finally announced that he should probably go freshen up a bit. His mother sneaked a hug around his neck as he stood up and he bent down to kiss her on the cheek.

"It's good to be home," he told her. He started toward the patio door, but glanced back at Kara and then smiled. "Good to meet you, Kara. Looking forward to getting to know you."

She nodded to him numbly as he retreated into the house.

It was obvious the patio gathering was over for now, and Kara helped Mrs. Jeffers and Betty gather up the glasses. But all the while, she couldn't shake this strange feeling that had come over her from the very moment she had met him. It left her completely unnerved.

While they quickly washed and dried the glasses, Kara concentrated on the task at hand, feeling suddenly self-conscious. She kept wondering if they had sensed anything peculiar. But if they had, they never mentioned a thing.

CHAPTER SIX

"Did you get enough cobbler, son? There's plenty more…"

"No thank you, Mom, I couldn't eat another bite."

"Well, if you're sure…"

His mother stood up and slowly began collecting the dishes while the rest of the family sat around the large table. Kara had been dining with them again, as usual, and she quickly jumped up after her.

"Please, you sit back down with your family, Mrs. Jeffers. I'll get these."

"Oh…well, thank you, Kara," and she hesitantly returned to her seat. "That's sweet of you."

Kara noticed that both father and son had started to rise from their chairs also, and for a second she had been confused. Then she remembered seeing similar scenes in movies. It was a gentlemanly manner she'd never had a chance to personally experience first-hand until now. She knew it was considered archaic to some, but the simple chivalrous gesture was endearing to Kara—a way of showing honor.

She went about collecting the dishes and cups, making a special effort to avoid becoming too near to the handsome young soldier as she reached for his plate. He handed it towards her before she could reach it, their fingers touching for one brief second. She kept her eyes from his and quickly retreated into the kitchen, her face aflame.

Enough of this! This is getting absolutely ridiculous, she scolded herself as she began filling the sink with warm water and dish soap. She knew she had to go back in there to retrieve the remaining dishes and silverware but for some reason, she couldn't make her feet move in that direction. Thankfully, Betty came in carrying them and set them on the kitchen counter.

"I thought you might like some help."

"Thank you, but you really don't need to. You should stay out there and visit with your brother; I can take care of these."

"It's okay, I don't mind. He told me he was going to take me for a soda after school tomorrow, just the two of us." She turned off the water that Kara had started and began placing the dishes into the sudsy warmth. "I'll wash, and you can dry. All right?"

"All right." She filled up the other side of the sink with hot rinse water. Directly above the sink, a breeze blew through the curtains that helped cool Kara's still heated cheeks.

The two proceeded to do the dishes in relative silence, with only the voices of parents and son being heard from the other room. Kara wasn't sure how to make conversation at the moment, nor did she understand her own general feeling of embarrassment. Perhaps no one even noticed anything strange at all and everything was just her confused imagination. But why wasn't Betty chattering, as usual? Kara plucked another glass out of the new rinse water and wrapped the dish towel over it, determined to shake this silliness.

"That will be nice....you and your brother going out for a soda tomorrow, I mean," she ventured.

"What was that? Oh... yes! It will be. Then tomorrow night is the party. It's not going to be a big party, though; we're just having a few friends over. That's all he says he wants, and it's so last minute, we doubt if everyone can make it. It still is going to be lots of fun! We're going to finish phoning people tonight."

At least Betty was talking again, Kara observed. She nodded and then searched for something else to say.

"I'm sure the party will be nice." She scooped up another plate and began wiping. "I know how happy you all are to have him home. Your brother seems really... nice." Kara winced. *Can't I think of any other adjectives tonight?*

"That's funny. He said the same exact thing about you."

Kara shot her a glance. "He did?"

"Yes, he went on about how nice you seemed. Of course, he was curious about where you came from and the whole mystery of how you ..." she stopped short and looked over at Kara, obviously embarrassed. "I'm sorry. I didn't mean it like that. I'm glad you're here, really I am."

Kara swallowed. "It's okay, I understand." She knew that her presence must seem shrouded in mystery to the whole family. Most of it, she didn't even understand herself.

"No, really! It's swell having you at our house. I know you haven't been here very long but it sort of feels like you're, well...kind of like my older sister. Only without the bossiness, of course," she laughed.

Kara smiled, warmed by the declaration. "Thank you. You know, I've always wanted a sister."

Betty beamed in reply. After a few moments, she added, a little slyly,

"I think my brother likes you.

Kara's dish slipped from her hand and landed with a splash into the rinse water. She quickly grabbed it back up.

"Well...I hope so. She hoped she sounded nonchalant.

Betty looked over at her. "No, I mean, I think he *really* likes you."

Kara held more tightly to her dish this time. "What do you mean? He doesn't even know me."

"I can just tell, that's all."

Just then, Kara nearly jumped as the subject of their conversation casually strolled into the kitchen. She quickly turned all of her attention back to the last two dishes left as if they required her deepest concentration.

"Mother wants to know who all is playing Rook. She's setting up the card table now," he said from behind her.

Had he heard anything? Their voices had been hushed so she doubted it. Still, she had the distinct desire to sink through the linoleum floor.

"Sure! How about it, Kara?" Betty asked.

"Rook? Oh... I don't think so. I don't even know how to play. But you all go ahead!" Kara replied without looking up, drying the last glass and setting on the dish rack.

"Why don't you join us and watch for a bit, then? It's pretty easy to learn," the masculine voice asked, warm and soft like honey from a few close feet behind her.

"I..." she slowly turned around. His expression was so earnest and gentle, she couldn't seem to resist.

"Well, all right." She wiped her hands on the dishtowel while he waited for her.

For the next hour and a half, Kara sat with the family, savoring the family atmosphere— despite the fact that Jerry sat all too close beside her. While the game continued, he'd try to explain the rules to her, leaning over to show her his cards on several occasions—his clean, masculine scent invading her space. She tried to follow what he was saying but for some reason, it was so hard to concentrate.

***

The next morning, Kara woke up on the mattress in the attic, slightly stiff and her mind attempting to focus. It took a moment to even remember where she was. Then yesterday's events came pouring in and the memories warmed her entire being. She sat up and stretched, sleep still embedded in her eyes.

She leaned back against her pillows, watching as tiny dust particles danced in the sunlight that poured from the attic window. They looked like delicate fairies performing a ballet, she thought, dreamily. She gazed around the room and then a new realization formed: *This was where it all started—right here in this attic.*

She had been so immersed in this new life lately she had almost forgotten. Her original life wasn't here at all but somewhere in the future.

Strange that she didn't miss it as much anymore...

Now that she was forced to face it once again, she began to wonder—just what was happening to everyone she had ever known? Her preschool class...Shannon... Was time marching on without her there, or did it have a different way of moving? If she was ever able to make it back to her original life, would it be as if no time had passed there? Was she being missed right now?

Kara shook her head as if to erase the muddle...there were so many questions. It was all too mind-boggling and she had no way of finding the answers, at least at the moment. Besides, none of it would matter if she was stuck here forever. She didn't even know of any way to go back. No way at all...unless...She bolted up and headed towards the place behind the wall. To the trunk where it all began.

When Kara had first found herself here in this time, the trunk and attic hadn't seemed to change. She supposed she had been in such a state of shock in the days that followed, she never thought rationally about returning to this spot. Now, she stepped over slowly, reaching out to touch the jagged crevices of the old trunk. It looked old even eighty years in the past. She tried lifting the lid, but just like the first time, the trunk was locked and the lid wouldn't budge.

Of course, she still didn't know if the contents would hold the secret to sending her back. But she didn't have many other options at the moment. She couldn't attempt opening it behind their backs—that would feel wrong, somehow. She had earned the family's trust and she couldn't risk losing that. She decided she would simply have to persuade Mrs. Jeffers to open it. She just wasn't sure how she should go about it.

Her stomach gave a protesting growl, reminding her that she couldn't stay up here all morning. She would have to think about all of this later. She padded back to her mattress and grabbing her robe, hoped she could discreetly maneuver her way through the house and up to the shower.

As she descended the attic stairs, she realized it was the first time she had done so since discovering her world had changed. *What if I was suddenly transported back to my original time as I reached the bottom step?* But the family's voices edged out that theory as she opened the door. Surprisingly, she felt more relief than disappointment.

Betty and her mother were busy in the kitchen and she sent them a hurried greeting as she rushed through.

"Good morning...I'll be back to help but if you don't mind, I just need to go take a quick shower first," she called over her shoulder.

"Yes, I know how much you like your morning showers. Go right ahead."

"Thank you!"

She hurried through the house and up the main staircase. Almost reaching the bathroom door, she ran smack into something and nearly toppled backward. She was caught by the arms in time and when she looked up, she found herself staring straight up at Jerry. Backing away, she quickly tried to regain what little composure she had begun with.

"I'm so sorry... are you all right?" he asked her, still trying to steady her.

"Yes, of course. It was all my fault; I wasn't looking where I was going."

Aware that she was still clad in a nightgown and robe, she hurried past him and into the bathroom. She promptly closed the door and leaned against it, trying to compose herself. Her breaths came out in rapid succession and her cheeks simmered once again.

What was she so worried about, anyway? It wasn't such a big deal. *So what if I bumped into him? Everyone here is like family—it should be just like bumping into a brother or cousin in the hallway.* So why was her heart racing now? And why had she turned into jelly when he steadied her, his face only inches from hers?

***

It had taken Kara a little while to shake the awkwardness—and to shake how it had felt to be accidentally in his embrace. She had successfully avoided the family during breakfast, claiming she wasn't hungry, and had grabbed a piece of toast when everyone had dispersed. Now she was determined to put this silliness out of her mind.

Earlier in the week, she had asked Mrs. Jeffers if she might be able to help tend the vegetable garden—or "victory garden" as they called, it. So now, a watering can in her hand and a kerchief she had borrowed from Betty tied around her head, she traipsed toward the back of their yard in the cool mid-morning air.

Strange how she had to remind herself that this was once her own yard. It seemed so different now. Perhaps it hadn't literally changed all that much, but the feel of it was certainly different. Other trees and shrubs grew all around now. The one very large pine tree she remembered that had towered over the rest, giving so much shade—it had to be that dainty little one in the same corner of the yard. She also had never known the beautiful cherry tree which now graced the other side.

Wearing borrowed garden overalls, she knelt and began pulling a few weeds that had crept up around the pea vines when a voice startled her.

"Mind if I help?"

She glanced up to see Jerry standing there, looking all boyishly handsome in his civilian clothes, and she wasn't sure what she wanted more—for him to stay or to leave.

CHAPTER SEVEN

Vibrant clouds covered most of the sky even as the sun pierced through their mist. Kara remained where she knelt in the soil, squinting up at him.

"Sure… you can join me," she finally answered. "It's your garden, after all." She suddenly realized she looked anything but glamorous and then wondered why she even cared.

He knelt beside her. "Pulling weeds?"

She nodded as she continued with her work.

"I used to come out here every summer growing up and helped my mother with the garden. We almost always had one, even before the war." As he talked, he began pulling up a few tiny weeds which had sprouted up here and there. "I remember I would always confuse the carrot tops with weeds and accidentally pulled up quite a few."

Kara smiled. "Was your mother upset?"

He laughed. "No, not really. But I do remember getting shooed out of the garden a time or two."

"Well, I've always liked working in gardens. Something about the feel of the earth and...I don't know...how everything smells so rich and alive."

"I know what you mean. I can understand why farmers love their work so much."

Nervously, Kara pulled harder at an extra thick weed, all too aware of his close proximity, as she searched for something else to say.

"They tell me you want to follow in your father's footsteps after the war," she ventured, looking up at him for a brief second before directing her attention once more on her stubborn weed.

"Ahh... insurance." He paused as he fingered the small leafy weed in his hand. "Yes, Dad and I have had some talks over that."

He didn't add anything further and Kara looked up in his direction. He was studying the weed as if engrossed in it, then suddenly caught himself with a rueful laugh. "There's so much going on now. None of us heading overseas are sure how long we'll be there, or what things will be like when we come back." After another moment's pause, he went on. "Dad's wonderful at what he does. He isn't the pushy sort; he just has a naturally cheerful personality. He's always honest and forthright and he loves people. I do too, but I've started to have second thoughts. I just can't see myself selling insurance all my life."

"What is it you want to do?"

"That's just it. I'm not quite sure, though I have several ideas. Most of the things I'm interested in take a college degree...and there isn't time for that now."

"I see."

He seemed deep in thought, but then looked back over at her with an apologetic smile.

"I'm sorry—I don't know why I rambled on like that."

"Don't be. I was asking," she told him.

"Well, it's not like me at all. Anyway, what about you?"

Kara swallowed. "Me?"

"Yes, you. What do you want to be when you grow up?" he asked her, a teasing in his voice.

"Oh...I don't know." A fleeting thought about the preschool job she left somewhere in time flitted through her memory. "I...I've always liked the idea of teaching. But for now, it looks like it will be the shipyard."

"Teaching? That's such a noble profession. I've had some wonderful teachers growing up." After a few seconds, his expression clouded again and he sighed, suddenly tossing the weed away. "But it seems Hitler's schemes for the world are interfering with all of our dreams and ambitions right now, doesn't it?"

She nodded but wasn't sure how else to respond. After a moment, she asked, "Does your dad know you aren't so crazy about going into the insurance business after all? I'm sorry...I don't mean to pry."

"No, it's all right! And that's a good question. I don't think I had even thought much about it until recently. But it doesn't matter, anyway. Uncle Sam has other plans for me at the moment."

She looked back down and pulled out another small weed. "Do you know where you'll be going?" she asked him, quietly.

"No. But I guess I'll know soon enough. I do know I'll be heading somewhere across the Atlantic."

Kara could feel a growing sense of worry for him. Strange—she barely knew him, but the desire for him to stay safe right here next to her simmered somewhere under the surface. She didn't like the idea of him leaving into the unknown…and into unseen harrowing moments somewhere across the world.

It was crazy, of course—these strange thoughts and feelings. She had only just met him. Yet once again, she couldn't tear her gaze away from the warm, dark eyes as they searched hers. He leaned in ever so slightly and she felt that strange, magnetic pulling again. A short lock of dark hair fell over his brow, and she fought the urge to reach up and brush it aside. Instead, she clasped the nearby watering can to keep her hand steady. For one breathless second, she was almost sure he would kiss her. But with a jagged sigh, he broke their gaze and looked downward.

"I suppose I should go." He slowly stood, then reached down to take her hand, helping her to her feet.

"Kara..." He glanced her way, almost shyly. "I...I know we've just met. And I don't want you to feel obligated. But would you consider writing to me?"

"Yes... of course. I'd be honored to write to you."

He still held her hand and she relished the feel of it but at the same time, the intensity terrified her. She wanted to pull away but she found she couldn't somehow.

It suddenly dawned on her that she had no right promising to write to him when this wasn't even her world. She didn't even know if she could stay. Yet, at this moment, she wanted to be able to keep that promise more than anything else.

"That will mean a lot to me," he told her. Pausing, he also seemed to gaze down at their hands but didn't let go. "Why is it...?"

"Why...is what?"

"Why do I feel like something incredible is happening here? Like I've known you so much longer than just a day?"

She stared at him. He had just echoed her feelings completely and had spoken them out loud. These strange stirrings hadn't been just her imagination.

She slowly nodded. "I know..."

Never in a million years would she have ever been so familiar with someone she barely knew. It was completely unlike her. Was it just because she was in a new and different world that didn't seem truly real? No, she knew it had to more than that. It was *him*. And in some ways, this world felt even more vibrant than the one she used to know.

There was a sound from the patio and she turned to see Mrs. Jeffers closing the door behind her. Kara pulled away suddenly, brushing the garden soil from her knees.

"Excuse me; I'm going to go wash up." She threw him a tentative smile, but then hurried away towards the house, with only a quick greeting for Mrs. Jeffers as she passed. She felt both giddy and frightened. How could she be falling for someone so quickly?

But there was no denying it; something strong and amazing was stirring and she didn't know quite what to do about it.

***

"I'm so glad the rain decided to stay away for a while."

Mrs. Jeffers had just taken the metal mold of strawberry Jell-O out of the icebox and placed it onto the counter. The colorful fruit inside the gelatin seemed to keep dancing indefinitely after she set it down. Kara stood nearby, slicing cheese while Betty set things out on the table.

"I know; it will be so much nicer for everyone to go out on the patio to dance. We can play records and turn up the music nice and loud!"

"Well...not too loud, I hope! We do have neighbors, Betty." Her mother was smiling, though, while she took a platter and began arranging the Ritz crackers around the edges. "Kara, when you're done there, you can bring the cheese slices and arrange them here in the middle, please. I think we're almost ready and good thing—the guests will start arriving in about an hour!"

Kara was relieved to be busying herself, helping for the party—glad to be here in the sanctuary of the kitchen with only Mrs. Jeffers and Betty for company. There didn't seem to be any awkwardness as they all chattered and went about their tasks...just like it had been at the beginning. No one else around to cause any strange emotions or peculiar stirrings.

"Betty, help me finish making the punch, dear. Then I think we'll be just about done," her mother directed. "The boiled sugar water is almost through cooling. Just juice the lemons and oranges while I cut up the pineapple."

As Kara continued to follow instructions, she noticed that it seemed to be a lot more trouble than her previous way of making punch—just throw together canned tropical juice with 7-Up and perhaps a little sherbet. She had to admit, it did seem special to have the fresh fruits mixed in. She watched as Betty began juicing lemons one by one, twisting them over a green-colored glass juicing dish.

"What else do you add to make the punch?" Kara asked them.

"Just the carbonated water. We add that last," Betty explained, as she began peeling an orange for juicing.

Twenty minutes later the punch was ready, glistening in a giant sparkling bowl on the dining room table. Betty and her mother had hurried upstairs to freshen up and change while Kara headed to the attic to retrieve her only stylish dress. Betty had promised to help her with her hair so she hastily grabbed the dress, along with her slip and shoes, and hurried back down the attic stairs. She dashed through the house and up the main staircase, managing to make it to Betty's bedroom without running into anyone else this time. Quickly, she knocked on her door, a bit out of breath.

"Come in!"

At the sound of Betty's voice, Kara scurried in.

"Oh, that's such a cute skirt, Betty!"

"Thank you, I just finished making it myself last week."

"It's amazing that you can sew like that!"

Betty glanced at the clock. "We certainly don't have much time to get ready. Oh, I wish school was over for the year and we could stay up extra late. But Mother told everyone that the party would be from six-thirty to ten."

"I was sort of wondering why you didn't wait and have the party Friday night."

"I guess I was so anxious to have everyone over! Besides, I think Daddy and Mama wanted to have him a little more to themselves this weekend. He has to take the train back first thing Monday morning and ships off right afterward."

Kara nodded. Her emotions took a momentary dive as she silently changed into her dress. Betty, meanwhile, was sitting at the vanity mirror, pulling back her pin curls. Kara finished dressing and then paused to admire Betty's quick style.

"You did such a nice job with your hair—it looks adorable!"

"Thank you," she replied, revealing a slight blush. "The curls I pinned last night turned out especially well this time—even if I do say so, myself! Are you ready for me to help you with your hair now?" She looked from her own reflection to Kara's.

They spent the next fifteen minutes working on perfecting Kara's hairstyle. She was glad now that her hair had a bit of natural wave and the many bobby pins helped to keep the swept upsides in place. When they were through, she smiled at the results.

"Wow, I love it, thank you! I know I couldn't have done this without your help. You know, you definitely have a knack for hairstyling."

"You do look beautiful, Kara. Do you think….Oh, yowza!" Her shriek came at another glance at the clock. "It's time! We should hurry and go down there—the guests will be arriving any second. Let me go tell Jerry…" She scurried out into the hall and banged on his bedroom door. In a flash, she was back, leading Kara by the arm. "No answer—he must be downstairs already. Come on, Kara, let's go!"

***

Kara sat outside at the umbrella table alone, nibbling at her cobbler while guests mingled and chatted throughout the patio and lawn. Several of Jerry's friends, including a couple of girls, were gathered around him. She could hear bits and pieces of conversation and they all were laughing now, apparently about something that happened their last year in school.

The party had become larger than Kara had envisioned—even larger than Mrs. Jeffers had expected, too, due to hearing her wonder aloud if there would be enough of everything. There had to be close to fifty guests, Kara estimated. It definitely appeared to be much more than "just a handful of Jerry's friends'. Besides the many young people around, there were also several families, a few parents of Jerry's friends, with a few relatives mixed in.

The group around Jerry stood about ten feet away, huddled together like intimate chums. She knew it was silly to feel left out. No one here knew her, though introductions had gone around. When it came right down to it, even the Jeffers family barely knew her themselves, she realized.

She looked up in time to see one of the girls laugh and whisper something into Jerry's ear as she touched him on the arm. The young woman's raven black hair was swept up into a flattering style—a sort of half up, half down look, complete with a side part and victory rolls. Her red lipstick was dark so that both hair and mouth contrasted sharply with her fair skin. She was strikingly beautiful, Kara had to admit, even if she was a bit overdone.

For some reason, watching her fawn over Jerry was leaving Kara with a bad taste in her mouth. Her fork scraped around at the cobbler for a few seconds before she finally pushed her plate away.

Her eyes began purposely scanning the backyard for someone else to focus on. But after a few moments, they disobediently seemed to drift back over to the group of friends. And just when they did, Jerry looked over and met her gaze.

Oh no. She quickly glanced away. Did she appear lonely and pathetic, sitting here by herself? The last thing she wanted was his pity. Besides, this was his time to enjoy himself. He would be facing some terrible unknowns soon—he definitely deserved to relax with his friends without worrying about some stranger sitting alone.

As if purposely ignoring her thoughts, he excused himself and headed over in her direction.

"Hello," he simply said as he pulled up a chair next to her.

"Hello." After a few seconds, she added, "Please don't leave your friends on my account." She inwardly winced. She hoped that didn't come out sounding petty—she actually hadn't meant it that way.

"I'm not. Well, all right, *I am*. But only because I was getting a little tired of walking down memory lane and would rather talk with you now."

Kara smiled, though wasn't entirely sure if he truly meant it or was just being kind.

"Your friends seem nice. It's obvious they all think the world of you."

"We've all known each other forever—or at least, it feels that way. Some of us go all the way back to first grade. Great kids, most of them."

Kara noticed the girl with the raven black hair eyeing them. She was still standing exactly where he had left her but Kara was unable to read her expression.

"Have you known all the girls here at the party just as long?" She couldn't imagine why she had asked that. "I mean—that's a long time to know anyone."

"If you mean those two girls there, then yes, I suppose so. At least all through junior high and high school."

She looked up at him and he seemed to see the unasked question.

"We're all just friends. A couple of high school dates—a malt or a movie now and then. But nothing serious." He paused, and then added, "None of them are what I'm looking for."

She didn't want to read more into his statement than she should, but she found herself at a loss for words. Then he cleared his throat, almost as if he was just as nervous as she was.

"I was wondering if you'd care to go for an evening walk with me after the party winds down."

Before she could give an answer, Mrs. Jeffers strolled past, pausing for a moment in front of their table. Kara instinctively reached for her cobbler and brought it closer.

The woman smiled; a gleam in her eyes. "Don't feel you have to eat that, dear, if you really don't want to."

"Oh…no, it's delicious, honestly. But I've already had some of the Jell-O earlier."

"Well, I'm glad I had both the desserts after all. This is quite the crowd! Nearly everyone we invited is here. And somehow," she added, leaning over, conspiratorially, "quite a few more."

Jerry reached out and slyly nudged Kara's plate over towards himself. "Here, let me help you with this, then," he said, taking a bite.

His mother laughed. "Let me know if he gives you any trouble, Kara. Excuse me; I think Mrs. Parker is trying to get my attention."

As she left their table, Kara shook her head at Jerry in amusement. "Your mother sure must have been right when she said this dessert was your favorite."

He slid it back to her. "It is, but I was also making sure she knew it. Sorry, you can have it back now."

"No, I was through." She held her hand up in protest, laughing.

"Well... if you insist." He slid it right back in front of himself again. His twinkling eyes suddenly appeared shy as he glanced back. "I think I was asking you something a few minutes ago..."

A shadow of someone else appeared and once again and they both looked up from their conversation. "Miss Raven-Hair" poised in front of their table, smiling demurely. Her expression seemed to form the ideal blend of fake innocence and determination.

"Excuse me, might I borrow you for a moment, Jerry? You don't mind, do you...Miss...I'm so sorry, I completely forgot your name."

Jerry rose politely, and with a strained expression, made introductions once again.

"What exactly is the problem, Patricia?"

The brunette first smiled and nodded coolly towards Kara. Her demeanor was grating but her style—as synthetic as it seemed—appeared quite polished and well-rehearsed.

"Oh, yes... Kara. That's right. Such an unusual name, isn't it?" There was a bite to her tone. She then turned her attention to Jerry. "It's...well...a bit confidential."

Jerry sighed before turning towards Kara. "Will you excuse me for just a moment?" He leaned down and whispered, "I'll be right back."

"Of course."

It had warmed Kara the way he had seemed reluctant to leave; still, she felt uneasy. She watched as the beauty slipped her arm through Jerry's and escorted him to the outskirts of the lawn.

CHAPTER EIGHT

Kara willed herself to stop staring after them. She stood and began strolling about the backyard aimlessly. The whole time, she kept chiding herself. After all, she had no right to feel even a twinge of jealousy. Everyone here had known each other for ages. She and Jerry had barely met.

She gazed off in the direction of the burgundy sun, watching as it sank deeply behind the hill. The vibrant colors were spilling over onto the patio all around her, casting a glow over the entire gathering. Music still played and the sounds of conversation lilted from every direction but the charm of it all was suddenly fading for Kara. Maybe if she simply excused herself to the family and ducked inside…she could grab a good book from the shelf and head up to the attic, unnoticed.

"Hello. Miss Michaels, was it?"

She had been so busy scanning the backyard for a sign of Mrs. Jeffers so she could make her excuses that she nearly jumped when a young man appeared directly in front of her. He stood just a few inches taller than her five-foot five-inch frame, with a slightly stocky build and a pleasant smile. She smiled back at him, trying to be polite.

"Yes...please tell me your name, again." She hoped she didn't sound too much like Miss Raven-Hair but it was hard to remember so many new names.

"Jim Stevens. A friend of Jerry's from way back." He paused. "Would you like some more punch, Miss Michaels?" he asked her, motioning toward the house.

"Please, call me Kara." She looked toward the house and hesitated, still feeling the need to escape. "And no...no thank you."

"You probably don't know many people here. Did you get a chance to meet everyone?"

"Yes, I think so. But it's hard to keep the names straight," she confessed, scanning the large group of guests. "Of course, it's different with all of you. You've known each other all your lives. That must be a nice feeling."

She glanced away from him for a brief second, her eyes falling on Jerry and his friend, Patricia, still deep in conversation at the very back of the yard.

"That's true. And yes, I suppose it has its merits." He shifted a bit where he stood. "But of course it's always nice to meet someone new."

She gave him another smile, though a bit absently, as her eyes strayed again to the back of the lawn. She forced them back to the young man in front of her and tried to think of something else to say so that she wouldn't seem rude.

"Are you also enlisted?" she asked him.

"Jerry and I enlisted together as a matter of fact. We're both shipping off next week."

"Oh…I see."

She looked at him a little more closely for a moment. She wished she had something glorious to say in response to his service but nothing seemed quite right. As much as she wanted to run up and retreat to the attic, she felt it was the least she could do to stay and talk with him a while.

"You know, I think I will take that glass of punch after all," she told him.

He grinned. "You got it. I'll be right back."

As she stood there alone, she quietly observed her surroundings. People—mostly young people—mingled and laughed in the waning sunlight, the lengthening shadows stretching across the patio and lawn. She took a deep breath, inhaling the fragrances of late spring. Despite the sweetness of the air in her lungs, though, it somehow ended up coming back out as just a long sigh.

She glanced around and noticed an empty chair nearby. She sank into it, relishing the cool breeze that played with her hair as she leaned back. She loved the relaxing feel when it tousled the strands, but then she instinctively touched her head to make sure her hairstyle was still in place.

Kara noticed Betty striding towards her then. She had been spending most of the evening giggling and sharing secrets with one of her best friends but she now headed over alone, carrying a bowl of pretzels and wearing a look of concern on her adolescent face.

"Why are you sitting here all by yourself? You should come join us," she offered, gesturing to where her friend stood, now chatting with one of the boys.

Kara smiled but shook her head. "I think I'll just sit here for a few minutes. Thank you, though."

"You must be so bored, not knowing anyone. Are you sure you won't come over with me?"

Kara appreciated Betty's graciousness but this image of being the lonely little wallflower was getting to be a bit much. Before she could say anything more, Jerry's friend returned with the punch, leaving Betty staring as he handed Kara the cup.

"Oh...I didn't realize. Jim, you keep her company now. She doesn't know anyone but us." And with that, she headed back over to her group of friends without further word.

Kara gave a little laugh as she thanked him for the punch.

"Honestly, I'm not as pathetic as she's making me sound!"

"On the contrary," he said, grinning. "But I would probably feel a bit out of place myself if I were surrounded by folks I'd just met—and who all knew each other." He took a sip of his punch, then pulled a chair over next to hers and sat down. "I hear you're staying with the Jeffers family for a while."

Kara shifted in her seat. "Yes," she said simply. She really hoped that he wouldn't probe any further...but her hope was premature.

"Are you a distant relative, by chance?" He stole a sideways glance, and then casually took another sip of his punch.

"No, not a relative. I didn't even know them or... anyone in town, for that matter. But we quickly got acquainted and they were very kind to invite me to stay for a while."

There. Keep it simple.

"You don't say? What actually brought you to our little town?"

Kara fought the urge to sigh in irritation. She knew the questions were fair ones, but they required too much thinking in each reply and her temples were beginning to throb.

As if sensing her hesitation, he added, "I'm sorry. I don't mean to pry. It's just that everyone's a bit curious. You see, not many young people come here by themselves. If anything, so many of us are leaving. Not that we aren't fond of it here. It will always be my home. But so many are leaving for jobs in the city, sometimes to get married, go to college... and of course, now with the war on..."

Kara relaxed a bit and nodded, noticing an opening to change the subject.

"You said that you and Jerry joined up the same time?"

"Yeah. But then, we've done a lot together over the years. We played baseball together as kids, got into a few scrapes...we even liked the same girl a few years ago," he added, laughing. "But our friendship managed to survive. So I guess it was only fitting that we joined up the same day. Of course, we don't know where either of us is heading and the chances of our ending up the same place are about slim to none."

Kara swallowed, forgetting why she had even steered the conversation in this direction.

"It sounds like you two have been through a lot together."

"Yeah, I guess so. Jerry—he's one of the good guys. It would be great if we could sign up to go the same direction for the duration but it doesn't quite work that way."

"It must be strange...not knowing where you will be. Leaving your friends and your family and ..." Her voice trailed off. She was going to say, "Not knowing when you'll see them again," but she decided against it.

"I guess it is. But not so strange when almost everyone is in the same boat. Besides, there's a big job to do so what other choice is there? Too much at stake." He took a quick sip from his glass and said no more.

Kara sat there quietly, his words ringing in her ears. She kept remembering the stories she had heard and all the thousands upon thousands of others who went off bravely to fight for something bigger than they were…"the greatest generation", as she once had heard them described. And Jerry and his friend were both a part of it. She had an overwhelming desire to tell this young man how much she appreciated what he was about to do but she didn't think she had the right words.

An instrumental that Kara knew well wafted out from the phonograph playing inside. She had heard "Stardust" in various versions throughout her life and she even remembered most of the words. The melody had always given her goosebumps, no matter the rendition, but now, in this time and place, it felt completely magical. If only another certain soldier was sitting beside her now.

Her companion didn't say anything more; they both seemed content to remain silent for the time being. She vaguely noticed a few young couples had begun to dance on the limited patio space, adding to the dreamlike ambiance. She must have been completely lost in it all because she didn't even notice that someone else had been steadily walking towards them. Suddenly she looked up to see Jerry standing in front of her, seemingly having come from nowhere.

"I see you've been getting to know this rascal, here," he said, grinning with a nod at Jim.

"Nice way to talk, when I've only been saying great things about you the whole time!"

"Wish I could believe that!" he laughed.

Kara smiled. "It's true. Although there was something about your both liking the same girl…"

Jerry took on the expected embarrassed expression. "I believe that was back in ninth grade. And isn't she engaged now?"

"Maybe. Probably on the rebound from her broken heart over you all those years ago," Jim teased, taking another sip of his punch.

Kara found herself laughing with them just as a new song began playing. She recognized the romantic sounds of "Serenade in Blue" and soon the enchanted feeling of the music and atmosphere began to wrap itself around her again. No one had said anything for several seconds and when she glanced back up at Jerry, he was gazing intently at her. Then he slowly reached out his hand.

"Care to dance?"

A moment later, she was in his arms, swaying to the gentle sounds of Glen Miller in the evening twilight.

His arms…she couldn't believe how it felt to have his strong arms around her. It was as if she were floating. She fought the urge to lean against him or place her cheek too near to his.

"A beautiful song…" he whispered.

"Mmm-hmm."

"I'm sorry I got pulled away just now. It wasn't even important but she tried to make it that way. Sometimes I wonder about that girl!"

Thinking of "that girl" was nearly enough to break the dreamy spell, so she quickly dismissed it.

"It's fine, really."

She wanted to add that he wasn't expected to stay with her all evening and in fact, this was his party to enjoy. But she didn't feel like speaking very much at the moment—not when she was dancing so close in his arms.

In fact, she didn't remember ever feeling quite this way before. *Ever.* It was as if a powerful undertow was pulling her off balance. A part of her knew she needed to be careful of her heart...she had just met him...*that this wasn't even her world...*

"Well, anyway... I'd much rather be right here."

Kara remembered being told similar things before, but they had never quite rung true before now.

"Really?"

He pulled back enough to look at her.

"Really."

She could so easily get lost in those dark eyes which were only inches from hers. She had never been *this* close to him. As they continued to dance, he gently pulled her just a little closer and her head leaned against his chin for the last few strains of "Serenade in Blue". All too soon it was over. He took her hand and led her back to their original table, which was now illuminated by a candle in the growing twilight.

As they found their seats, Glenn Miller's upbeat "String of Pearls" began playing, and two other couples began the easy swing moves on the patio nearby. For a quick moment, she had a flash of the swing dance class she had taken a few years before, but knew she probably wasn't confident enough to try it now. Kara leaned back into her chair to watch the swing steps but soon felt Jerry's eyes on her.

"What?" she asked, turning towards him.

He seemed to be embarrassed for a second. "Oh, nothing."

"No, what?"

"You…you just look so beautiful."

Kara stared at him and before she had time to reply, he reached over, his hand gently covering hers. His words and his simple gesture…they stole her breath.

Kara felt as if they were the only two people here in this time and place, yet she was keenly aware of all the guests milling around them. Should she pull away? Did the others around them even notice and if they did, could they read her feelings? She was thankful that the music would at least drown out the pounding of her heart.

***

Kara blinked the sleep from her eyes. She stretched her arms overhead with a yawn, and then turned over on the mattress, letting all the memories from the night before come flooding back to her. And with them, all the tender emotions, as well.

Because of the late hour the night before, she and Jerry had only taken a short stroll after the party had ended but the time had felt sweet. They talked a little and during their stroll, he had held her hand.

She sleepily basked in the images of the evening for a few more minutes before finally forcing herself to sit up. She wasn't sure what time it was exactly. Mrs. Jeffers had told her she would try to find her an extra alarm clock soon. Straining her ears, she listened for sounds of the family stirring but all she heard was an occasional trill of a bird.

She looked around for her robe, wishing she didn't have to creep past everyone to get to the shower each morning. She spotted it a few feet away and quickly slipped it on. *Strange that no one seemed to be up yet.* She noticed by the way the sunlight slanted through the windows that it must be late in the morning.

As she tied the robe more tightly about her, the thought shot through her once again that she might come down the attic stairs and find herself back in her original time. But there was a difference this time: now, this thought was teamed with a jolt of panic. What if the family she had almost come to think of as her own suddenly vanished from her life? And she had no chance of saying good-bye?

But more than that, the idea of never seeing Jerry again filled her with a strange loneliness—too deep to even try and define. A part of her wanted to scurry down to relieve her fears and the other part was too afraid it might be true.

Still… hadn't she resolved earlier that she should at least try to return to her original time? It almost seemed an obligation of sorts. After all, this wasn't where she belonged.

Kara tried pushing all the recent warm memories of Jerry away and thought back to the moments when everything first changed. She knew it had happened the second she had slipped on the watch. She had assumed that it must be inside the trunk now, here in the past. After all, that's where she'd found it. But now she was beginning to wonder...to remember...

She had thrown it off as everything had gone spinning around her. Even though she was now in the past, perhaps it could be laying somewhere outside the trunk. Why hadn't she thought about this before now? But then, there had been so much to think about and take in…

She moved towards the area behind the partition, her feet like lead. What would she do if she actually found the watch now? Almost reluctantly, she scanned the floorboards where it might have landed but she saw no sign of it. Kara let her breath out. She knew she should be feeling disappointment, not relief.

As she walked toward the attic door, she wondered, though...what if the stillness of the house meant she had already returned to her time? It suddenly seemed all too possible and her heart began to beat faster. She headed toward the door, nearly tripping on the steps as she hurried down. Peering around the corner, her robe tied tightly around her, she looked for any signs of life and then took a few faltering steps inside.

"Jerry?" No answer. "Mrs. Jeffers, are you here?"

Trying to stifle the growing panic, she kept moving. She was just passing through the...*the kitchen*!

With a wave of relief, Kara stopped and looked around. The kitchen looked just as she had left it the night before. She nearly collapsed with relief right into the nearby chair. She thought there couldn't be a lovelier red, vinyl dinette chair in all the world!

But where was everyone? She promptly stood again, intent on searching the other rooms. She glanced up at the ticking clock on the mantle in the living room and saw that it was a little past seven. Today would be a school and workday, and usually Mrs. Jeffers was even up by now. But then, they *had* just entertained a huge gathering last night, Kara remembered.

Satisfied that everyone must be sleeping in, she decided to at least begin getting ready for the day.

Heading up the staircase, she was continuously relieved as she passed pictures that the Jeffers family kept on the walls. She still hadn't heard a sign of anyone yet. She would feel so much easier if she'd just see someone...

A crazy thought hovered on the edge of her brain. *Had the house returned to the present day without them?* A shudder passed over her shoulders. At the top of the stairs, her feet quickened their pace. She stopped short at all the closed doors, too afraid to knock on any of them.

Then—like music to her ears—the sound of a shower could be heard from the bathroom. She felt her lungs fill with breath again just as a bedroom door opened and Mrs. Jeffers appeared in the hallway.

"Oh, Kara! Sorry, but you startled me!" Then she looked into her eyes quizzically. "You look a little pale; is everything all right?"

Kara nodded. "Yes...it is now."

"Are you waiting for the shower?"

"I...no. Yes. I mean, there's no hurry."

The woman studied her a moment longer. She wore almost the same expression her grandmother used to have when Kara was little and had turned down her homemade brownies. For a second, she almost expected her to feel her forehead with the back of her hand, but instead, her face relaxed into a smile.

"Well, we're all a little slow this morning, I'm afraid. I'm just now going to start breakfast," she said, heading downstairs. She paused on the second step down. "It was such a nice party, wasn't it?" She seemed to be thinking it out loud as much as she was asking Kara.

"Yes, it really was." Kara's heartbeat began finally settling down.

Mrs. Jeffers nodded and continued down the stairs.

"I'll be right down to help you in a few minutes after I've freshened up a bit," Kara promised.

About twenty minutes later, she was back in the kitchen, true to her word, though her mind still felt a little dazed as she went about the tasks. Pouring hand-squeezed orange juice into glasses, carrying plates from here to there...There had been little time to reflect on all of her mixed emotions.

"Good morning," a voice said behind her.

Kara jumped, sending a platter piled with toast nearly careening to the floor. She was able to steady it with only one piece sliding off. It landed down by her feet, butter side down.

"Oh, I'm so sorry, Kara..." Jerry bent down to retrieve the wayward toast as she carefully set the platter onto the dinette table. "I didn't mean to startle you like that!

Too embarrassed to say anything, though she wasn't sure why, she simply stood there, feeling like an idiot. His face wore a kind and tender expression which should have helped—but it didn't.

"It's...it's okay, really," she muttered. "I guess I'm just feeling a little jumpy this morning."

He paused for a second, then said,

"I was thinking of taking a little walk by the creek today. I wondered if you might like to join me."

Kara blinked. Off to the side, Mrs. Jeffers seemed to be busying herself, leaning over the skillet of scrambled eggs, but she couldn't help but wonder if she was all too aware of their conversation.

"I...I'm not sure if your mother will need me..."

Without even looking up from her task, his mother replied, "No, you two run along after breakfast. It's too nice of a day to go to waste."

Kara looked from her direction and then back again to where Jerry stood waiting. His expression remained quietly hopeful.

"Well, I guess that settles it!" she laughed.

"Good." His smile melted what was left of her previous awkwardness. "How about we head over there right after breakfast."

***

Past one and two-story houses, they stepped beside each other down the sidewalk, while the occasional automobile motored by. As they made their way through the residential district, rose and hydrangea bushes entangled gates and trellises and their fragrances seemed to greet them welcomingly.

Kara was wearing a simple little blue checkered dress that his mother had quickly made over to her size. She had done so in nearly a matter of minutes before presenting it to her that morning. Kara thought there seemed to be no end to her sewing capabilities, or her kindness.

Meanwhile, Kara was learning to style her own hair more easily for everyday wear. Today she wore it with a simple side part and upward sweep— a sort of modest victory roll.

"I'm glad you decided to join me," Jerry was saying. "It's not often I get to show someone the creek for the first time. Not that it's anything special, really…but it is pretty. Peaceful."

She sent him a sideways glance. Something in his voice was missing. *Was he acting just a tad bit distant with her now?* Maybe it was just her imagination.

"How far away is it?" she ventured.

"Just a few miles out, on the other side of that hill."

Her eyes followed to where he was pointing and noticed the grassy slope in the distance.

"There are some farms out that way, some orchards and meadows." He suddenly glanced down at her shoes. "I'm glad you're not in high heels. Say, they look familiar... aren't those Betty's saddle shoes?"

She gave a sheepish laugh. "Yes. When you left the room, she and I were finishing up the last of the breakfast dishes and she offered to loan them to me. We seem to wear about the same shoe size. I guess I should have suspected then that it was going to be a bit of a hike!"

A small rumble of a laugh escaped his throat.

"Well, not really a hike, exactly. But it's a bit grassy and hilly in places."

He didn't say anything more for the moment. She wasn't sure why, but the lull in their conversation fell thick and heavy over her shoulders as they continued plodding down the sidewalk. She glanced down to the little basket consisting of fruit, crackers, and cheese she was carrying. His mother had thrown it together, insisting they take some food along. Now, she wasn't so sure she'd have much of an appetite.

As if on cue, he reached for it. "Here, let me carry that."

She relinquished the basket and glanced over at him. He kept looking forward, refusing to meet her gaze. She noticed his eyes seemed vacant of any real expression. She looked back to the road ahead and tried to focus on the scenery. If her hopes for the day had been a balloon, then it had been pierced by something unknown and the air was seeping slowly away.

By his demeanor now, she felt as though she might as well have been a cousin from out of town he was showing around. Had she imagined anything more between them? Her thoughts drifted back to those moments in the garden…and the dance. No, there had been something special going on—something real—she was sure of it!

She felt him glance her way for just a second but no words followed. Were they just going to travel all the way to the creek like this— in distant silence? She tried to think back…had she done or said something terribly wrong? Originally, she had even thought he might take her hand as he did the evening before…but now, he acted as though he barely knew her.

They were heading away from most of the houses as he led the way down a simple dirt path. It was situated between an orchard of budding pear trees on one side; on the left, a billowing weeping willow stood, surrounded by lush meadow. A few farmhouses lay off in the distance and the faint bellow of a cow rose from somewhere out in the field. The landscape only occasionally seemed familiar. She knew it had not been like this in her time or she would have remembered it clearly.

Scents from the pear blossoms floated lusciously in the air as they strode past them. Kara could hear the contented hum of bees drinking their fill. They hadn't even reached the creek yet but the spring-covered countryside was so beautiful. *Excruciatingly* beautiful.

So much so that Kara couldn't take this strange silence anymore. She suddenly turned towards him, the words tumbling out.

"I don't understand. Just why did you ask me to come along on this walk, Jerry?"

He looked over, appearing as stunned as she felt at her bluntness.

"I…I just thought you might like to see it. You've been helping so much around the house and had never been shown around…"

Indignation began to coil up in her throat. "You mean you felt sorry for me?"

Silence followed for the next minute. It was unbearable silence. Just the sound of their footsteps on the hard ground beneath them and the occasional breeze stirring the leaves. Then, unexpectedly, he stopped in his tracks and swung around to face her.

"Listen, Kara…" He looked down and roughly ran his hand through his hair. "I'm making a mess of this, I know." He lifted his gaze back to hers. "Feel sorry for you? I suppose, a little. The way you ended up here with no family…it's only natural. But that's not why I wanted to walk with you to the creek."

She stood silently waiting for him to continue, her breaths shallow.

"I wanted to be with you today. I don't know...it's crazy how little we know each other. And yet...I feel as though I've known you for years. But I..." He paused and took a deep breath before continuing. "But I'm leaving. I did some thinking this morning. I'm *leaving*, Kara. I'd be selfish....it's not fair to you— or to me—to start anything."

Hope and despair each swirled inside and seemed to tangle in mass confusion as she stared back at him. He was just standing there—looking just as she felt— vulnerable and confused.

Without even thinking, she heard herself say it, barely audible even to herself.

"But it's too late...we already have."

CHAPTER NINE

She couldn't believe she had actually uttered those simple, bold words. But then, they had only been a whisper. Maybe he hadn't heard her...

Only she knew he had. He stood, staring incredulously at her and she realized she was holding her breath. Then, ever so slowly, he gently reached over, brushing the hair from her forehead.

"You're right, Kara," he said gently. "I don't think I can ever forget about you now."

For a moment, she felt sure he was going to kiss her. But he didn't. Instead, he took hold of her hand and they continued once again along the wide pathway. If she had felt any twinge of disappointment, it was eclipsed by other things—his words and the way he had looked into her eyes. There was a different kind of silence now, a comfortable kind that no longer felt uncertain. The soothing warmth of his hand covering hers made the countryside beautiful again—the same beauty that only moments ago had felt agonizing.

They turned off the dirt road and began climbing the grass-covered hill. Tiny wild daisies dotted the green here and there, with a few small trees that grew up the side of the slope. The warm sun was rising higher overhead, making the occasional breeze welcome.

"Tired yet?" He broke the silence.

"No, not at all." She glanced his way and smiled. "Springtime seems to give me energy. And it's so beautiful out here."

He nodded, looking over at her with what seemed like admiration, still holding her hand. "Well, I'm glad you think so. I've come out here as long as I can remember. My friends and I would play in the creek every summer when I was growing up. But lately, I've taken to coming out this way alone to think. Sometimes to pray."

As they reached what looked like the top of the hill, he stopped.

"Turn around, Kara, and look behind us."

The plateau they were standing on was just high enough to present a serene view below, reminding Kara of some of the beautiful paintings she had seen in a museum. From where they stood, she could see most of the small town below them. It was *her* town, but it hadn't expanded and sprawled out as of yet. It was nestled between outlying farms, their plowed fields dotted with sprouting green color. To one side was the orchard they had passed and off in the distance, what looked like wild fields interrupted by a grove of oak trees. Farther out on the horizon, she could see evergreens and beyond that, mountainous terrain still holding onto the sprinkles of last winter's snow.

"So beautiful..." She felt a poignant tug towards this pristine landscape of farmland. If only it had looked this way in her lifetime.

He nodded. "You would think I'd be tired of seeing this same countryside all my life. Well, maybe I did take it a little for granted a few years back. But not anymore. And now...I just wish I never had to leave it." He let out a hollow laugh. "Maybe if I stare at it long enough, it will become imprinted on my mind. Like a photograph on a wall."

She tore her gaze away from the valley to look back up at him, forgetting all about herself. His expression pulled at her heart.

"It must be so hard to say good-bye to all this."

After a few seconds, he turned back to look at her, his eyes lingering on her loosely back-swept hair that fell over her shoulders. He once again reached over to tuck a strand gently behind her ear.

"You don't know the half of it."

Kara couldn't seem to move. A part of her wanted to turn on her heels and run. Run as fast as she could from him and all this emotion pummeling through her.

And run from this world—a world that was so much more real and colorful than any other world she ever remembered...yet couldn't quite fully live. She told herself to break away from this spell and tear off down the hill while she still could.

But she didn't. He leaned slowly toward her and his lips lightly touched hers. A tender, delicate, brief kiss and then he was looking into her eyes again.

"Kara, I...I'm sorry. I didn't plan on this... on any of this."

Her emotions reeled. "What do you mean?"

But instead of turning away as she suddenly feared, he pulled her close, his voice a husky whisper. "I never meant to fall in love with you."

When she heard him say those words, she realized that the same was hopelessly true for her. But it *was* hopeless! In so many ways, *it was all hopeless.* What future could they possibly have?

The two of them remained holding one another at the edge of the view for the longest time. It was as if they both felt the unknown to be so vast that they were too afraid to let go. Only she knew he didn't understand just how big a chasm actually separated them—it was so much more than the war itself. And how could she even begin to possibly tell him?

As they continued slowly heading down the other side of the hill toward the creek, Kara's mind whirled softly, gathering and spinning like autumn leaves caught in a tiny whirlwind. There were so many things to consider that she couldn't seem to hold onto just one.

Several thoughts persistently rose above the others. She owed him the knowledge of where she had come from. It just wasn't fair to him otherwise. More than that, she wanted him to truly know and understand the real her. How could that ever happen when she always had to be hiding and evading the truth?

Then, the practical questions followed. What would happen to her after he left in a few days? What would she do? Worst of all, what if something horrible happened and he never came back? That possibility was the hardest to face of all, but she knew she had to.

"We're just about there. You might be able to hear the creek now." He glanced her way, warmly.

She was grateful for the interruption from her jumbled thoughts. Even with the comfort of him by her side, the whirlwind of different scenarios had begun to swirl with intensity. Deep down, she knew she couldn't decide anything right now. They had this day together; she should try to quit fretting and simply enjoy it. At least nothing could ever take this time away from them.

She let the crazy whirlwind fade as the leaves inside her head floated softly back to the ground...at least for the time being.

"Hear it now?" Jerry asked, expectantly, and she realized she had never replied.

"Yes, is it behind those trees?"

He nodded. "Right inside the woods."

When Jerry had first asked her if she wanted to come with him to see the creek, she hadn't given the location very much thought. Everything here in this time seemed so different to Kara; it was sometimes easy to forget this was truly where she had grown up. Now she began to study her surroundings as if trying to remember what she had known.

A realization dawned on her that this creek—the one Jerry loved so much— must be the same little creek behind the condos on the outskirts of her town. It wasn't much of a creek that she remembered, but then, she rarely saw it. It wound behind the backside of the two-story condominium, making a picturesque setting for the residents there. Kara had seen it just a few times but there were never many reasons to go that way.

All of this…it was barely recognizable to her. Kara swung around, briefly glancing in each direction. A connection began to form. *Right here would be Callen's Market, with the coffee shop next door… and all the other little businesses that clustered around it.* She stared with wonder at the serene countryside, hardly believing it could be the paved roads and businesses she knew.

"What are you looking at over there that's so amazing?" Jerry asked her.

"Oh...nothing, really. Just admiring all the natural beauty here."

He smiled. "It does have that." He was holding her hand as they walked and she realized just how wonderful it felt. "And what's the place like where you're from? You've never really told me."

She swallowed. "Oh, nothing like this. Well...perhaps a little."

"How so?"

"Well...there are distant hills there, too...and we have our share of flowers and trees, of course. But there's much less farmland and wilderness. The town is busier and more populated. It's still considered a small town but nothing like this. It spreads out and takes over the land around it."

"I suppose this town isn't much, is it?"

"No, just the opposite! I like it much better this way."

"Where is this town of yours?"

Kara hadn't lied since this whole thing began and she wasn't about to start now. Especially to Jerry. She realized that withholding the truth— especially something this incredible—was still a deception, but she didn't know another way.

"It's here... in Oregon. But..." She looked over at him. "I'm sorry, Jerry. I don't mean to be so secretive. It's just that...well, there are a few things I'm not quite ready to talk about yet." She paused, and then added, "And you don't need to worry, I'm not running from the law or anything." She gave a slight rueful laugh but he didn't join in.

"That thought never even crossed my mind."

An uncomfortable few seconds passed between them before he added,

"Kara, I don't want to be nosy. Honest. If something is too painful to talk about, then, of course, I understand. But with the way things are...well, I just want to get to know you better. You see, I feel as though I've known you all my life but at the same time, I don't know anything about you."

He looked so earnestly at her. *Why did he have to tug at her heart so much?* If he only knew how much she wanted to tell him everything! For now, though, the wall had to remain.

"I'm sorry, Jerry. Give me a little time."

He gazed straight ahead for a few seconds and then turned back to her with a reassuring smile.

"Okay," he said simply.

Kara smiled back at him but felt his brief exchange had left a hollow feeling inside. She knew that his wanting to know her better was only natural and right. How could they ever have a normal relationship? She remembered all the stories of soldiers going off to war...how couples didn't know if they'd ever see each other again. This was a million times worse.

Before she knew it, they had arrived at the creek. Alone in this woodsy setting, it seemed so much more substantial and lovely than she ever remembered. And more robust; it rumbled over the rocks as if it had purpose, sparkling boldly in the filtered sunlight.

"I really love your creek," Kara said, simply.

"I hoped you would. In the last year, I've done so much thinking and praying here. It's so secluded and peaceful in this spot. Of course, others like to come here sometimes, but I can always find a place to be alone when I want to be."

He took her hand and led her to some smooth boulders near the bank, motioning for her to sit beside him. The area was partially shaded, with dappled sunlight escaping through the leaves.

"Are you hungry yet?" he asked her.

"Maybe a little. Do you want something?" She opened the basket and began rummaging through it, pulling out a couple of small apples.

"Sure, thanks," he said, taking one and immediately biting into it.

"It was so nice of your mother to pack this for us."

He nodded. "Yes, she's one in a million." After a moment, he asked, gently, "So Kara...Is there anything you *can* tell me about yourself?"

She had just taken a bite of an apple herself and quickly swallowed, looking over at him.

"Don't be upset, Kara. I just mean, is there anything at all that you can feel comfortable telling me? Wait, I know!" He held his apple out in front of them, his eyes suddenly twinkling. "We can start with this."

"An apple?"

"Well, in a way. What is your favorite food?"

A relieved laugh escaped her. "Okay…well…spaghetti. I love spaghetti."

"Now we're getting somewhere!" He was grinning. "Spaghetti, is it? We don't usually have that at home but I hear there are a few Italian restaurants in Portland. And your favorite books?"

She thought for a moment. She did love books. Thankfully, most of them happened to be old classics so she wouldn't run into trouble.

"Let's see… I love Jane Austen books. And Little Women…Anne of Green Gables. Oh, and Dickens."

"Which one is your favorite?" he asked, right before taking another crunch of his apple.

"Hmm, out of all of them? That's hard to say. I do have a favorite Dickens book, though."

"Which one is that?"

"David Copperfield. Did you read it?"

He smiled. "I own it. It's one of my favorites too."

For the next twenty minutes, they sat dining on their picnic and talking about everything—as long as it didn't include her past. She savored their conversation and the warmth of his shoulder near hers as the minutes turned into hours.

If only things could stay like this forever.

Willing her mind not to think too deeply, she watched the ever-changing creek skip and dance over the rocks as it moved past their feet. It was indeed ever-changing…yet as it continued moving and flowing on, it somehow always seemed to remain the same.

The idea of this felt strangely comforting to Kara.

CHAPTER TEN

If only she was free to write.

Back in her old time, she would have tried to process everything by scribbling in her journals. It had always helped to put her feelings down into words. However, even if she borrowed pen and paper now, she didn't feel it would be safe to mention anything she was going through in writing.

She was lying on her mattress, a thin blanket pulled up to her chin in spite of the warm afternoon. She had gone up to the attic after their walk to change, but had suddenly felt exhausted. Maybe her fatigue was due to their long hike that morning, but she suspected it was a bit more complicated than that. Although their time together had been wonderful, the weight of everything pressed down upon her again now that she was alone. There were just too many emotions for her to even begin to sort out—and too many unknowns.

Her eyes roamed the attic space and they once again fell to where the trunk stood silently behind the wall. Maybe if she tried one more time… if she asked Mrs. Jeffers about it, she might even open the trunk for her. And then, if the watch was inside...if it could send her back...maybe she could somehow escape having her heart torn into a million shreds.

What would it be like to stay here forever?

It was something she had to truly think about. Would she miss those left behind? The closest relative she had left was her dad. It was true, they were never very close, but she would like the chance to at least tell him good-bye. And her best friend...there was no denying she would miss Shannon.

Kara's thoughts then began to analyze the practical side. Would she be able to give up all the modern conveniences she had come to know? Actually give them up forever? There were so many recent advances—too many to even count. Internet and cellphones came to the top of her list. To think—if she stayed, she might never experience these and other advances in technology ever again. As she thought over the inventions of the decades, she realized with a start— she might even have to wait a while before owning a simple black and white television set!

Kara had to admit, it all would be a sacrifice. However, the more she considered everything, the more she knew she could do without any of it. She found she rarely missed technology anymore. Especially when had been so much more to think about...

In fact, she knew she could probably live without a lot of things... *if she had Jerry.*

Although this thought should have been comforting, she instead found the realization unsettling. If she stayed—and something did happen to Jerry—how could she remain here without him?

Only hours ago, when Jerry admitted trying to protect them both, she had stood outside and obstinately told him that it was already too late. She almost wished she could take those words back now. Perhaps he had been right when he said it wasn't fair to either of them, even if he was only thinking in terms of the war.

Yes, it was true—they were already falling in love, but if she could somehow leave now, maybe they could each salvage a bit of their hearts. After all, she really didn't belong here...*did she?*

Before she could change her mind, she quickly bolted up from her mattress and resolutely headed down the narrow staircase. Mrs. Jeffers was not in the kitchen when she opened the door, but Kara found her standing on a wooden stool in the living room. A knotted kerchief tied around her hair, she was reaching up with a feather duster toward the top of the bookshelf.

Kara cleared her throat and the woman glanced down with a smile.

"Oh, hello, Kara. How was your walk this morning?"

"It was...very nice."

The memory of the kiss and their conversation flooded her and she hoped his mother wouldn't see the blush she felt burning her cheeks. But thankfully, she seemed too busy to notice.

"Good. How do you like our little creek? I haven't been up that way in a while. It must be really flowing this time of year, even if we are due for some more rain..."

"Yes, it was. It's beautiful there."

"Jerry has loved going over there all his life. But I suppose he probably mentioned that." As she spoke, she lifted a small porcelain statue of a girl clutching a basket of flowers. She delicately brushed the feathers of the duster over her, followed by a quick brush of the shelf before gently setting her back in place.

Kara nodded absently, though she wasn't sure it could be seen in the woman's peripheral vision. Fearing she might lose her nerve, she plunged ahead.

"Mrs. Jeffers, I was noticing there's a trunk in the attic."

A few more sweeps of the duster and then she looked down at Kara.

"Why, yes."

"I...I was just curious about it."

Kara knew she had to tread carefully. After all, they still knew very little about her. She'd hate for them to think she was trying to snoop for valuables or something! Kara remembered all too well how she had first been seen coming down from that attic. She hoped a similar memory might not cause any concern in Mrs. Jeffers now. She cherished their trust and growing friendship too much.

"It's just that… it's the only thing stored up there so I couldn't help but be curious. I don't mean to be nosy…if it's personal…"

Mrs. Jeffers carefully stepped down from the stool. "No, Kara, not at all! It's just I hadn't thought about that trunk in a long time. I was trying to remember just now what was actually stored in there." She picked up the stool and headed into the kitchen, motioning Kara to follow as she went on. "I'm afraid that it really isn't storing anything all that special, though. At least from what I can recall."

Kara paused at the threshold of the kitchen, watching her place the stool and duster in the closet before wiping her hands on her apron.

"Let's see…I think there are some old dishes that belonged to my great grandmother in there for safe-keeping. A quilt she made, too. Maybe a few odds and ends from Mr. Jeffers' side of the family."

"Oh…I love things like that…things from a long time ago."

"Sometime maybe we can go up and rummage through there if you like."

She picked up a few bowls from the counter and placed them up in the cupboard, looking somewhat distracted. "Now then..."

She glanced back at Kara as if suddenly remembering their conversation. "Oh, the trunk. Maybe we can look through it this evening if we have time. But I'll have to locate the key...I'm not even sure..." She glanced at the kitchen wall clock. "Oh, I nearly forgot! I have an appointment I need to get ready for in a jiffy! Would you mind terribly sweeping the kitchen now, dear? Oh, by the way, Jerry went to get a few things at the market for me. I should be home in a couple hours and we can start supper then." And then she hurried off.

Kara moved the broom across the floor in a mechanical fashion. She wasn't exactly sure how to feel at the moment. For one thing, it seemed so sneaky, trying to have Mrs. Jeffers open the trunk for her.

Kara sighed. It wouldn't even matter what she wanted in the end— not if it wasn't possible to go back. The thing was, she wasn't sure what she wanted anymore. She only knew that the idea of leaving now left her feeling cold inside. Maybe her feelings didn't matter, though. Did she even have a right to stay in this world she wasn't born into?

Kara finished sweeping, then placed the broom and dustpan in the kitchen closet. She wondered vaguely if Jerry's parents had any special plans for this last weekend with him. She hadn't heard anything mentioned.

How tempting it would be for the two of them to try to spend every last minute together these next two days...so much had happened between them and their time together was so frantically short.

No, it would only make things harder on us both. Better to try and stay out of the picture as much as possible...let Jerry's family have him now.

"I'll be back in a little while!" Mrs. Jeffers's voice called out, followed by the sound of the front door shutting behind her. Kara realized that Jerry would be back at any time now. And the less she saw of him, the better for everyone. There was already a strange ache inside her and she knew it would only grow deeper in the coming days.

She stood in the kitchen a minute, trying to think. If she headed into town, as well, there was too great a chance they'd run into each other. *Maybe I should just grab a magazine or two and hibernate in the attic for the rest of the afternoon.*

This idea appealed to her somewhat. As she ducked into the living room and began scanning the coffee table for reading material, the front door opened. Jerry appeared, carrying a bag of groceries—and just like that, her plans for a quick escape were defeated.

He smiled when he saw her and she couldn't help but smile back. *Oh, why did he have to look so endearing?*

"I picked up some things at the market. I would have asked you if you wanted to come along, but I heard you were resting," he said, closing the door and heading toward the kitchen.

"Would you like some help putting everything away?" She wasn't sure why she offered when she knew she should simply grab a magazine and retreat as far away from him as possible.

"Thanks!" He set the bag onto the table and, eyes twinkling, proceeded to thrust a large bunch of carrots a little too close to her face. She snatched them, giving his arm a little playful punch. His laughter warmed her.

"What is your family planning on doing this evening?" She placed the carrots into the refrigerator and moved aside so that he could add a few more items to its shelves.

"It beats me. They didn't mention anything. But I did run into Jim in town just now. He asked if we might like to join a few of them for sodas tonight around nine."

"We?"

He closed the refrigerator door and turned to look at her. "We—as in, you and I. At least, that's what I was hoping. In fact, I was thinking… maybe you might want to go see a movie with me first."

He was standing too close for her to think. "I...I don't know. Your family...they probably want to spend time with you." She backed up a step.

He looked slightly bewildered. "Of course, and I want to spend time with them, too. I have the rest of the weekend, though. Mom even suggested I go spend time with friends tonight."

"Oh...I see." She struggled for some kind of excuse but nothing seemed to form.

"Kara, what's wrong?"

"I...nothing. Nothing is wrong."

"Yes, there is. Did I do something? What is it?"

"No, you didn't do anything. I'm just a little tired."

"Oh...I see."

Only he looked as if he didn't see at all!

A part of Kara wanted desperately to spend the evening with him—to spend every last second with him while she could. It was obvious to her that he was feeling the same way. This noble idea of avoiding him at all costs was breaking her in two.

"All right, Jerry," she heard herself say. "I would love to go with you tonight."

CHAPTER ELEVEN

"So, what did you think of the picture?"

They had just exited the theater, the heels of Kara's stylish new pumps making a lovely staccato sound as they clicked onto the sidewalk. She gazed out past Main Street and noticed how the sun had begun fading behind the silhouette of the hills. It cast a golden haze over everything and seemed to mirror the glow she was feeling at the moment.

"It was so fun!"

She grinned over at him, suddenly realizing that she hadn't paid all that much attention to the plot. Maybe this was because at some point during the movie, he had reached over and taken her hand. Or maybe, it was hard to concentrate just being near him.

If she hadn't exactly followed the plot of the movie all that well, at least she recognized the leading actor—even though he appeared much younger than she had ever remembered.

"I really like Donald O'Conner, too," she told him.

"He's pretty entertaining, all right. To think, I read he's even a little younger than I am! If only I was that talented."

"We all weren't meant to be movie stars. You certainly don't see me on the big screen, either."

"Well, if looks mean anything, you certainly could be."

His innocent flirtation made her cheeks warm. The way Jerry had shyly made this comment let her know that he meant it. She felt sure she was blushing so she quickly laughed to cover it up.

"Oh, you're too kind, sir."

As they kept strolling, she absently reached up and touched her curls, as if to make sure they were still in place. It was still a bit of an effort, but whenever Kara styled her hair now, it became just a little bit easier each time. This evening, she wore it down and pulled back with barrettes, with plenty of curl above her forehead and at the ends. She knew she was hardly movie star material, but she felt truly lovely tonight.

The simple, lovely floral dress she wore probably helped, too. Sporting fashionable shoulder pads, the fabric gathered on one side of her waist and the length fell just barely below her knees. Between her dress and her hair, she did feel a bit like one of the starlets she had seen cavorting up on the screen with Donald O'Conner.

Perhaps, when everything was said and done, this whole evening might turn out to have been a terrible idea. For now, though, she couldn't help but bask in it. Here she was—in this completely amazing time in history! And most of all, Jerry was right beside her. If she had hidden away, she would be missing so much.

"Jer-ry!"

The voice seemed to come out of nowhere. As the two of them approached the soda fountain, a rather shrill voice pierced the air above the low rumble of a car ambling by. Kara turned her head and spied a young woman standing across the street, waving at them.

"Jerry! Over here!"

When he finally saw her, he gave a polite wave. The girl then briskly crossed the street and it was then that Kara recognized her. Miss Raven-Hair was suddenly in front of them now, wearing an exquisite red print dress and a large white flower that pulled back one side of her dark hair. Any previous imaginings Kara had had over her movie star image quickly evaporated.

"Hey, Patricia. You remember Kara?"

"Yes, of course, hello. Jerry, are you heading over to the soda fountain now?"

"Yes, that's where we were headed."

"Me, too. The whole gang is there. I couldn't miss the chance to see you boys one last time before you ship off." Her voice was no longer shrill but had returned to the cool tones Kara remembered. They all began moving along the sidewalk once again, Patricia falling in beside Jerry on the other side.

"Well, that's nice. I wasn't sure who all was going to be there tonight."

"Oh, just about everyone from the gang—nine or ten of us at least! Counting *you*, of course, Kara," she added, leaning over to give her a special acknowledgment. Her tone oozed of condescension and Kara stiffened.

The special glow she had felt only moments ago was starting to subside a little. Though Patricia had just intruded on them, she had a subtle knack for making Kara feel as if *she* was the one doing the intruding.

*But then again, maybe I am... after all, Jerry and his friends have all known each other for ages...*Kara gave herself a little inward shake. *No, Patricia definitely horned in on our date!* Something about her mannerisms set Kara's teeth on edge; she could see right through all her maneuvering.

Jerry opened the door to the soda fountain, holding it politely for both the girls. There were loud greetings above the music that poured out from a jukebox over in the corner. To the right, a sprinkling of young people—mostly teenagers—rested upon round, candy-apple red stools in front of the soda counter. A few of them turned to glance their way as they entered but then quickly went back to chatting or sipping their sodas.

Jerry returned his friends' greetings and the three of them headed toward their booth.

"You remember Kara?"

Everyone nodded and smiled, then squeezed in to try to make room. Jim suddenly stood up and offered his seat to Patricia, and to Kara's unabashed relief, she scooted in. He then motioned for Jerry and Kara to join him at the empty booth nearby.

"How was the movie?" he asked them as they settled in.

"Great! How long has everyone been here?"

"Just a little while." Jim glanced at Kara and back to Jerry. "Did Patricia come with you?" he ventured.

"Uh, no. She was just on her way over here when we...sort of ran into her."

Ten minutes later, Kara was sipping a chocolate soda and feeling her mood rising once again. A song had just begun lilting from the jukebox, a beautiful melody she somewhat recognized. "There are such things", the vocalist crooned. There was no mistaking the young Frank Sinatra's smooth, romantic style.

As Jerry and his buddy chatted for a while, she was content to melt into her surroundings and sort of render herself dreamy. Being here in this nostalgic time and place...Jerry sitting beside her at the booth...it was all too wonderful. She relished the sound of his warm voice, his shoulder pressed to hers...

"...and the train pulls out at 8:30."

The phrase jolted her ears like shrapnel, piercing her beautiful reverie. Jim was speaking, but she knew he referred to the train both he and Jerry were taking Monday morning.

"Are you coming to the station, Kara?" Jim asked, as if suddenly aware that she was listening now.

"I...I want to."

Jerry had been staring at the glass in front of him, then slowly turned to look over at her. "Are you? I was afraid...didn't you say you were starting your new job that morning?"

The job at the shipyard. The whole idea had kind of unnerved her from the beginning. She had just gone through the motions of securing it because, well, what else could she do? But since then, she had almost completely put it out of her mind. Especially when other things began to take over her thoughts soon afterward. Talking of it now felt so strange.

A thought flitted through her brain. What if she found the watch and it actually sent her back? Her job at the shipyard might not even come to be. *Wait! What am I doing, acting so carefree...playing at romance and nostalgia tonight?*

Maybe her feelings were all too real, but she was still playing at happiness, wasn't she? Perhaps she should have kept her resolve to keep her distance, after all. They were just putting off the inevitable. One way or another, she and Jerry would be parted in a few days—and there was no guarantee they'd ever see one another again.

She could feel Jerry looking her way so Kara forced herself to finally answer his question.

"Yes, I start work that day, but I don't have to be there until ten o'clock." She slowly turned to meet his gaze and he seemed to mirror some of the turning emotions inside her. Still, he managed a small smile.

"I'm glad. You don't know how much I was hoping you'd be there."

All too soon, the sweet song was ending and just as quickly, a slightly upbeat melody took its place. And with it—Patricia.

"It's 'Tangerine'... remember this song, Jerry?"

Kara wasn't sure how she had managed to leave her booth so quickly, but she was now extending her hand over Kara's soda toward Jerry, her red nail polish glistening.

"Care to dance with me? For old times' sake— before you ship off. It will be just like that time last summer. You don't mind, do you?"

The last question was for Kara but she felt too stunned to reply.

"I'm afraid I don't feel very much like dancing at the moment. Maybe Jim, here..."

"Oh, I'd love to dance with Jim later, but this one's ours. Don't you remember, Jerry?"

He looked a bit confused, so she went on, with confidential tones.

"Jerry…last summer, at the party…we danced to this song and you told me how much you loved the scent of my perfume?"

Kara felt a wave in the pit of her stomach. She could hardly believe the blatant way Patricia was carrying on. With a sudden move, she stepped out from the booth.

"Please, Jerry…go right ahead."

He gazed at her momentarily before finally sliding out and taking Patricia's outstretched hand. Kara then sat back down, thankful they were behind her view.

Jim cleared his throat. "Would you like to dance, Kara?"

"No….No, but thank you." She twirled her straw around in her soda just a little too briskly. The word *brazen* popped into her mind.

It wasn't like her to seethe like this; she had just never been the jealous type. She closed her eyes and took a slow, deep breath, desperately trying not to picture how Jerry and Patricia might look together on the floor directly behind her.

Meanwhile, a male singer on the record first crooned the lyrics, followed by a female vocalist. The song was all about some gorgeous flame of Argentina who had all the guys swooning. The other girls could all see through her charade…and the only girl she was fooling was herself.

That's about right! Kara gave her soda another aggressive swirl with her straw.

Meanwhile, she was aware that Jim was trying valiantly to make small talk with her. She appreciated the gesture and tried to focus, but it took most of her effort as the music blared on. She suspected her lack of concentration wasn't simply because this *old friend* of Jerry's had whisked him away. Oh, it was partly that. Mostly, though, it was...everything.

Finally, the song mercifully ended and Kara looked up to see Jerry walk his dance partner back to her booth. She thought Patricia's eyes seemed to actually sparkle in triumph as she gave a quick glance her way.

Kara scooted in so Jerry could sit on the end this time. As he slid in next to her, his eyes seemed to be searching hers apologetically. But though she had been annoyed, she wasn't feeling angry, exactly—at least not with him. It was all too obvious he hadn't wanted to dance with Patricia at all. And Kara *had* insisted, after all.

Her expression softened and she answered him back with a smile, which he returned gratefully. Whatever happened in their past was past, Kara told herself. And she suspected it had been much less flirtatious on his part than *little Miss Tangerine* had implied.

"I was just telling Kara about my kid brother. He's always getting into some kind of scrape, isn't he?"

Jerry looked his way and then nodded, appreciatively.

"Remember that time he almost fell in the ice?" Jim went on.

Jerry shuddered. "And how! That one was a little too close a shave for me."

Kara was interested now. "What happened?"

"Well…" Jim readjusted himself in his seat. "It was a few years ago. Jerry and I were still in high school and Sam was ten. It was just a few of us—Jerry and I, Sam and my other brother, Johnny. He's just a little older than Sam."

"And a few other guys had come along, too," Jerry broke in.

"Yeah, Stephen and his little brother, right?" Jim turned back toward Kara. "Anyway, we had all gone up to the hill to go sledding. I remember it was January and we had a couple of feet of snow that week. We hadn't had that much snow in ages so we were all having a pretty great time. After a while, I noticed that Sam wasn't around. I mentioned it to Jerry and the two of us left the others and went looking for him. At first, we couldn't find him anywhere."

"You must have been so worried!" Kara absently took a sip of her soda, momentarily losing herself in his story.

"I was getting a bit nervous, I have to admit. But we kept searching. As it turned out, he had gone to check out the creek. That stinker didn't even tell anyone where he was going! It's not really that far from where we were sledding, but not easy to get to in the snow. Maybe a hundred feet away. We couldn't tell which direction he had gone at first because the snow where we were playing had been trampled over. Finally, we headed toward the woods and found his tracks. And then we found Sam. He had gone to see how the creek had frozen over in places and decided it might be a great idea to find out if the frozen places could hold his weight."

"Oh no…"

"When we came through the trees, we spotted him just as he was taking another step. I hollered at him and he turned. That's when one of his feet broke through the ice and he started to go down."

"We ran like the dickens and got to him just before everything around him gave way," Jerry added.

"Yep, we grabbed him up so fast he didn't know what had hit him," Jim laughed.

Kara let out her breath. "Wow, it's good that you two went looking for him when you did!"

"You're not kiddin'! The water was pretty deep in that part of the creek. As it was, we had to hurry and get him home. His whole leg was soaked with the frigid water. But he was fine…he got a big scolding from Mom and Dad and came down with a cold, but otherwise, he was just fine."

Kara shook her head. "Tell me he never wandered off to play in a frozen creek again."

"Well, no…not a frozen creek. But he's gotten into just about every other kind of trouble!" Jim laughed.

"Sounds like he's been a handful!" she laughed sympathetically and turned toward Jerry. "He was just telling me earlier about the time his brother tried climbing a big tree and then couldn't come down."

"Oh, I remember that! The summer before last, wasn't it?" Pointing at Jim, he added, "I think you and another friend of yours had to climb up and rescue him, right? If someone from town hadn't happened to walk by that way and hear him calling, he'd be up there still." Light laughter followed.

"It seems you're always rescuing your brother," Kara remarked to Jim.

Before answering, he took one last long sip of his soda, draining the glass. His expression had changed. "I guess so. So far, he's survived to the ripe old age of thirteen and hopefully past the worst of it. But I guess he's on his own for a while."

No one had anything more to add. The whole place was strangely quiet at the moment with a gap between jukebox numbers. Just the sounds of muffled chatter, glasses and silverware clinking and then the sound of a soda being made.

Jerry abruptly excused himself and slipped out of the booth. Kara wasn't sure what to make of this and glancing behind her, watched as he made his way over to the jukebox. She turned back toward Jim, who gave a half shrug, so she focused on the glass of soda in front of her. Music began playing again from the corner and a few seconds later, Jerry was back, standing beside her.

"Would you care to dance?"

Kara felt her heart lurch. The strains of a gentle Glenn Miller tune lilted from the jukebox. It was beautiful and strangely familiar. She looked past him and hesitated.

"But there's no one else on the floor right now." She wasn't sure of the protocol, but she was suddenly self-conscious at the idea of their being the only couple dancing.

"Please?" he asked, gently.

She slowly rose and he took her hand, leading her just a few feet away. Then she was floating in his arms again, just like those moments at the party when everyone around them seemed to blur into the distance.

She was vaguely aware that several sets of eyes had turned to watch them, but she no longer truly cared. One... then two more couples joined them on the floor. Then she caught sight of the raven-haired friend watching, her mouth slightly open and a look in her eye which Kara didn't want to try to decipher.

As the purely instrumental portion gave way to the male vocalist, she recognized the melody completely now—"At Last". She had first heard it, listening to music with her grandfather, but never had it sounded more beautiful as it did at this moment.

"Hey, I'm sorry about what happened a little while ago. I just wasn't sure what to do. About Patricia, I mean."

Kara looked up at him. "I know. I could tell you were just trying to be polite."

"Well, that and I didn't want her to cause a scene. I wouldn't put it past her. But after I sat back down I kept thinking —she has some nerve! Who acts like that when a guy is with another girl? I hadn't even thought *she* was capable of it."

"Well, now that you mention it, that's exactly what I kept wondering. But then, you know her better than I do."

"Not in the way she…no, not really. Just a longer time. That comment she made? There's never been anything between us."

Relief flooded her veins in spite of herself, but she tried to answer, coolly, "It's fine. You don't have to explain anything to me."

"I want to, Kara. I've never even had any interest in her. The funny thing is, she's acted like that around me off and on, yet she's always going out with some Joe. A different guy all the time. I guess maybe she's mad that I'm one of the few who never wanted to ask her out. I don't know… I may have wanted to be a gentleman a little while ago, but I should never have let her get away with being so pushy. And most of all, it wasn't fair to you. I'm sorry about that."

She smiled. "It's all right." And suddenly it was. "So…you're not completely perfect, then?"

He gave a small laugh but then studied her. "No…I'm honest and I'd like to think I'm a decent guy, but I have a very long way to go before being perfect. So, are you saying you forgive me?"

"Yes, Jerry." Then glancing back up at him coyly, she couldn't help but add, "But as for her—if she tries to dance with you one more time tonight, well… I just may not be so lady-like myself."

He threw her a startled, amused look before once again pulling her back in his embrace. She let her head rest on his shoulder and everything but the two of them seemed to evaporate again.

CHAPTER TWELVE

All she could do for the longest time was stare down at the key.

Before Kara had gone up to the attic, she and Jerry had said their good-nights in front of the main staircase. It had been eleven-thirty when they had arrived home and it was obvious that everyone else had already gone to bed.

"I had the best time tonight," she had told him as they stood by the banister, his hands reaching for both of hers.

"Good. Because I did, too." Their voices were barely above whispers in the dark entryway.

"Are you sure your parents were all right with our going out tonight? I mean, I don't want them to feel as if I'm taking their time away from you."

"I don't think they feel that way at all. Remember, they wanted me to have a carefree evening out with friends before I left. Spending it with you made it better than I could have ever imagined. Besides, we can spend the day with them tomorrow. I heard it might rain so maybe we can all relax here at home...maybe play some cards or something."

The idea of staying home with all of them sounded warm and comforting to Kara. Still, she honestly didn't want to intrude on their time. As if reading her thoughts, he added, softly,

"They think of you as family, Kara. I can tell."

She smiled. "I hope so. I feel the same way about them."

He lifted her chin with his fingers. "And me?"

She hadn't been sure how to answer that, but a moment later he had held her close and kissed her tenderly.

"There are so many things I want to say to you." His low voice had been a whisper over her shoulder. "The way things are for me now...I just don't know if I have the right. But I think you know how I feel."

Her heart was in her throat and she had only nodded. She leaned her head on his shoulder and he held her close, neither saying a word for a long time; the only sound had been the clock on the mantle ticking faithfully from the other side of the room.

Finally, he had slowly let go of her and cleared his throat.

"I'll see you in the morning," he had told her and then he waited as she had rounded the corner to the kitchen. From there, she had walked up the attic stairs, turning on the little lamp near her mattress.

And that's when she had seen the note lying on top of her blankets. It was just a little scrap of paper with a few simple lines scrawled across.

Kara,

After you and Jerry left this evening, I went looking and found the key to the trunk hidden in one of the drawers. I placed it on top of the trunk for you. I don't think there's much of interest in there but feel free to look through it whenever you'd like and I'll get the key back from you later. I'm off to bed now,

Mrs. Jeffers.

Kara had numbly stepped over behind the partition where the key, indeed, lay on top of the trunk. For the longest time, she could only stand there. It was what she had wanted, wasn't it?

Don't back down, now. Even if it's not in there, you have to at least look. She began inching closer to the trunk as she lectured herself. *You can't live in limbo like this forever, keeping up this pretense and living with secrets. The longer you stay, the more deeply you will fall for him. He's leaving and this isn't where you belong.*

With her heart galloping in her chest, she picked up the key. Her shaking fingers fumbled with the lock and finally, she felt it click; then she slowly lifted the heavy lid until it stayed open. She took a deep breath and plunged ahead. Her fingers moved over the bundle of cards that were tied with a string...the linens...she could feel the old dishes stacked underneath.

Tears began to form behind her eyes, like thick clouds ready to burst. She kept them at bay, trying to focus in the dim light. She didn't need tears! Her hands fumbled through various items. Some she recognized some she wasn't sure of. Her heart nearly stopped when she felt something underneath a blanket. Her hand froze. Forcing herself to take hold of it, she pulled it from the trunk.

It wasn't the watch at all! She stared at the object in her hands. It was small and round and seemed to be made out of pewter or silver. *A napkin ring— only a napkin ring!*

Her pounding heart began to slow back to a normal pace and she continued her search. She carefully pulled out nearly every item from the trunk, exploring the corners of the trunk with her fingers. But there was nothing. The watch wasn't there.

***

The next morning the gray daylight crept in through the attic window slowly, almost cautiously. Kara could now hear the soft patter of raindrops on the roof becoming a bit more insistent as she turned over on the mattress. She had slept fitfully and was now feeling the effects. A dull headache crept up from the side of her stiff neck and she sat up slowly, carefully stretching.

What time was it, she wondered? The small clock that she was using in the attic had stopped and it was impossible to distinguish between dawn and noon by the dark, overcast weather. Slipping on her robe, she gave her sore neck a rub. Maybe a hot shower might help.

Gathering up a casual skirt and blouse on loan from Betty, along with her underthings and make-up bag, Kara scuffled downstairs and glanced at the kitchen clock. *Almost Eleven!* She had no idea how she could have slept for so long.

Peeking around the corner, she was relieved to see no one was there and quickly hurried up the stairs to the bathroom. The thought flitted through her brain once again at the sight of the empty house: what if she had gone back to her time?

But no, everything here— the furniture, the décor—it was all the same. As she showered and got ready, memories of the evening replayed in her mind. She would find herself smiling, her face warm, at one moment...then the next, she'd remember her troubled thoughts as she had tossed and turned all night.

It had touched her that Mrs. Jeffers had trusted her enough to simply loan her the key, but there were so many unanswered questions. Why wasn't the watch in the trunk? Would she be trapped in this time now for the rest of her life—with no way back? Strange…in so many ways, she knew she didn't want to leave. Yet, when faced with the reality that she might not have a choice, she now felt a bit cornered.

Deep down, though, Kara had felt a tremendous sense of relief. She didn't know what she would have done if she had actually found the watch and had been faced with the possibility of really leaving.

For about the hundredth time, the relentless tug of war pulled inside her. The overpowering need to run away before her feelings became too strong…the overpowering need to stay and be with him for every last minute he was here. It seemed to be a never-ending war lately.

She heard movement from outside the bathroom door now, reassuring her that the Jeffers family was still there, safe and sound—though, for whatever reason, she had never actually worried this time. She quickly finished a few touches to her hair, fastening an extra bobby pin in place and then smoothed down her skirt. The smell of hash browns and eggs greeted Kara as she entered the hallway and headed downstairs. Mr. Jeffers sat at the dining room table looking over the newspaper. He glanced up and smiled.

"Good morning, Kara! Or should I say, good afternoon?"

Embarrassment warmed her cheeks. "I'm sorry I overslept this morning."

"Not at all! I only came down myself."

She smiled gratefully and hurried into the kitchen to see if she could be of any use.

"Kara!" Betty grinned up at her as she stood, pouring orange juice into small glasses. Mrs. Jeffers greeted her, as well, as she dished up the eggs and hash browns onto a large platter.

"I'm so sorry to leave you with all the work. What can I do to help?" Kara briskly snapped up a spare apron from the kitchen closet as she spoke. "But…I didn't see anyone when I first came down."

"Betty and I were in the garden for a little while. I decided last night that it might be nice to have a late Saturday brunch."

"We just picked these! The first of the season." Betty presented a bowl of fresh, juicy-looking strawberries. The sight of them made Kara's mouth water.

"They look delicious! But I feel so guilty, sleeping in. I guess I had a little trouble falling asleep. Anyway, what can I do now?"

"You can just help carry everything to the table, dear. And don't worry, I made the muffins last night, as well as shredded the potatoes." Mrs. Jeffers handed her a platter of warm muffins. "I've kept the hash browns in cold water in the icebox all night so everything this morning was a snap."

Kara set the muffins on the table, wondering where Jerry might be but too embarrassed to ask. As if reading her mind, he came in through the living room, just as she was placing the pitcher of orange juice onto the table.

She looked up and he smiled at her, his expression filled with affection. It also had a look that made her feel as if he knew her well and the idea of that warmed her.

Only he didn't know her well, she suddenly realized. Not *really*.

She looked down, pretending to straighten the napkins. *He doesn't know me or my story at all.* She hurried back to the kitchen to see what else she could do. *It's not fair to him. Not even fair to me.*

She couldn't avoid him on his last weekend, could she? Not after all they had said to one another. She couldn't...not even if she wanted to. And the truth was, she really didn't want to.

"Well, everything's all ready. There you are, Jerry!" His mother was untying her apron when she saw him peering through the entryway. "Did you have a nice walk?"

"It's a bit wet out there. Don't worry, Mom, I left my boots by the door and changed." He caught Kara's eye and added, softly, "I had thought about asking if you wanted to walk with me, but I couldn't find you and thought you might still be sleeping. Besides, I didn't think you'd want to walk in this weather."

She didn't have time to reply because they were ushered to the table and everyone found a seat. For the first time in a long while, Kara sat across from Jerry, rather than next to him. For the next few minutes, the family conversed casually over the delicious spread. And it *was* delicious. Kara hadn't realized just how hungry she was, despite her tumble of emotions.

Banter came easily for the family, but Kara didn't feel much like entering in at the moment. She found herself avoiding eye contact with Jerry whenever he looked her way.

"...and don't worry about the rations. I did splurge a little while you were here, but we'll get by just fine afterward."

"Well, you shouldn't have, Mom."

"Son, you should know by now how well your mother does when she has to cut corners."

"I know, but the last thing I want to think about when I'm gone is the rest of you sitting around, cutting corners."

"I think I can do with a bit of corner-cutting." His father patted his stomach for effect. Kara thought this might have worked better if he had actually had a substantial belly to show. What he did have was unimpressively trim. Still, Jerry gave a relieved laugh.

"Who all was at the soda fountain last night? Any of my crowd?" Betty took a sip of her orange juice but before she could get an answer, she continued, "And how was the movie?"

There was silence for a few seconds before Jerry answered. "Good...it was good."

Kara immediately sensed the tentativeness in his voice. She couldn't help but glance up and sure enough, he was peering back at her with a questioning, almost wounded expression. She knew instinctively why. She hated seeing that look in his eyes.

"Yes, it was a wonderful time," she heard herself say. "The movie, the time at the soda fountain...all of it."

She felt like such a heel, now, for avoiding Jerry. After all, nothing was his fault. She looked back up at him across the table with what she hoped was reassuring warmth. He eyed her a bit quizzically at first before returning it, but he appeared somewhat relieved.

Betty had been looking back and forth between them curiously before finally adding, with a slight shrug,

"Well, Molly wants to see that movie, so I was thinking of going with her. I'm pretty sure she has a crush on Donald O'Conner."

Jerry cleared his throat. "Well...there's just no competing with that guy!"

Kara half laughed but it came out more of a gasp and she nearly choked on her last bite of scrambled eggs. She quickly recovered, though, and threw Jerry a knowing smile. He met her gaze with a twinkle in his eyes and it seemed that whatever tension she had caused to fill the air was now melting.

An idea began to take hold inside Kara at that moment: pain would come, whether she tried to avoid Jerry or not. Hiding away for the next two days...would that actually keep their hurt away? If anything, she'd probably feel more regret for losing precious time with him. Because the only certain things were these moments.

"I had hoped we could all go on a picnic this afternoon, but it's entirely too soggy out there," his mother was saying. "What would you like to do today, Jerry?"

"Well, since you ask...I thought it would be fun just to relax here, playing games. Cards...or charades?"

"Terrific!" Betty's face lit up. "I've been wanting to try to beat you for some time now, big brother."

"You have?" Jerry laughed.

"And how!"

"Well, sorry to burst your bubble, sister-dear. There's not much chance of that," he teased.

"All right then," their mother laughed. "Why don't we all gather back here in about an hour? I'll have beverages out and warm up the coffee. "

They all began gathering their plates and as they entered the kitchen together, Jerry nudged at Kara's shoulder with his. "Just how good are you at charades?"

"Me? Probably not very good at all. I haven't played in ages."

"Fine. You'll be on my team."

"What? Why?" she laughed.

"Well, there are five of us. Betty isn't that great, either, so we'll all team up against my parents. My dad is right up there with the champs. Mother is just fair and since I'm a close second to Dad, it will all be even, see?"

"Uh, I'm not sure...but whatever you say."

She was smiling up at him in an amused, bewildered way. The uncomfortable mood now lifted, she had a feeling she was really going to enjoy this family time. She suddenly wondered if she should apologize for acting distant earlier. Maybe take him aside and try to explain. Or perhaps it wasn't necessary now...maybe she should just leave it alone?

Besides, hadn't he behaved in almost the same way—and for some of the same reasons—at the beginning of the walk to the creek?

Before she could decide if she should say anything, she noticed Mrs. Jeffers loading a stack of dishes into the sink. "Please let me do those. It's the least I can do for sleeping in this morning and leaving all the cooking to you and Betty."

"Thank you, dear. Betty, will you dry, then?"

Betty was already putting on her apron for the task.

Jerry gave Kara's arm a gentle squeeze before retreating. "See you in a little while."

There was so much tenderness in his voice. Warmth shot through her, right down to her toes. As for bringing up her earlier behavior, she decided she might as well leave it alone.

CHAPTER THIRTEEN

Outside the rain continued to pour with a steady rhythm, but inside, no one seemed to care. Between several rounds of various card games and two intense hours of charades, laughter filled the house while the overcast skies darkened over time. Lamps were lit and there was a cozy, wintery feeling, in spite of it being the middle of May. Kara never remembered having as much fun playing family games as she was having this evening.

"Sounds like…" Jerry shouted.

Betty pointed to her arm.

"Harm!"

"Farm!" Kara tried. Betty motioned to lengthen the word. "Farmer?"

Betty touched her nose to indicate it was correct, nearly dancing with excitement.

"The Farmer in the Dell!" Jerry burst out before Kara could even think anything through.

"That's it!" Betty squealed.

While their team was celebrating, their dad stood up and stretched. "No fair, everyone. That was too easy."

Betty was still nearly bouncing with victory. "Well, maybe, Daddy, but we still won!"

"Yes, yes, I suppose so. Congratulations to all of you, and all that." His tired eyes twinkled. "But if you'll all excuse me, I think I'm going to get another cup of tea and go lie down with a good book for a while. I know when I'm licked. Good game, son…ladies." He smiled at each of them in turn.

"Good game, Dad. Even I have to admit, we did get most of the easier ones."

The rest of the group helped carry in stray cups and Kara volunteered to wash them.

"I'll dry. Gotta' get ready for KP duty." Jerry was already reaching for the dishtowel.

"Well, all right. I think I might go rest and read a magazine for a while, myself, before starting supper." Mrs. Jeffers paused on her way out and looked back at him. "Remember, son, you're to take it easy this weekend and relax. You only have another day here, you know. Then... well, then you'll be doing more than your share of work, I'm sure."

"Pretend I'm on a little vacation here at home, is that it, Mom?"

"That's it." She reached over and hugged him impulsively. He bent down, giving her a peck on the cheek before she disappeared into the living room.

"You aren't a bad little Charades player," he told Kara as they worked side by side on the dishes a few minutes later.

She laughed. "Oh yes, I am, actually. But as I said, I haven't played in years. How often does your family play Charades?"

"Oh, every now and then."

"Your dad honestly is a great player. How he got a few of those titles, I'll never know."

"Yeah, normally he beats the socks off of the rest of us."

After a moment, Jerry spoke, hesitantly. "Kara? You've never really told me about your parents. All you've said is that your mother died a few years ago."

Kara pushed a cup around slowly through the warm suds, making a swirling pattern in the water. Finally, she answered,

"My mom...she was so special. She was always there for me; always a shoulder to cry on." Her mind drifted, remembering more and more little things. "She was gentle. Maybe a little shy. But strong in a lot of ways."

She hadn't talked about her mom to anyone in a long time. Memories came flooding back and they suddenly seemed so near, she could touch them.

Jerry answered gently. "She sounds wonderful. You must really miss her."

Kara opened her mouth to answer but no voice came so she simply nodded.

"And your dad?" His voice was tentative as if edging his way along a narrow cliffside.

She swallowed the ache in her throat. Placing the cup into the rinse water, she swished it slowly before handing it to him.

"My dad was—is—a decent man. He always went to work, came home and gave me allowance and advice." She paused, thinking. "He was nothing like your dad, though. He wasn't one to play games or do fun things very often. He was always a little distant. And after Mom died, he became even harder to talk to. But then... he suddenly met someone. Just months afterward. He's married again now and lives across the country. I never see him."

He turned to look over at her. "He just deserted you?"

Kara felt stunned. *Deserted?* She had been supporting herself at an early age but Jerry didn't know that. She was as much as homeless in his eyes and that thought made her inwardly wince.

Thinking back, she realized she had never wanted to give in to feelings that her father chose someone else over her. That would feel petty and immature. After all, she was able to take care of herself now. Maybe she *was* still young and most of her peers still relied on their parents in many ways, but hadn't the gift of the house made her somewhat self-sufficient?

Yet, she supposed that in some ways, her father had indeed deserted her. She suspected, deep down, she had always felt it. He rarely called to make sure she was doing all right. In fact, she could only remember one time he had been the one to phone—and most of that conversation had revolved around the cruise he and his wife had just taken. *Had he even asked how I was getting along? How I was feeling? If I needed anything?*

The truth was that her father hadn't been there for her in a very long time. Facing this realization was like opening a wound she had tried to ignore. She took the last cup and bathed it in the fading bubbles. "He...I think he thought I was grown up enough to get by. You see, I used to have a job. I think he just became wrapped up in his own life." The excuse fell terribly flat. And Jerry's lack of reply afterward only emphasized it.

To think she hadn't wanted him asking about her personal life simply because of the strange secrets she had to keep. She never dreamed that his innocent questions about her family would feel so searing.

"I'm sorry, Kara," he simply said.

She couldn't tell if he was sorry for her situation, or that he sensed he had brought up painful feelings. Or both. She handed the last rinsed cup to him to dry and she drained the sink. There was a basin of rinse water to empty but he took it from her when she started to lift it and he poured it out.

Kara just stood there, feeling suddenly tired. She wondered if maybe she should excuse herself now and go up to the attic to get her bearings. Silently, she took off her apron and hung it up, but before she could make her getaway, Jerry slowly stepped towards her. The concern in his eyes was obvious. She certainly didn't want him worrying about her on his last weekend home. The pain behind her own eyes throbbed with the strain of keeping her tears in check.

"Hey," he whispered. "Are you all right? I'm sorry about stirring up anything. But I want you to know, you don't have to pretend around me. I want to know the real you—the good, the bad...all of it."

Kara blinked back the stubborn tears.

"And see this shoulder? It may not be as special as your mom's but you can cry on it anytime you want."

It was the last straw. She fell into his arms and she let the tears fall.

***

For the last hour, the rain had grown stronger. It now occasionally pelted the windows as if it were in an angry temper, but inside, everyone seemed oblivious.

"Betty, hand me my knitting needles, would you, please?"

The whole family had gathered back in the living room once again as the Boston Pops orchestra lilted from the radio. Betty brought her mother the basket of yarn and needles from the other side of the room, stepping over her father's feet while he lounged with a crossword puzzle.

Meanwhile, Kara was relishing sitting next to Jerry on the divan. She dared not sit too close—she still felt too self-conscience—yet close enough to feel the comforting warmth of his shoulder next to hers. Tiredness was closing in. She had been taken aback by her loss of composure a few hours earlier, but somehow, she had felt a strange comfort in it, too.

She realized she had been holding on so tightly to so much. The unresolved issues with her parents were only part of it, she suspected. That topic may have been the catalyst for her falling apart, but there were so many things that had been building up inside. It was falling in love…and saying a slow good-bye. And all the strange happenings beyond that.

And so, the dam had finally burst. All Jerry had done for her was stand there and hold her close, but it had been enough for the time being. If the rest of the family had heard her crying in the kitchen, no one mentioned it.

"*Your Hit Parade* is starting soon. Just ten more minutes!" Betty made this announcement as she thumbed through a movie magazine, eyeing the clock.

"Oh, I know, but this music is so relaxing, don't you think?" He rustled the newspaper which hid the twinkle in his eyes but not in his voice. Still, Betty didn't seem to catch on.

"But Dad! You always let me listen to *Hit Parade* on Saturday nights!"

Everyone glanced at her and then she sheepishly looked over at Jerry. "Oh, sorry…we should leave it up to Jerry this time."

"Hey, anything is fine with me." Jerry then glanced over at Kara and she knew he felt just as content as she did.

"Now, when hasn't your father let you listen to *Your Hit Parade?*" Mrs. Jeffers asked, smiling and shaking her head.

Despite it being nearly summertime, the harsh rainstorm outside had brought a decided chill to the house now that the sun set. Kara fought the urge to lean against the warmth of Jerry's shoulder and close her heavy eyelids. Instead, she allowed herself to lean back a little more against the cushion and stretch her legs. After a little while, she realized she must have somehow dozed off. The radio had suddenly been turned up and the blaring of brass jolted Kara's eyes open. She stole a sideways glance at Jerry, who smiled down at her.

"Have a nice rest?" He leaned in close as he spoke so she could hear above the music.

"I didn't mean to fall asleep," she murmured, scooting into a more upright position.

"Don't worry. It probably was just what you needed. But I'm afraid there's no sleeping now. It's like this every Saturday night, nine o'clock on the dot."

As the show continued to do a countdown of the most popular songs, Kara kept recognizing many of them. It felt kind of exciting to listen to them this way— as brand new numbers at the top of the charts.

Several songs into the show, Mr. Jeffers extended his hand to his wife.

"Care to dance, dear?"

Kara was taken aback and completely entranced by the scene.

Mrs. Jeffers smiled demurely. "A pleasure, sir."

As Kara watched them, she was struck by the obvious love they still had for one another. She could never envision her parents doing anything remotely close to this.

"Well, would you do me the honor?"

So mesmerized by the scene before her, Jerry's soft voice startled her. He had stood up and followed suit, extending his hand toward Kara. She suddenly felt a bit shy at the thought of dancing alongside his parents but he coaxed her with his expression. She slowly rose and took his hand.

Trumpet notes from Harry James floated eloquently from the radio, swirling around them where they stood. Seconds before, the announcer had just mentioned the song's title and it dawned on her how well it described her feelings now—"I Had the Craziest Dream." Just as the song conveyed, arriving here had been like a wonderful, crazy dream—one she wished would never end.

Still, she knew that even if she stayed here in this wonderful, dreamy place, she couldn't stop Jerry from going off to war. As they danced, she let her head rest on his shoulder and closed her eyes, relishing his nearness. *If only we could dance like this forever...* As the music played on, she wished, more than anything in the world, that they could bottle up this moment for all time. But she knew that was impossible.

CHAPTER FOURTEEN

The next day should have gone by more slowly. It was Jerry's last full day at home and therefore, Kara thought it should have crept by, allowing each second to be held and savored indefinitely.

But it didn't. By afternoon, Kara anxiously realized that the day was racing by. Even though she tried to keep the impending departure as far away from her thoughts as possible, it loomed over her anyway. She had a feeling that she wasn't alone in this, as the whole family seemed to emit a quiet sense of foreboding.

Kara managed to treasure the morning, though. After breakfast, with the sun's rays peeking out for a while, the family had decided to leave the car behind and walk to church. As she had sat next to Jerry in the service, she listened intently to the message which had been all about facing questions and the unknown. She still felt so confused about everything, but she had breathed a silent prayer for God to somehow find her in all of this.

After they all returned home, Kara helped prepare a light snack for everyone. Mrs. Jeffers had planned a large Sunday dinner later with ham she had purchased just for the occasion, using the last of their meat rations. The snack of fruit salad and crackers would tide them over until then.

Rain showers had soon returned and now Kara had gathered with the family in the living room while raindrops pattered outside. It seemed to be a sort of Sunday afternoon in-between lull; the dishes had been washed and dried and it would be almost another hour before they'd have to start preparing dinner. Kara wondered if the family always stayed together like this on Sunday afternoons or if it was because they wanted to spend every last moment with Jerry. She gave a reluctant glance up at the clock—already almost two o'clock.

"Kara...what time did you say you needed to report for your first day of work tomorrow?"

Jerry was sitting next to her on the divan, his fingers aimlessly ruffling through a magazine as he spoke. More dread wormed itself around her heart. She knew it wasn't just typical new job jitters. Beginning this job also marked the act of firmly planting her feet into this time—for better or for worse—and most of all, it meant Jerry would no longer be here with her.

"Not until eleven. They said it would be mostly orientation and training."

Her voice came out sounding flat. She supposed she should start preparing herself for the next day's training, but all she could concentrate on was how quickly the moments with Jerry were ticking away.

He nodded in response but offered no further comment. Everyone seemed in limbo at the moment, Kara observed, glancing around the room. His parents sat in chairs near one other, looking at sections of the newspaper in silence while Betty sat on the floor, her back resting against the sofa on the other side of Jerry's feet. She had a book, but strangely, she wasn't even reading it now. Outside, rain beat a steady rhythm against the window. A sudden clap of thunder jolted everyone out of their reverie. Betty visibly jumped, while Mr. Jeffers set his paper down and gazed out the window.

"I heard this rain was going to last a couple days. Hopefully, it will let up a little by tomorrow," he commented, still watching the darkening skies.

"Well, no need to water the garden for a little while." Mrs. Jeffers glanced out the window before setting her paper aside and picking up her knitting. "I think I'll do a few more rows before starting dinner."

Kara still sat motionless. She had been momentarily startled by the thunder but her listless mood remained. Apparently, so had Jerry's. When she finally stole a glance at him, his eyes were clouded over with an expression that seemed to mirror the storm outside. He was watching the rain pelt the window and she knew a hundred thoughts must be swirling inside.

After several minutes, he abruptly stood.

"I think I'm going to sit out under the awning and watch the storm."

His family stared at him but he didn't seem to care. He gazed down at Kara now. "Would you like to come with me?"

She looked into his troubled eyes and she knew that she had to.

"Jerry," his mother broke in after another small clap of thunder sounded. "Do you think it's safe to go out right now?"

"Don't worry, Mom. The storm seems to be moving away already. We'll be right on the other side of the patio door." He looked back at Kara. "That is...if you want to."

She nodded and he held out his hand as she rose from the divan. Another clap of thunder sounded, this one farther away. When he opened the back door, the air felt slightly chilly, but the moisture on the budding earth smelled fresh and inviting. The rain was still coming down in sheets as he closed the door behind them and they huddled close together. She waited to see if he would say anything; yet, she was perfectly fine if they stood there without a word. She knew he had been feeling just as troubled as she was, but in his own way and for his own reasons.

His hand let go of hers and then slowly slid around her shoulders so she leaned in close to him. She couldn't help but wonder if this would be the last time they would be alone together like this. The moments went by without any conversation, just the sounds of the downpour around them. It felt comforting to be facing the storm together. The pounding rain splashed little droplets onto their hair and faces, despite the cover of the awning, but she didn't care. She felt content wrapped up next to him.

Finally, after a while, the storm seemed to calm a bit. The rain softened and became gentle.

"Thank you for coming out here with me," he said, quietly.

Kara looked up at him. "There is nowhere else I'd rather be right now."

He had been continuing to stare out at the rain but looked over at her then. "I don't want to leave."

A knot formed in her throat. She just nodded and tears began to pool in her eyes without warning. He slowly looked back into the rain.

"Don't get me wrong. I want to serve. But I'd be lying if I said I was looking forward to what I might face out there. Leaving my family, wondering when— or if— I will see them again."

"Please don't..."

"I'm sorry, but it's something everyone has to come to grips with right now." He turned back to her. "But adding to all of this is how I have to leave you...now that I've found you."

A tear spilled over onto her cheek as he pulled her even closer. Then more followed, one after another, until they seemed to blend into the rain. After a moment, he pulled back to look at her and to her undoing, she saw tears in his eyes, too. Then he kissed her and she returned it, not caring if anyone could see.

As he held her he said, raggedly, "You might as well know, I love you. I don't know if I have the right to ask you to wait for me. But if I come back, I know I would want to spend the rest of my life getting to know you. And I'd love to be able to hold you like this for the next sixty years."

***

She wasn't sure how she had ever gotten to sleep the night before. Opening her eyes, Kara stared blankly from her mattress on the attic floor, the dim, cloudy skies making shadows on the walls. She glanced at her clock and saw that it was already almost six-thirty. *Only a few more hours and Jerry will be gone.*

When he had told her he had loved her, she seemed to melt and dissolve as if joining all the rain puddles at their feet. She knew there was no denying it now—her love for him was completely real. As she stood, huddled beside him, she had wanted to promise right then and there that she'd wait for him forever. But how could she truly promise that? All she could do was hold tightly to him and let her tears flow...and tell him she loved him, too. For the time being, it had seemed to be enough for him.

Now her eyes fell onto the outfit she planned to wear today to the shipyard. Instead of the dresses and skirts that she was growing accustomed to, this outfit consisted of pants, a boyish shirt, and a bandanna to keep her hair out of her face. She wished she could have dressed more elegantly to see him off, but she supposed none of that really mattered.

How am I going to make it through this day?

She wished that remaining here on her mattress would mean that time wasn't ticking, but she knew that wasn't true. Since she needed to grab a shower before dressing, she reluctantly got up and gathered her things. Stepping down into the kitchen, she saw Mrs. Jeffers was already there, but instead of her usual bustling around, she sat alone at the dinette table, slowly sipping a cup of coffee. She barely noticed when Kara entered, and then slowly looked up, trying to smile a greeting.

"Good morning, dear. I was just taking a moment before starting breakfast. Would you like a cup?"

"No thank you, not just yet. Do you mind if I take a quick shower before helping you with breakfast?"

"No, go right ahead." And then, Mrs. Jeffers averted her gaze and took another sip.

Kara had never seen her quite like this and her heart wrenched a little. Making her way up to the bathroom, she refused to think about anything and focused simply on getting ready as quickly as she could. After dressing, she applied her makeup and took one last look at herself in the bathroom mirror. She could certainly pass for a WWII factory worker poster, she thought. But there was no novelty or joy in the realization. She knew she wasn't simply playing dress-up today...or even simply starting a new job. The reality of what this morning really meant felt like a heavy weight that she couldn't throw off.

She took a deep breath and slowly went downstairs. When she returned to the kitchen, she saw that Mrs. Jeffers had now started breakfast, though her motions appeared robotic and stiff.

"What can I do to help?" Kara asked as she reached for an apron.

"You can set the table and pour the orange juice into glasses. Betty, help finish the rest of the scrambled eggs while I see to the pancakes."

Betty had just entered, and she, too, appeared pale and reticent, as she silently followed directions. They all dutifully went through the motions of readying breakfast without anyone saying very much. Before long, Jerry wandered into the kitchen and they all abruptly looked his way.

"Is there anything I can do to help?" he asked.

"No, dear. It's all about ready. Just go in and sit at the table." His mother turned quickly back to her task, hiding her face from view. He met Kara's gaze and softly smiled before he turned and left.

Just get through this. Follow his mother's lead and just get through this. Kara took off her apron and swallowed back the tightness in her throat.

Breakfast went by quickly and quietly. Mr. Jeffers was the only one who tried to make light conversation occasionally, but even he fell silent towards the end. As everyone excused themselves, he cleared his throat and asked if they could pray for Jerry's safety together. The idea startled Kara but at the same time, soothed her heart. She hadn't been around a family who prayed together like this, but it was comforting to think they weren't in all of this alone.

***

The blurred scenery moved past as Kara sat in the back seat gazing out the side window, the glass still streaked by the earlier rainfall. The clouds were now beginning to break away and streaks of sunshine tried persistently to push in between them. Everywhere Kara looked, light danced on droplets of water resting on leaves or blades of grass.

But inside the automobile, the sunlight didn't matter; the blackening skies and thunderclouds could have easily remained and Kara was sure no one would have noticed. She glanced over at Jerry next to her and he returned her gaze, again attempting an encouraging smile. He gave her hand a squeeze and she tried to smile back but her cheeks felt so stiff. She leaned in and let her head rest on his shoulder. She knew his parents had to realize by now that there was a full-blown romance brewing and wondered what they thought. Today there was no sense in remotely trying to hide her feelings.

In the front seat, his parents were still unusually silent, and on the other side of Jerry, Betty solemnly stared out her own window. The only sounds now were the rumble of the engine and the breeze through the driver's half-open window. Kara wasn't sure how long it would take to get to the train station. Unless there had been another station in the past she wasn't aware of, she presumed they were heading to the depot in downtown Portland. She wanted to ask how long the drive would be— yet, she didn't want to, either. Time seemed to be looming over all of them enough as it was.

Jerry broke from his thoughts and leaned in closer to her. His voice was barely a whisper and she strained to hear.

"You know...there's so much I wish I could say to you before I leave. I...I just can't seem to form a logical sentence at the moment. But do you know how much you'll be in my thoughts every day that I'm out there? Because you will, I can guarantee it."

Kara looked up at him. "Jerry, I..." She swallowed. "I know you'll have more urgent things to think about than me..." She felt so muddled and her heart began to ache. She could relate to his not being able to form a logical sentence.

He gave a half-smile. "Well, my mind will have to be focused, that's for sure. But you'll never be far away."

She was searching his eyes, wanting to somehow soak him in these last few moments...his expression, his scent, the sound of his voice. "I'll miss you more than I can say," she whispered.

He reached over and covered her hand with his. The car came to a slow stop; her heart lurched for a second but then she saw they were only at a stoplight.

"When do you think you'll know where you'll be going?" she hesitantly asked.

He took a deep breath. "From what I've been hearing, it will probably be as soon as we get to the next base. They'll probably brief us then. The talk is that I probably should have brushed up on my Italian, though."

They turned a corner and headed down a two-lane highway. They rode in silence again for a moment and then he added, "You know, my dad was in the first war. He was just about my age when he was sent overseas for two years."

She glanced up at his father in front of her, silent in the driver's seat, wondering if he was hearing their conversation.

"I didn't know that." She let the information sink in as the car rumbled along. "Did your mother know him then?"

"No, they met soon after he returned. But she...she lost a brother in that war."

His voice was nearly a whisper but as if Betty had heard, she looked over their way, her eyes clouded with worry.

"Jerry, when will we know where to write you?"

"I'm not sure. But hopefully soon," he said, turning toward her. "I'll write just as soon as I can. I promise." He reached his arm over and hugged his sister around the shoulder.

All too soon they were pulling into the train station and the car eased into a parking space. As they all got out, Jerry and his dad went around back and grabbed his gear from the trunk. Kara then followed the family to the platform, hanging back just a little. As much as her heart seemed to be dissolving by the minute, she felt she needed to let his family say their proper good-byes.

She glanced around, noticing several other servicemen already at the platform. Then she spotted

Jerry's friend, Jim Stevens. He was talking with a middle-aged couple while two boys hovered nearby. She realized they must be Jim's family, including the incorrigible Sam. Kara's heart went out to all of them, too.

As they kept walking, Jerry was arm in arm with his mother, talking about something she couldn't quite hear. Suddenly, he swung around and held out his hand toward Kara. She hesitated for just a second before hurrying forward to catch up with them. When she reached him, he pulled her to his other side and the three of them walked the remaining steps together. His father and sister joined them and they all clustered together. Mr. Jeffers stole a glance at his watch.

"Well, it looks like you have about fifteen minutes, son."

Jerry nodded. "Hey, I was wondering. I wanted to speak to Kara for a moment alone. Would you all excuse us? I promise…it will only be a few minutes."

He took Kara's hand and she numbly followed him about fifty feet away, to the other side of the depot. Standing close, she looked up at him and without warning, she suddenly couldn't hold back the swirl of tears pooling and clouding her vision. She swiped at them frantically and he handed her his handkerchief.

"Kara, don't, sweetheart."

He had never called her that before. It sounded like music.

His arms went around her and his voice was filled with emotion. "I know I said that it didn't seem fair to ask you to wait for me. But..."

A sob escaped her throat before she could stop it. "Jerry... there could never be anyone else in the world for me. Only you."

The words had been impulsive. Why did she let them spill out without thinking? Yet, she knew she meant them; there could never be anyone else. Even if she returned to another time....

They kissed then; a long, tender, yet desperate kind of kiss and then they held each other tightly. Her fingers touched the back of his hair, trying to memorize how real he was. If there was ever a time she might forget, she had to know now that he was flesh and blood, completely alive and true.

After a few moments, he gently pulled away and reached into his pocket, pulling out a small box. Kara's heart beat frantically.

He cleared his throat. "I...I'm not asking you to promise me your life...yet. Though I might as well promise you mine. I don't know how long I'll be away...what kind of shape I might come back in. And you've only known me such a short time. But Kara, I love you so much. I want to give you this as a way of a promise...a way of holding me close to you while we're apart."

She took the beautifully carved box from him and it looked strangely familiar. Before she could think, she opened it with shaking hands. It took a few seconds for her mind to wrap around what she was seeing. It was an exquisite jeweled watch, sparkling in the ray of sunlight overhead.

No, no....it couldn't be! Her mind was reeling. But as she stood gazing on it, she knew it was the very same watch she had slipped onto her wrist up in the attic. The same watch that began everything.

Her vision began to swirl and her legs refused to hold her up any longer.

CHAPTER FIFTEEN

"What is it? Kara…are you all right?"

She blinked, realizing Jerry was now holding her steady in his arms. Everything felt a little fuzzy.

"Kara?"

"I… just felt a little strange for a moment, that's all." She took a few seconds to try to gain her bearings. "I think I'm all right. I guess I'm just feeling overwhelmed by everything."

"Are you sure?"

She nodded and tried to smile.

"You had me worried there for a moment."

He pulled her into a gentle hug and she felt herself relax a little. Until she remembered what he still held in his hand. He let go of her and brought the box back up between them.

Giving a nervous laugh, he said, "I'd like to think you almost fainted because the watch is just so beautiful." He was gently teasing…only he couldn't know how it tormented her. "I know it's probably not worth all that much monetarily, but it's special to me," he told her. "It belonged to my grandmother. We each received some of her belongings when she passed away a few years ago. Betty had chosen something else—a necklace, I think. So, even though this was a woman's watch, well, I took it to...to perhaps give away someday."

She could barely look at it. Her head was down, hoping for the appearance of admiring it, but she focused instead on the rugged cracks in the platform near their feet. She knew he was waiting for her to say something. Finally, she forced herself to look up at him.

"Thank you, Jerry... it's beautiful. Really." She took a deep breath. "And I'm honored. I just don't know if I should accept it...it's so special...a family keepsake."

"I really want you to have it, sweetheart." His voice was tender. "Yes, it is special...but you're a hundred times more special to me. I guess it's my way of saying that no matter what happens, I'm always going to love you. I thought you might like to have it to remember me by."

Forgetting her fears for a moment, her arms went around him. She clung to him tightly, breathing in his scent. "I'll always love you, too." Her voice came out in a raspy whisper.

He gave her one last, long kiss before gently placing the box into her hand. Then he led her back to the other side of the platform where his family stood waiting. A male voice called out, then, and she turned to see Jim darting over. For the next couple minutes, he spoke with all of them, the conversation warm but hurried with hugs and handshakes as they all wished him well.

"Tell your mother I'll be calling her soon," Mrs. Jeffers told him as he turned to leave.

"I will!" Then he quickly headed back toward his own family. "If I board first, I'll hold you a seat!" he called over his shoulder to Jerry.

Then suddenly the "all aboard" sounded and there was a general nervous energy moving throughout the platform. Loved ones were embracing all around them...a few families and sweethearts...a young wife holding a baby. The sounds of muffled tears were everywhere.

"Son, you know we'll be praying for you every day. Write just as soon as you can." His father started to shake his hand and then suddenly pulled him into a strong hug.

"I will, Dad."

His sister embraced him next as tears streamed down her cheeks. Then lastly, his mother. It was obvious that she was straining to keep her emotions reined in. Her face was pulled taut but Kara glimpsed the tears pooled in her eyes.

It was so hard for her to watch—all of it. The heart-wrenching good-byes everywhere fell upon her own grief until she wondered how she was even able to breath. She had been hanging back again slightly, but Jerry sought her with his eyes. She ran over and he took her into his arms one last time, just holding her tightly for a few seconds before giving her one last, quick kiss. Then, just as suddenly, he picked up his bags and covered the short distance across the platform before boarding the train.

Kara and his family stood, staring after him until a moment later, he appeared at an open window, waving. Soon, nearly every window was filled with soldiers. One leaned out so far that it seemed he might fall out, trying to give his girl another passionate kiss good-bye. Then another girl ran to her soldier...then another.

Kara could only stand there numbly, along with Jerry's family. She felt as if her emotion was too deep to even move or speak; otherwise, everything might shatter into a million tiny pieces. The train now gave a lurch. She stepped a little closer and waved while his face became blurred through her tears. To her surprise, he suddenly motioned her over and she blindly hurried to him. He reached out to her through the window and she grasped his waiting hand.

"Good-bye, sweetheart." He said it quietly to her despite the chaos all around them.

The train car was moving and she squeezed his hand before having to let go.

"Jerry…" she breathed as hot tears streamed down her cheeks.

He sent her a tender expression as he continued to move farther from her grasp. The train jaggedly edged along the tracks while servicemen hollered last farewells and waved, leaning from the windows…it twisted around the bend…fading until it was gradually out of view.

***

Making her way up to the attic, she knew she had less than an hour before she and Mrs. Jeffers had to leave again. Reporting for her first day…learning new duties. *Just as if I had no other thoughts or feelings of any kind. Just as if I had no heart.*

Collapsing onto her mattress, she let all the stifled emotion now pour out freely. She hid her face in her pillow, sobs shaking her body as she cried with abandon. She wasn't sure if anyone could hear her, but if so, she knew they'd understand. And maybe she wasn't the only one in the house crying right now.

So strange, she thought…she had known him such a short time but somehow, it seemed closer to a lifetime. She had finally found the one she had been searching for and then suddenly— in the blink of an eye—he was gone from her life. She knew she still had his love but he was no longer beside her. It was as if a light had gone out all at once and now she was trying to feel around in the dark.

She caught sight of the box she had let fall onto the bed beside her. With the pain of saying good-bye, she had almost forgotten it again. Or else it was too strange and terrifying for her mind to lay hold of.

Slowly sitting up and taking it into her hands, she thought about how she had searched in vain to find this very watch, thinking it might be able to take her back to her own time. Was this a sign that it was now time for her to go?

Her heart ached at the very thought. How could she leave him now, after what they said to one another? At least if she stayed here, there was the chance she could be reunited with him. If she left, that chance would completely disappear.

I could stay here and work...maybe even continue to live here with the family. Perhaps pay a little rent and keep helping them around the house...

Her hand fingered the box.

But this isn't my original time, the time I was born into...And I'd never again see those I left behind.

Her fingers played with the small latch on the box.

Even if something happened to Jerry, perhaps I could still learn to live here in this time...But, no, he has to come back...

The latch opened beneath her fingers.

As she stared down at the ornate watch inside, she remembered Jerry's tender expression when he gave it to her, only a few hours earlier. He longed for her to wear it while he was away, but staring at it now, she was afraid to as much as touch it, not knowing what it had the power to do. She remained there on the mattress for much too long. How could she decide her whole future in a moment—especially in this vulnerable state she was in?

She inhaled a jagged breath; then snapped the box closed.

Not yet...I can't make any decisions yet...

She walked over and placed the box on top of the trunk and turned to go. For now, she'd report for work, just as she had planned. She'd go through the motions and maybe in the process, her time working might serve to occupy her mind. She dried her wet cheeks, and then resolutely headed downstairs.

In the main part of the house, the only person around was Mr. Jeffers, who sat at the dining room table, sorting through some papers. He glanced up to say a quiet hello as she came through, but then he quickly went back to concentrating on his work. Kara continued upstairs to the bathroom, taking time to freshen her makeup before returning to the kitchen.

She wasn't hungry but decided she should probably pack a little something to eat later at the shipyard. She had just finished placing a sandwich and a small apple into a sack when Mrs. Jeffers came over.

"Oh, Kara, I'm glad you thought of packing that. It completely slipped my mind."

"It's my responsibility—you shouldn't have to worry about me…especially right now," Kara answered softly. She couldn't help but notice how red and puffy the woman's eyes appeared. *I wonder if mine look the same...*

"Are you all ready?"

Kara nodded. She just wished the grief and longing didn't keep washing over her in waves every so often. It was obvious that Jerry's family was struggling, too, but somehow they seemed to be managing better. Maybe they weren't facing a brand new job on top of their pain as she was, yet, Jerry was actually their son. And then she reminded herself that—along with all of this—she was also facing something they would never believe possible.

She gathered her things and the two of them headed toward the front door.

"Good luck with your job, Kara!" Mr. Jeffers called out, looking up briefly.

Kara turned and smiled. "Thank you."

A few minutes later, as the car pulled out, Mrs. Jeffers finally spoke again, not taking her eyes off the road.

"Are you going to be all right, Kara?"

"I think so."

The woman nodded and after a moment, continued, "I hope so. I have seen how much you and Jerry obviously mean to each other."

Kara wasn't sure how to reply. She knew that if there had been any doubt about their budding romance, it had become obvious today. But Kara had never addressed the subject with Jerry's mother before and she felt her cheeks begin to flush.

"We...it all happened so fast. But yes...he means so much to me." She knew she was stammering and if she wasn't careful, her voice might start wavering just talking about him. "Did...did Jerry say anything to you?" Kara asked.

"Just a couple things. But even before today, it had been plain to see what was happening between you two."

"What exactly did he say...if you don't mind my asking?"

"He said that you had become very special to him. He knew it had happened quickly but he felt quite sure about his feelings. He spoke briefly about it a few days ago to his father and me."

Kara suddenly realized how much their approval meant to her. "And is it all right? With you and Mr. Jeffers, I mean."

The woman glanced over at her for a second, her expression softening, before returning to focus straight ahead. However, her words weren't at all what Kara expected to hear.

"It's interesting...we've known you such a short time—and known so little about you, too. On top of that, remember, we met you in kind of strange circumstances."

Kara pulled her jacket more tightly around her chest. Hearing her words, she realized she couldn't blame his parents at all if they didn't approve, yet she wanted their blessing more than anything. All this time, Mrs. Jeffers had never shown any real suspicion—only kindness. Had it been a pretense?

"So, when we saw what was happening between you two," she went on. "And then Jerry spoke to us, I'll admit we might have had a few concerns. Only...I don't know...I guess you could say, we felt as if we *should* have concerns." She glanced over at Kara again briefly. "However, our instincts tell us you are a genuine, kind person and we've all come to care about you a great deal. It's obvious that the feelings you and Jerry have for one another are very real. So, yes, Kara...it's all right with us."

Kara realized she had been partially holding her breath. "That means the world to me."

She wanted to say so much more. She wanted to tell her how she completely understood their concerns, yet how grateful she was for their acceptance. How she had never before believed in love at first sight but knew with all her being that her love for him was real.

However, she couldn't seem to articulate very much at all today so all these thoughts remained unspoken.

"It's such a terrible, uncertain time right now," Mrs. Jeffers went on to say. "It's so hard to plan anything, much less let romance bloom naturally. Just when love has begun, you're suddenly parted. It seems to be happening everywhere." She stole a sideways glance as she drove. "I hope I'm not interfering but…did the two of you talk much about the future?"

It wasn't that Kara minded confiding in Mrs. Jeffers and besides, she did have a right to know. It was just that she couldn't trust herself to talk very much about Jerry at the moment without completely unraveling. She was trying desperately to hold herself together as she headed for her first day of training.

"We didn't really say very much at all. He…he did say that he didn't think it was fair to ask me to wait for him. But still, he hoped I would. And that he…" Kara couldn't seem to find the voice to continue. "Oh, I can't! I'm sorry, Mrs. Jeffers…this is so hard!"

Her sudden emotion seemed to surprise them both. Mrs. Jeffers threw her a sympathetic glance and

Kara fumbled for her handkerchief just as the car rumbled over a few bumps, causing her lunch bag to topple to the car floor. Quickly snatching it up, she was relieved to find that nothing had spilled out. Then she quickly blotted her eyes, hoping it would keep any more rogue tears from forming.

"It's all right, dear... I know..." Her voice sounded as if she was trying not to cry as well. "All I can say for now is that if it is meant to be, you two will be together again one day."

If only she could believe this. She wished it were that simple, but none of it felt that way right now.

"I know this is a hard time for you and your family, too," she offered.

"Yes, very hard, I'm afraid. Oh, I'm proud of him and what he's doing but he's our only boy, after all. I keep telling myself, though, that I'm in the same situation as nearly a million other mothers." She took a deep breath before continuing. "And it's not the first time in history that parents have had to send their children off this way. You see, my own brother, Benjamin....he was killed in France in the last war.

"I know...I'm sorry. Jerry told me. That must have been so hard," Kara murmured.

"Well, it used to seem like a lifetime ago but this has brought all the memories very near again. And all the fears...." She cleared her throat. "Yet, I have to believe—*we all* have to believe— that Jerry will return to us safe and sound. We have to keep praying and put him in God's hands."

"I know." Kara blotted some more at the stubborn tears that kept forming.

"I don't know why my brother wasn't able to make it home. Some things we just can't see right now. But I guess, in a strange way, it helps me to remember that my husband was in that very same war with my brother. Of course, I hadn't met him yet then. But he fought in the same areas of France—maybe even the same trenches—that my brother did. And for all we know, it could have even been at the same time! Yet, my husband came home. He made it through. So, I have to have faith that Jerry will too."

She looked back over at Kara for a second. "And so do you. If you both have the kind of love that lasts, it will make it through all of this. It's true; you haven't known each other very long. But sometimes, real love transcends time."

Kara stared at her, absorbing her last words.

Finally, she slowly turned her attention to the scenery moving past them. The secluded farmland and occasional forest they had been driving through at first had long ago given way to a more urban setting and heavier traffic. She could see the skyline of Portland looming in the distance, though much different than she remembered. If she hadn't been so nervous and emotional, she might have been more fascinated by the changes in everything. As it was, though, she barely noticed them.

"I nearly forgot to tell you," Mrs. Jeffers was saying now after a long stretch of silence. Kara glanced in her direction, waiting for her to continue. "Actually, I haven't even told Jerry this, yet. After talking it over with Mr. Jeffers, I've decided to look into taking a job at the shipyard myself!"

"You?"

"Yes, me." She laughed. "I want to do my part, too, especially with Jerry now enlisted. I don't need to be home all the time, anymore. Oh, I know I was already volunteering at the Red Cross but with his going overseas, I suddenly wanted to do more. I kept hearing how women of all ages everywhere are working in factories and shipyards. So I thought why can't I? Anyway, I'm going to inquire about it this morning when we arrive."

Kara stared over at her, incredulously. "I had no idea, Mrs. Jeffers. I think it's…it's a wonderful idea!"

"Thank you. And of course, it makes sense, now, doesn't it? Both of us going to the same place for work every day."

Kara had wondered how she was going to manage the transportation back and forth to work. She knew Mrs. Jeffers couldn't continue to do this—it was much too far. Unless they had planned to loan her the use of the car. She just hadn't thought that far ahead and no one had even discussed it. But knowing, now, that Mrs. Jeffers might be working at the shipyard with her made her feel a little less uneasy about it all.

Before she knew it, they were pulling into a parking space. Kara stepped out of the car, pausing to look around as the noise of machinery echoed nearby. Everyone seemed to be going about their business and all of them appeared to know exactly what they were doing. Kara knew she was supposed to go to the personnel office but had no idea what the rest of the day would look like. The clanging against metal and jolts of machinery seemed to both clash, yet strangely blend with the calls of seagulls overhead.

She couldn't help but feel a bit like a little girl on her first day of school. As if reading her mind, Mrs. Jeffers assumed the motherly role and smiled, reassuringly.

"You'll do fine, Kara. Come on; let's go help Jerry win a few battles."

CHAPTER SIXTEEN

Every muscle was sore and her feet were throbbing. Besides the physical demands, Kara had spent the last six hours trying to learn and absorb a thousand things—all on the heels of saying good-bye to the one she loved. There didn't seem to be anything left of her now. She had just been able to eat a few bites of dinner before dragging herself up to bed. Now she was lying, sprawled on the mattress under a blanket, while sleep began closing in.

Somehow, Kara had made it through the entire day. It had been extremely hard in some ways but mercifully distracting, as well. At first, everything had seemed so intimidating. She soon realized, though, that many had never even worked outside the home before. Yet, by the time their first training shift had ended, everyone in her small group had actually learned to weld.

Kara knew she should have had the advantage over the other women, having grown up in a completely different era. In her case, though, it didn't make the slightest difference. Working with tools had never remotely interested her; she barely knew a monkey wrench from a hammer.

She had often wished she was mechanically inclined, though— especially as a home-owner at such an early age. Only a few weeks after moving in, a pesky leaky faucet had caused her to call on Shannon's dad for help. Then later, it had been a call to long-time family friend, Mr. Perch, to check on her temperamental dishwasher.

Now here she was, about to be a part of a team constructing massive ships. It was all too amazing to comprehend! And not just any ships—Liberty ships, they were called. Despite her exhaustion, it had been one of the highlights of the day, learning just how crucial these ships were and the role she would play in building them.

During orientation, they were informed that Liberty ships were emergency cargo vessels, used to transport needed supplies between the U.S. and Britain. They could carry nine thousand tons of cargo, which included ammunition, jeeps, tanks and even planes. Kara realized she would be just a tiny cog in the wheel, yet each part was crucial. She learned that a quarter of a million parts were prefabricated around the country and then welded together in mere days. That's where she would come in. It was mind-boggling to think she would get to contribute to something so vital to the war effort.

It wasn't exactly going to be all glamour and excitement, though. Besides all the hard work, there were other issues to take into account. During training, their supervisor had recited all of the safety precautions and hazards. He was a short, gruff-looking older man whose voice seemed to drone on monotonously. But despite his manner, Kara had hung on his every word as she took feverish notes. Her palms had perspired just hearing of all the potential ways a worker could be injured—or worse. She had never fathomed she could be walking into a virtual death trap.

They had also been given an eye-opening tour of the shipyard. All the various employees of all races, male and female, were working in different departments, going about their duties faithfully among overhead cranes, dangerous swaying steel and the loud clamoring of machinery. At one point, they were shown a nearly finished childcare center that would accommodate the many mothers being recruited. As Kara and her group had paused at the site, images of the class of preschool children she once knew flashed through her brain. Their sweet faces darted swiftly in her mind's eye, but there had been no time to dwell on them. The tour moved on so she quickly pushed the memory aside.

Eventually, she and the others in her group were each handed a large welder's mask. It seemed monstrous, at first. They each practiced placing the huge metal contraption onto their heads and raising and closing the latch. The mask had felt just as heavy as it appeared to Kara. She wondered if she'd ever get used to being enclosed inside it for long stretches. To her relief, she learned they would only be required to wear it for certain tasks while other times, they'd only need safety goggles. It was just so hard to believe that all this would somehow become second nature to her.

She was a bit disappointed to learn she wouldn't actually become certified—that apparently took special training. Kara's job would be to place small welds into slabs of steel so that the actual certified welders could come along and complete the job. Her role would be crucial, though. It was all like an extensive assembly line.

Towards the end of the day, she and the others in her group were told to don their heavy masks again and begin practicing. To Kara's surprise, she actually started to get the feel of it after a while.

Throughout the whole day, Kara had been vaguely aware that she was witnessing an amazing slice of history. Yet, everything required so much concentration that she had little chance of this being more than a fleeting realization as she went from hour to hour.

Finally, after the first shift of training was over, her group had been dismissed for the day. Kara reported back to the office where assignments were given out and she'd been relieved to see she'd continue working the rest of the week under a supervisor. She knew this would give her time to hone her skills before being thrown out on her own.

Her brain had felt so foggy on the drive home that she could barely concentrate on any real conversation. But she did remember one thing—Mrs. Jeffers had told her she was hired at the shipyard, too, and would be starting immediately to be trained as a pipe fitter.

A pipefitter. Before today, Kara hadn't even heard of the word. Mrs. Jeffers had mentioned something about it requiring extensive training and that she'd be starting as more of an apprentice. Kara must have dozed off in the car because she didn't remember much of anything else. For now, she was just grateful she wouldn't be starting this new journey alone.

Kara wasn't sure what time it had been when she finally collapsed into bed. She only knew that it was still light outside as she drifted off now. The birds sang an early evening serenade outside her attic window, the sound of it like a balm to her overworked mind and emotions. As far as the evening robins were concerned, there was no shipbuilding work to learn, no loved ones out of reach....no war. And definitely no strange plummet through time. They only seemed to know this sweet, content music. Within minutes, their lullaby lulled her into a deep sleep.

***

By the next morning, Kara didn't feel like budging. She turned over, pulling the blanket up over her eyes to shield them from the glaring sunlight. She supposed she should be thankful that she wasn't due back at the shipyard until ten o'clock all this week. Still, she dreaded leaving her warm bed at all. A part of her longed to stay and hide under the covers indefinitely.

She knew hiding here wouldn't do her any good, though, even if she could. She'd only spend it thinking and crying a little too much. At least, at the shipyard, she reasoned, she'd be doing something useful—and in a roundabout way, for Jerry.

She glanced at the clock. Only about seven-thirty but her stomach was beginning to rumble and she realized she hadn't eaten much the day before. Besides, she felt a strong need for a long, cleansing shower, so at last, she slowly forced herself up. She grabbed her things and trudged down the attic stairs with aching muscles.

After showering, she put on a clean blouse but had to re-wear the pants she had worn yesterday. She still didn't have many clothes; Mrs. Jeffers had promised to make a few things over for her. But now that she would be working, too, she wondered how she would ever find the time.

One thing that motivated Kara about her new job was that she could buy some material with her first paycheck—maybe even another outfit or two. More than anything, she'd be relieved to finally pay the Jeffers' back a little for all their expenses.

She paused and stepped back before leaving the bathroom to make sure she looked presentable for the day. She sported a bandanna tied around her hair to keep it safely out of her eyes. There was no denying that she truly looked the part of Rosie the Riveter. She smiled with satisfaction.

And then, something inside her faltered. Kara leaned back against the wall, staring at her reflection. *Just how long am I going to keep up with all of this? This charade… as if this is truly my time?*

She had more than just fooled those around her, she realized…she was now fooling herself right along with them. She was almost beginning to believe she actually *did* belong here. Maybe she had successfully put off her decision—but for what? To keep working day in and day out at the shipyard with no guarantee of ever seeing Jerry again?

What am I doing? A headache began to creep up her neck as she tried to think this through. True, she could stay with this family she had now grown to love…but what if she was supposed to go back to her original time?

Jerry had placed the elusive watch back into her hands. She hadn't wanted to think about this—it had been so unsettling and confusing. But she couldn't keep avoiding the obvious sign staring right at her.

Oh, she had to stop torturing herself like this, she thought, desperately. Teetering between two places in time...She had to make a decision once and for all.

But when? Now? A week from now?

Memories of Jerry's warm voice and the way he always looked at her filtered through her thoughts. She already missed him more than she had thought possible.

One month. Just one month. She would give herself exactly one month from today to decide what to do. And then, if she wanted to stay, she truly would *stay*. With her whole heart. She would embrace this time and make it her own. And if not, she would try to return. *If that was even possible.*

A knock on the bathroom door jolted her.

"Kara?" It was Betty's voice. "I'm sorry, but are you almost through?"

"Yes...sorry." She opened the door and then mumbled another apology for taking so long. She hurried past her and down the stairs.

Mrs. Jeffers wasn't in the kitchen so Kara decided to see how she could best get breakfast started. She gathered eggs and margarine from the refrigerator and set them on the table. Then she caught sight of the small calendar on the wall. She stepped closer...today was the 25th—*May 25, 1943.*

Okay. I have until June 25th. Until then, she'd allow herself to live in this strange state of limbo.

For the next three weeks, life became a blur of the sights and sounds of the shipyard. Kara's waking hours were consumed with learning to master welding techniques, finding her way through the maze, meeting fellow workers and long drives to and from Swan Island with Mrs. Jeffers.

By request, they had both been given the day shift, which began by their rising at 6:30 every morning and clocking in by 8:00 am. Getting used to this routine wasn't nearly as tough as it could have been, Kara observed. Summer was around the corner; the early mornings were becoming brighter and warmer. She also had the companionship of Mrs. Jeffers, who rose early with her. On the rides home from work, they'd talk about their day, compare notes and laugh at some of their stories. Kara realized they were becoming friends.

The family told her she should have Jerry's room again, rather than sleeping on the attic floor. The hot weather was coming and his room was just sitting empty while he was gone. Their offer made her feel even more a part of the family—as if she truly belonged. Of course, she insisted on paying some sort of rent and they had all agreed on a small percentage of her paycheck. Still, she grappled with twinges of guilt when she had first put her things back into Jerry's room. She kept wondering what he might be enduring while she slept in comfort, yet she knew he wouldn't want it any other way. And she had to admit, being near his things made her feel that much closer to him.

It was a beautiful Friday in early June when she and Mrs. Jeffers drove home from work, the windows rolled down and the warm breeze blowing through. Fresh air had never felt so inviting to Kara since beginning work at the shipyard.

Many times, especially in the beginning, she had to practice her welding skills in small, closed-in areas. Doing detail work in tight quarters while wearing her heavy welder's mask began quickly losing its charm for her.

However, today had been a little different. She had been given her first opportunity to work out in the fresh, open air. It had felt exhilarating to be out in the sunshine for a few hours, working on the top deck of a Liberty ship. Kara's mood was bright as she described this new aspect of her job on the drive home.

"So, will you get to do this all the time now?" Mrs. Jeffers asked her.

"No, not every day. But I got the impression that it will be happening often. I had almost forgotten just how good fresh air feels—even if it is mixed with a little diesel smell," she laughed. "In fact, everything went pretty well today. I think I'm getting the hang of things now. After two weeks, I feel like I can actually call myself a welder!"

"That's wonderful. And I'm happy to say, I had a pretty fair day, myself. Pipefitting is a bit complicated, I'm afraid, but I think I'm starting to figure it all out. My supervisor is even finally saying a few positive words to me now and then."

Kara laughed. "That's a relief! She seemed to be giving all the newcomers in your division a hard time."

Kara's arm had been leaning over the open window and she lifted it to let her hand lazily catch the open breeze. "Aren't you glad it's the weekend, though, Mrs. Jeffers?"

"Kara...I've been meaning to mention this lately. You needn't always call me Mrs. Jeffers. It seems so formal now. You can call me Marjorie if you like." She glanced cautiously over at her.

Kara stared back in surprise. "But...I mean, thank you..." She tried letting the idea of it roll over in her mind for a moment. "Honestly, I don't know if I could. I've known you as Mrs. Jeffers for so long."

"Well, of course, either is fine," she laughed cheerfully. "But I just wanted to let you know you're welcome to call me Marjorie. We're fellow workers now, after all! Besides, you're also a fellow adult. I may be old enough to be your mother, but I'm not exactly ancient yet. Although I sometimes feel like it by the end of these workdays!"

Kara smiled. "All right, I'll try...*Marjorie.*" It felt so foreign and she hesitantly glanced over at her. Then they both burst out laughing. "Well, I suppose it will take some getting used to!" Kara admitted.

After a few moments, she asked, "Have you decided to let me take turns driving with you?"

Kara had asked her about this soon after they began working but had never gotten a definite answer.

"Oh, yes...well, I was talking to Mr. Jeffers about it the other day." She paused. "Or should I refer to him as Ray?" She glanced over at Kara mischievously.

"No, calling one of you by your given name is about all I can handle, at least for now," Kara laughed. She hadn't remembered seeing Jerry's mother in such a jovial mood before, especially since Jerry had shipped out.

"Well, Mr. Jeffers then. He said it was fine but that you should probably give it a practice run around the neighborhood first. How long has it been since you've driven a car?"

Kara clearly remembered driving home from teaching preschool on the Friday when everything changed. She swallowed, trying to answer the best she could.

"Not very long....not long before you met me." She eyed the dashboard as she spoke, taking note of the various knobs and buttons and the strange, long stick which snaked up from the floorboard between them. Even the foot pedals seemed peculiar.

But, then...how hard could it be? The basic concept was the same. As for the looks and style of the automobile, she had a feeling this would be a sought after classic in her own time—the kind gracing the car shows she used to attend with her grandfather.

"But Mr. Jeffers is right," Kara added. "I may even need a lesson first since this isn't the kind of car I'm used to driving. What is the year and make of it, Mrs. Jef...I mean, Marjorie?"

"Let's see...it's a Chevy Coupe. 1938, I believe. We got it used about three years ago and I remember it was just two years old then."

"You've kept it very nice."

"Thank you, but we don't always need to drive where we're going in this small town so it hasn't gotten much wear and tear. Thankfully, Mr. Jeffers doesn't mind walking the short distance to work so we can use it. He actually enjoys the walks in this fine, summer weather.

"Did Jerry learn to drive this car?"

"No, that was with the old black Model T we used to have. The styles of automobiles have changed so rapidly in the last decade, haven't they? We had that old car for years, though. It took us through most of the Depression."

There was a topic Kara hadn't explored. "Was it very difficult for your family during the Depression?"

"Hmm. There were some hardships, but we didn't have it nearly as bad as so many others. Mr. Jeffers was out of work for a short time. Jerry did just about every odd job he was able to get as a young boy and I took in sewing whenever I could. Oh, and just as we have the victory garden now, I was able to raise plenty of vegetables and do a lot of canning for the winters." She paused, seemingly lost in her thoughts for a moment before continuing. "One season, our whole family worked for a farmer a few miles away, picking fruit along with the migrant workers. That whole time was a bit humbling, but God was looking out for us...we always had enough to eat and never had to lose our house. For that, I'm so grateful. Still...we had to make do with what we had—which meant walking almost everywhere and trying to keep that old 1927 Ford running."

Kara hadn't thought much about what the family endured before the war. Imagining Jerry as a young boy doing odd jobs during the Depression was a new picture for her and it was endearing, somehow.

"What about your family, Kara? Did you struggle much during those years?"

Kara stared over at her for a moment, then away. A strange, hazy guilt fell slowly over her, though she couldn't articulate why.

"No...not too much. We did all right," she answered quietly.

***

"Mama, look! Kara!"

They had just closed the front door when Betty accosted them in the entryway, grinning and waving an unopened letter. Kara knew in an instant what it was and though excitement surged through her bloodstream, she couldn't seem to move.

"From Jerry?" Mrs. Jeffers quickly took the letter from her, scanning the return address. Her eyes lit up. "Is your father home yet?"

"No, not yet. But it was all I could do to wait for you to come home and not tear it open!"

Mrs. Jeffers glanced at the clock and finally over at Kara, her eyes softening. Kara realized she must have looked peculiar. She was still standing near the door, staring wide-eyed and most likely looking a little flushed.

"Mr. Jeffers should be home any minute. It's the first letter, after all...We really should wait..." she hesitated.

"Oh, please, Mama. He can read it himself just as soon as he gets home. I've been holding onto it for *two hours*!"

"Oh, very well!"

After retrieving a letter opener from the writing desk, she led the way to the sofa and carefully tore open the envelope as Kara and Betty sat down beside her. Two separately folded papers were inside. As she lifted them out, they appeared to be photocopies of original writing.

"This one has your name on it," she told Kara, smiling.

Kara took it, embarrassed that her hand was shaking a little. She also felt a sense of awe that Jerry would actually write to her separately. Oh, he had implied that he would but it still filled her with warmth. She was puzzled, though, by the copied look of the paper.

"This doesn't look like it was his original letter, does it?"

Betty leaned over, touching it. "Oh, it's V-mail. I've been hearing all about them but we've never gotten one before now! They say it's much faster."

"And it saves room on the cargo planes, too. I admit, it would be nice to hold the actual paper he had written on, wouldn't it? Still, it *does* hold his thoughts! Did you want to wait and hear what he wrote to us, Kara?" Mrs. Jeffers asked her.

"I...I think I'd like to go somewhere and read mine first. Do you mind?"

"Not at all, dear, you go right ahead."

Kara excused herself and hurried away, clutching the letter. She could vaguely hear Mrs. Jeffers' voice as she began to read Jerry's letter out loud. A part of her wanted to hang back and listen, and at the same time, it made her feet move even faster. She nearly flew up the stairs and then flung herself onto the bed. With trembling fingers, she unfolded the letter.

CHAPTER SEVENTEEN

June 2, 1943

Dear Kara,

How are you, Sweetheart? How is everything at the shipyard?

As for me, I'm doing all right so far. It's strange to be on foreign soil for the first time, especially somewhere that feels as foreign as this place. I never envisioned ending up in Africa, but the word is we won't be here long. I hear some guys have been able to do some sightseeing in other places, but nothing like that is in store for me at the moment. Maybe someday in the future, I'll be able to come back under better circumstances...visit Rome, Venice—maybe even Paris. After it's out of German hands and restored to all its former splendor, as they say.

The trip over here was mostly uneventful. I was definitely glad to be back on land by the time it was over, though. We just arrived the day before yesterday and things are gearing up, I'm not sure exactly where they'll send up from here. I have a general idea where, but as you know, I can't talk too much about that right now.

Although I know you would probably want to hear about some of these things and be assured I'm here safe and sound, I guess I'm buying time with small talk because there's something important that I have to talk to you about.

You see, ever since I left you standing at the train station, I have been doing a lot of thinking. About you... and about us. I had nothing to do but think, sitting in the train car, watching the country pass by the window for those first two days. Of course, some of my thoughts were about where I was heading to and what was in store. But even then, those thoughts were still surrounded by you.

I told you I didn't think it was fair to ask you to commit a lifetime to me when you've only known me for a short time. Or when I didn't know how long you'd have to wait or what might happen to me. It's strange, because I know so little about you, too. I suppose it seems like we should know one another so much more before making such a big commitment. All of these things make perfect sense. But the more thinking (and praying) I did, the more I realized that I could know you five years and still not be any more convinced that I want to spend the rest of my life with you.

If you still want to wait to give me the answer, I will completely understand. But in times like these, with everything so uncertain, I think there are two ways to look at things. Either run from love because of the uncertainty or run TO it.

So, Kara, I'm asking you now if you will do more than wait for me. Sweetheart, I'm asking you to be my wife.

I'm sorry that I'm asking you such an important question in a letter. I really regret not saying all of this to you at the train station. If I could go back in time and change that, I would.

There's so much more I'd like to write now but I have to go—I have just enough time to address this and put it with my family's letter before the mail goes out from here.

Remember, when you write, please be honest with me. If your answer is no, or not yet...if your feelings have changed or you're just not ready or sure, I'll understand. But as for me, I am completely sure and I knew that waiting until some unknown time in the future was just not going to work the way things are now in this messed up world.

Please write to me soon, Darling. I love you with all my heart.

Yours, Jerry

Her eyes filled with tears until she couldn't see the page anymore. She didn't know what she had been expecting to read in his letter but she knew it wasn't this. Her heart was beating a mile a minute. The letter so beautiful, though he had composed it with just moments to spare. And she could hardly wrap her mind around it—he had asked her to marry him.

Just for a brief second, she had almost feared that he might be about to tell her the opposite of what he did. Though he had addressed her as "sweetheart", the tone seemed so uncertain at first. When he had said he was putting off telling her something important, she had almost stopped breathing.

But he's asking to spend our whole lives together!

The idea thrilled her to the very core. But could she *really* marry him? Since she didn't belong here, did she even have the right?

As she leaned back on her pillow, she let her mind wander to what life might be like for the next sixty years or so with Jerry by her side. It seemed too wonderful to even comprehend! It was a lifetime commitment, though. She had to think…She had to keep herself from jumping headfirst. As much as she loved him, this was no ordinary situation. She gazed out the window, barely seeing, as she strove to look past her heart to the practical.

She'd be living through decades she would never otherwise have seen—this felt both exciting and a little terrifying. Strangest of all was that she might not ever see the decade she left behind. She knew her youth wouldn't be taken away; she'd just be living it in a different way.

She couldn't hide from him any longer, though. If she married him, she had to tell him *everything*. It would be such a risk….but there was no way she could live the rest of her life with him in pretense. If she agreed to marry him, she knew she'd have to take the chance that he would still love her— and believe her.

But when and how?

The war would rage on for another two years. If Jerry was gone for the duration, could she wait that long to tell him everything?

This was not anything she could ever explain in a letter—even if there wasn't a censor board. Waiting for him would be difficult enough…waiting to explain everything and hear his response would be torture.

On the heels of these thoughts, another strange concept struck her. She knew what Jerry didn't know about the war. In fact, she knew almost the entire course of history from now until the twenty-first century! Could she just go merrily along, trying to live a simple, happy life with Jerry, when she could forecast the next world event before it ever happened? This new train of thought troubled Kara; it seemed to strip away any sense of normalcy she hoped to have here with him.

All of these problems wound around each other to form a sort of boulder in her mind's eye. It had slowly rolled onto the path between them and she had to decide if she was willing to go around it. Or turn back…

Her eyes fell back to Jerry's letter. Part of her was anxious to write him this very minute. *But not yet.* She'd better wait until the morning. It seemed wiser to sleep on all of this. She needed to be able to tell him her answer with no reservations at all.

One thing she knew beyond a doubt by now, though—she *did* love him. That part was something she didn't need to think through. The idea of going back to her original time without him seemed too painful to even comprehend anymore.

She folded up the letter and placed it gently under her pillow. She had a feeling she'd be reading it again and again.

***

That evening, after she and Betty had finished washing the supper dishes, Kara finally sat down to read the letter Jerry had written to his family. Mrs. Jeffers had told her that she was more than welcome, but that they didn't expect to read her private letter in return. Kara wasn't quite ready to reveal to them just how special that letter actually was.

"I'm going to go do a little yard work before the sun goes down," Mr. Jeffers announced as he came through the room, having changed into casual clothes. He glanced at the letter in Kara's hand as if he was about to say more, then changed his mind. He gave her a half-smile as he headed out the patio door.

"He usually does the yard work on Saturday mornings. I think he's feeling kind of restless this evening," Mrs. Jeffers commented softly.

"He did seem a little quiet at dinner," Kara replied. "But I'm sure he was glad to hear from Jerry, wasn't he?"

"Oh, yes, of course. I suspect things were tough at the office today."

Kara quickly turned her attention to the letter in her hands, suddenly eager to read more of his words.

June 2, 1943

Dear folks,

Well, it's hard to believe I'm actually here, across the ocean and on foreign soil. I bet it's hard for you all to believe it, too—the farthest I've ever traveled was to Texas! I still remember that road trip when we went to see Aunt Pauline, Uncle Will, and all the clan. I sure had a lot of adventures that summer, and most of it was a lot of fun. Well, except for the heat and scorpions!

Betty, I know you don't remember much about that trip— and you had to miss out on most of the fun since you were so little. Funny, how I thought I was such a big shot at the ripe old age of ten.

Anyway, enough of reminiscing...you probably want to know how I'm doing. Our trip over here was pretty non-eventful. Although the sea was a bit rough, there were no other real troubles—at least not the kind you sometimes hear about in the newsreels. Some of the guys got a little seasick, though, and I have to admit, being on the ship made me kind of glad I didn't join the Navy!

We arrived two days ago but it looks like I won't be staying very long. I'm ready, though. I'd rather get right down to business instead of just sitting around, waiting.

I know I'll miss your cooking, though, Mom. I've talked to someone who's been out here for a while and he said that's one of the things he misses the most so far— home cooking. K-rations just can't seem to compete.

Dad, I keep wondering if I'll see some of the same places that you saw back when you were here. After all, I don't know where all I'll end up before this war is over. I guess I should have asked you more about your time here before I left. As time goes on, I'll be sure to describe it all.

I don't have a lot of time to write before the mail goes out. But know that all of you mean so much to me and I'm grateful for everything you've done. Try not to worry. I'll write again just as soon as I can and I look forward to hearing from all of you.

One more thing... Mom and Dad, I know I mentioned it briefly before I left, but our conversation had been so short. Still, I'm sure by now, you all may have guessed my deep feelings for Kara. I know we've only just met, but I can't explain it. I'm very serious about her and I think she feels the same way. At least I hope she does. I just wanted you to know.

Take care of yourselves and thank you in advance for all those letters you're going to write...and for praying for me.

Love, Jerry

She folded the letter and took it over to where Mrs. Jeffers still pored over the new one she was writing.

"Thank you for letting me read it," she said, softly, handing it to her.

Mrs. Jeffers looked up, taking it from her hand. "Have you've been crying, dear?"

"Oh...just a little." She smiled apologetically. "It was a beautiful letter."

"Yes." She paused, laying down her pen for a moment. "Strange, how a letter like that can make you feel happy and yet a little melancholy at the same time." She seemed to be thinking out loud.

"I know exactly what you mean. It's...it's like you long to hear from them but when you do, it makes you miss them even more. And... it's hard not to worry."

She wondered if that was how Jerry's father was also feeling—maybe with a few memories of his own thrown in.

"We wouldn't be human if we didn't worry but we're not alone in that right now. All we can do is wait, pray, and try to keep busy."

Kara nodded and left her to finish her letter. She could hear the staccato clipping sound as Mr. Jeffers trimmed the bushes outside the open window, probably lost in his own thoughts. Heading into the kitchen, she poured herself a glass of water and sat down at the dinette table. She was tempted to run back right this very minute and tell Mrs. Jeffers about Jerry's proposal, but she knew she couldn't say anything until she had time to fully give herself to the answer.

She took a last sip of her water before plunking the glass into the sink, just a little too hard. She was thankful it hadn't broken. She could feel her own sense of restlessness growing and she suddenly turned, heading straight for the entryway.

"Marjorie?" The first name still felt so foreign as she said it. "I'm going for a little walk before it gets dark."

"But...so late? It gets dark pretty quickly."

"I just need to get some fresh air. Just around the block, I promise. I should only be gone twenty minutes or so."

"All right, Kara…"

A few seconds later, she was rounding the corner, passing the peaceful looking houses she had driven or walked by so often. Some she even remembered from her previous time, which had still stood faithfully, decades later. However, right now she had no desire to think about where she had come from. As she kept walking, the early evening spring air was still warm and heavy with scent, while long shadows stretched before her in the waning sunlight.

How she longed to have Jerry walking by her side again! She could almost feel her arm through his...hear his warm voice. How could she possibly endure another two years without him?

She looked ahead, noting that Main Street was now just a few blocks away. She didn't want Mrs. Jeffers to worry, but she wasn't ready to head back home just yet. She kept striding on, picking up her pace until she was going at a fairly brisk speed. The fast jaunt seemed to ease her anxieties a bit. It felt so refreshing to stretch her legs and breathe in the fresh summer air after the smells of metal and fumes all week.

As she turned onto Main Street, she could see Amberton Bijou and the soda fountain entrance up ahead. Memories of her date with Jerry flooded back. She couldn't help but notice there weren't many young men left in town anymore. Of those still around, most were teenagers.

At the soda fountain, Kara stopped short. As restless as she might be feeling, she had no desire to go in alone so instead, she peeked in the window. The sounds of the music and lively chattering seeped right through the windows and doors. The images of the young people inside seem to fade from her view when scenes of her dance with Jerry came swirling into their place. Kara stood there, entranced by her memories for a moment. All too soon, the scene faded and Kara turned to leave. Before she could escape, Betty caught her eye and hurried over.

"Hi! What are you doing here? Is everything all right?"

"Yes, of course! I just went for a little walk."

"Oh, okay. Come over and have a soda," She led Kara by the arm and brought her to their booth before she could object.

"Kara, you know Janie. And this is Susan, Paul, and Tommy. Oh, sorry, *Tom.*"

"Hi, everyone," Kara said, feeling somewhat awkward. "I don't mean to intrude on all of you...I was only out for a walk."

Betty's friends greeted her and then she was invited to squeeze into the booth. Maybe she could still make it back before dark if she didn't stay long, she thought, hesitantly sitting down next to them.

For the next twenty minutes, Kara sipped a cola while listening to the banter of the high school crowd.

Though she didn't exactly fit in, she had to admit it was a nice distraction for a while. She absently glanced around her. Two young girls in their early teens were sitting and sharing secrets at the soda bar. The one in the ponytail turned to look out the window when Kara noticed she looked a bit familiar. Of course, she knew she had seen lots of kids around town off and on in the past month, but there was something especially familiar about this girl. She tried for a moment to pinpoint it. It was the kind of half recognition that Kara sometimes got from time to time that wouldn't let up until she finally figured it out.

She leaned over towards Betty. "Is that one of your friends? Or was she at the party for Jerry? She looks so familiar."

Betty followed Kara's gaze. "No, that's Beth; she's pretty nice. She's two years behind me in school."

"She wasn't at the party?"

"No...why?"

"It doesn't really matter," she sighed, looking up at the clock. "I promised your mom I wouldn't be out wandering around after dark alone. I'd better go. How are you getting over to Janie's?"

"Her father's picking us up in about a half an hour. Do you really have to go?"

The young girl and her friend got up from their stools just then and began sidling past their booth towards the main door.

"Beth...Sharon, come over and meet Kara." The girls paused and stepped over to their booth. "This is Kara—the girl Jerry is sweet on."

The girls giggled then, along with Betty's other friends in the booth. Kara wasn't sure if she wanted to laugh with them or slink under the table.

"Pleased to meet you. I'm Beth Morrison and this is Sharon Carter."

"Nice to meet you both." Kara paused. "Did you say, *Morrison*?"

The girl nodded.

"Her mother works at the shipyard, too. Maybe you've seen her there and that's why her daughter looks familiar. A family resemblance or something," Betty offered.

"Oh...yes, maybe that's it."

"Mother's been working there for months now. Just part-time, though. She says she doesn't worry so much about George if she keeps busy."

Kara wished that the back of her neck wasn't bristling. "Who's George?"

"My brother. He's in the Navy over in the Pacific."

Kara felt a bit dizzy. "George... Morrison?"

"Do you know him?" Betty asked. "He's about your age—twenty, isn't he, Beth?"

"Twenty-one. He's been gone so long—over a year, now. I write to him all the time and we've gotten dozens of letters from him."

"Do you know him, Kara?" Betty asked again.

"I...I don't know." She tried not to keep staring at Beth but she couldn't help it. Suddenly, there was no doubt in her mind.

"Well, I'd better go. I'm supposed to be home now. It was nice meeting you," Beth said, politely, and her friend echoed the sentiment.

"Nice meeting you both." Kara numbly stared after them.

"Kara, what's wrong?" Betty leaned over. "Her brother isn't an old beau of yours or something, is he?"

"No, of course not! It's just...I just need to be going now. It's getting dark and I promised your mother." She felt so shaky, but she tried to give Betty a reassuring smile. "Thank you for inviting me to sit with you and your friends a while." She put down some change on the table for her cola. "And nice meeting all of you," she said, addressing the others in the booth. Betty's friends had been immersed in their private chatter for a while, and for that, Kara was thankful. They paused from their conversation to return polite good-byes.

Was she outwardly pale or shaking, she wondered? As she slipped out of the booth, she could feel Betty's concerned eyes staring after her. When she emerged outside, she noticed dusk settling in. Only a small pink glow remained on the horizon. At the sight, another memory of her evening with Jerry flitted across her heart.

As she quickly began retracing her steps toward home, she looked up and saw the same two girls walking just ahead; they all appeared to be going in the same direction. The girls were walking a bit slowly while they chatted and she'd be passing them any moment. They glanced back as she approached, and Kara tried to throw them a friendly smile. A part of her yearned to talk more to Beth, and still another part wanted to hurry as far away as possible.

"Hello again," she greeted them, forcing herself to sound casual. "I'm staying at Betty's house."

"Yes, I know where the Jeffers family lives. We're heading to my house. It's about a block before you get to the Betty's," Beth answered. "Sharon, here, is staying the whole weekend with me since her parents are out of town," she added, proudly.

"Is Betty's brother really sweet on you?" the girl named Sharon asked.

"Well..." Kara hesitated, caught off guard. "Yes, I suppose he is. He's in Europe right now."

"My older sister also has a sweetheart overseas," Sharon said. She stopped for a second to readjust a wayward barrette in her brown curls and then hurried back in step with them.

"Beth..." Kara ventured. "You must really miss your brother, too."

"Yes. Our whole family does."

Kara nodded. "Are there many in your family?"

"No, just my parents, my little brother and me. And George, of course. "

The strangeness of these circumstances was overtaking Kara again and she couldn't pretend and make small talk much longer. She needed to get home to get her bearings. *If only there was someone I could confide in!*

Before she could say her good-byes again and hurry past them, a woman's voice called from up the street. Kara looked ahead to see a woman leaning over a porch railing, waving toward them.

"Oh dear, I hope we're not in trouble!" Beth said, picking up her pace.

"We're only a few minutes late, aren't we?"

"We have to hurry, now. Good-bye!" Beth called back to Kara. The girls started running, Beth's ponytail bouncing frantically.

As Kara hurried closer, she caught only a glimpse of the woman's face as she ushered the girls into the house. As the door closed behind them, Kara stopped and stood there on the sidewalk, staring after them.

There was no denying it now. It was actually him…all of them.

CHAPTER EIGHTEEN

Finding them should have felt wonderful, but instead, it had sent her reeling. It tore down even more hope for any kind of normal life for her here. Seeing them also tugged at her heart in a way she couldn't explain.

Grandpa, I missed you…

That night after everyone had gone to bed, Kara couldn't sleep for the longest time. She knew she had remembered hearing Grandpa George had lived briefly here in Amberton when he was young. It was only for a short time and Kara had never even been sure of the years. She had a dim memory of her Grandpa taking her to the street he had once lived on, but she must have been quite small at the time.

Her mom once mentioned something about his family living here for a year or two before moving to Portland. But no one from her family ever returned until years later, when Kara's parents moved here in the 1990s as newlyweds. Her father had gotten a job nearby and they had wanted to settle down in a smaller community, so they had found a little bungalow on the other side of town. By the time Kara had arrived on the scene, they had moved into a larger house in a new development.

Why hadn't I thought about all of this before? I shouldn't have been so side-swiped by seeing them now! Frustrated, she rolled over onto her side, tugging at her sheet as it tangled at her ankles. Yet she had to be fair to herself. How could anyone expect to have all the angles figured out when they were suddenly thrust back in time?

Still, other things bothered her. Would she keep coming face to face with her own ancestors and family? She had always had so many unanswered questions about this leap backward in time, but now she had even more. What if she somehow altered the course of time? Changed events because of her mere presence? She would never want that kind of responsibility.

She always remembered hearing about Great Aunt Elizabeth, who had died of cancer before Kara was ever born. It was Beth...

And then, Kara had lost her mother to the same disease just a few years ago. Secretly knowing the destiny of family—some of whom she might meet— seemed a heavy burden to bear.

So much of it was all too mind-boggling to Kara as more questions tumbled over each other. *Mom...* If she stayed, would her own mother, yet to be born now, not give birth to her anymore? But then, she *had* to be born to be alive now! *It was all too impossible to understand!*

Kara suddenly sat up, propping her pillows behind her back and switched on the lamp. She reached over and picked up the pad and pen she kept on her nightstand. She had discovered long ago that drawing or doodling, while she wrestled with problems, helped to calm her. It was times like this, though, that she especially longed to put everything down into writing. Or at the very least, have someone around she could confide in. But there was no one she could share this secret with right now...not even Jerry.

As she drew little ovals with her pen, transforming them into petals of flowers, her mind drifted toward this young man whom she was ready to leave her whole world for. His genuine heart, the way he would look at her...Sometimes it seemed so simple just to want to stay here with Jerry for no other reason other than the fact that they loved each other. *Would it be enough?*

Kara wrestled with all of these jumbled thoughts for half the night. Finally, she reached under her pillow for Jerry's letter. Leaning against her propped pillow, she unfolded it, letting his words pour over her heart like a salve.

She *truly* loved him. She knew it was much more than infatuation—it was real. She knew it to her very core. It was more real than anything thing she had ever known. And what was even more amazing, he loved her, too. But she had to decide if this was enough.

If Kara had hoped to come to some sort of resolution in the wee hours of the morning, she was sadly mistaken. She finally fell asleep shortly before dawn, the letter still in her hand.

The next morning, the glaring sun rudely nudged her awake. Frowning at the clock beside her bed, she saw it was almost 9:30. Even at this late morning hour, she still didn't feel rested. Her sleep-filled eyes blinked against the sunlight.

What was Jerry doing this very minute? What was he facing now?

She had gathered from his letters that he was heading directly into action. There was no sugar coating what he might have to endure now.

"Please...be with him. Keep him safe." She let the whispered prayer from her heart fall from her lips. "I just don't understand any of this, God... and I don't know what to do. But I love him..."

How she wished she could see him again now, or even just hear his voice. If only the two of them could sit down and talk together as they used to. Then, everything might seem so much clearer...it might put some of her never-ending questions to rest.

She looked over at the letter, slightly crinkled on the side of the bed. He'd be waiting for a reply from her. She tried to wipe the grogginess away as she sat up, and taking the wrinkled paper, read it over, once again. When she finished, she gazed out through the bedroom window for the longest time. Slowly...and then a little more clearly...a new thought emerged out of the recesses of her overworked brain.

I don't have to figure it all out.

It was such a strange concept to Kara. *Was this really true?*

As the idea began to take hold, it felt like an epiphany. All her life, she always felt she had to figure everything out. Maybe sometimes, it was impossible to do. And maybe some things were simply out of her hands.

Earlier, the disturbing questions of the night had tumbled in, one on top of the other. Now, these new, fresh thoughts did the same—only with these thoughts, came a sense of hope.

I didn't purposely come to this time; I was brought here for whatever reason. And I don't have to understand it all right now. The last idea still seemed so foreign to Kara, but with it, came incredible relief.

I might not have Jerry with me at this moment, but I did have his love...

And perhaps, even the promise of their lifetime together—if she'd just take it. A new stirring began to grow within her. Nothing had changed outwardly, but Kara slowly began to look at everything in a different light. One by one, all of the positive realities of her current situation became clearer to her: She lived in her own house—the difference was that she now lived with a loving family who cared about her...She was doing a valuable job, crucial for the war effort and seeing, first-hand, an amazing time in history...Most of all, the man she loved had just asked her to spend the rest of her life with him.

"Yes... I'll marry you."

It was only a whisper. But she hoped these words could somehow catch a breeze and find him somewhere across the Atlantic.

***

After breakfast, Kara spent the rest of Saturday morning tending the victory garden, which was now bursting with peas, beans, and luscious-looking strawberries. Betty and her mother were also helping weed and harvest, and they seemed to mirror Kara's cheerful mood. The weather was nearly perfect, too, as they worked in the soil, warmed by the late morning sun.

The three of them chatted as they plopped green beans into their baskets. Kara planned on writing Jerry right after lunch and in the meantime, she kept waiting for a good time to tell his family the news. She couldn't wait until after she penned the words to him, as she originally planned—she was nearly bursting inside!

"I have something to tell you both," Kara began, and then suddenly felt a shyness warm her cheeks. They both looked her way rather quizzically. "You...you hadn't asked me about Jerry's letter..." she went on.

"We didn't want to pry," Mrs. Jeffers said, gently.

"Well, I appreciate that, but..." She decided the best way would be to simply blurt it out. "He's asked me to marry him."

Betty jumped up and squealed while Mrs. Jeffers just smiled, remaining where she sat in the garden dirt, clad in overalls and gardening gloves.

"And do you have an answer?" Mrs. Jeffers asked her.

Kara nodded happily. "Yes. That is, with your blessing."

"Of course! You have our blessing, Kara!" Mrs. Jeffers reached over and hugged her neck. "I had a feeling," she said confidentially. "Welcome to the family."

Kara knew she was beaming and tears were close to forming. Having her approval meant more than she ever realized.

"I knew it, I just knew it! This is so exciting!" Betty was actually hopping on the grass beside the garden. Kara laughed, her own joy about to bubble over now, too.

"Betty," her mom good-naturedly scolded. "Calm yourself, dear. You're jumping around like a little jackrabbit!" But she too was laughing, now.

"I can't help it!" She swooped down and gave Kara a hug. "I'm so happy for you both! And it's going to be great having you as a sister."

"That's one of the nicest compliments ever. I'm going to love that, too!"

Mrs. Jeffers stood up, brushing off the pieces of dirt from her overalls. "Well, I think we're about done here in the garden for now. Let's go celebrate with some lunch, daughters—what do you say?"

***

June 12, 1943

Dear Jerry,

I hardly know where to begin. It was so wonderful to come home yesterday and find your letters. When Betty greeted us by waving the envelope, I just can't describe the joy I felt. But I was not expecting what was in mine.

Before I go on and on, I won't leave you wondering....YES! My answer is yes, sweetheart.

Now I need to tell you that—just like you—I had a lot of thinking to do. I didn't have to think twice about how much I love you, though. But pledging our whole lives to each other is one of the most important decisions we can make and I don't think anyone should make it lightly. In the end, though, I knew that I didn't want to spend the rest of my life without you. In fact, I don't think I ever could.

I'm sorry that you know so little about me, my family and my past and I promise to make that up to you when we are face-to-face again. You do know, though, that I lost my mother a few years ago. And I cannot tell you how wonderful it feels knowing your mother has welcomed me with open arms into the family. Everyone has! And most of all, I am so happy thinking about spending my life with you.

Have I mentioned that I love you and miss you? Because I do. I hope and pray that you are safe right now. I know you can't tell me everything but you seemed to be saying you were heading straight to the front lines. Is this true? Please let me know what's been happening and that you're all right.

It seems so insignificant to talk about my life, compared to what you might be facing, but I know you want to hear about it. So I'll start with my job at the shipyard. It took a while to learn everything, but I finally feel confident now. As I think you know, my job is welding and yesterday, I was able to work out on the open ship deck for the first time. It was so nice, breathing the fresh air. Of course, most of my hours there are pretty tedious. We're usually inside with the heat and noise.

It's nothing compared to a battlefield, but I'm finding out that it can be a little dangerous at times. One man was seriously injured the other day when he was hit by the heavy steel plate that was swinging from the crane. Everyone was talking about it. And a few weeks ago, a young woman I met suffered burns.

I'm being very careful, though. And now that they've promised me that I'll get to keep working on the deck once in a while, I think my days will go even better. It's nice to finally be earning my way again and repaying your folks for some of my expenses. Of course, it also helps keep my mind off of how much I miss you every day. I know your mother is writing you so she'll tell you a lot, herself. But it's been so nice riding to work with her every day.

Spring is turning into summer here and the weather is beautiful. We picked some scrumptious strawberries today and I think we'll be making shortcake. I'm also going to be helping your mom and Betty do some canning next weekend.

Anyway, Honey, I think I've read your letter about five times already since yesterday and I will probably re-read it a few dozen more until your next one arrives. Not worrying is hard in times like these, but I'm really trying. In the meantime, stay safe and know I'm thinking of you every day and love you, too—with all my heart.

Kara

CHAPTER NINETEEN

The next couple of weeks came and went without any more letters. Kara tried to heed his advice and not worry, but sometimes it wasn't so easy, especially as time wore on. It wasn't too difficult to read between the lines. She knew Jerry was right smack in the middle of things. Sometimes she'd be going about her normal day and suddenly wonder if he was burrowed in muddy trenches, just trying to survive the next hour.

She didn't wait to hear back from him before she wrote again. She'd heard that sometimes mail on both ends could be delayed, then suddenly come in bunches. The important thing was to keep writing. She'd begun her second letter to Jerry days ago but kept pausing, adding a little more to them each day. On this drizzly Saturday afternoon, she decided to finally try and finish it. Mr. Jeffers said he was mailing his letter downtown today and would take any others that were ready.

Despite the clouds and misty rain, the air outside felt warm and smelled of fragrant greenery. Kara sat at Jerry's desk near the half-open window, reading over what she had already written before continuing.

June 22, 1943

Dear Jerry,

Well, life goes on here, though it seems I miss you more with each passing day. My job continues to go well, except for a few moments here and there. I've only been able to work on the top deck twice since that first time I mentioned, but I'll take what I can get.

There was a bit of excitement at work yesterday—but not the good kind. We've had some very warm days for this time of year and yesterday it reached about eighty-five degrees. Inside some of the rooms at the shipyard, though, it was much hotter—maybe even twenty degrees more. Several people passed out briefly and were taken to first aid. They think it was due to heat exhaustion but thankfully, I think they're all going to be fine. I heard they were treated and sent home. I didn't see any of this happen and don't know them personally, but I did see some of the commotion right afterward and everyone was talking about it. At the end of the day, we were all reminded to take our salt tablets at the stations.

Other than that, life is mostly peaceful and it's nice to ride with your mother each day and then come home to your family. I don't know what I'd do without them!

Speaking of riding home from work, your father gave me a lesson in driving the family car. I finally had my turn behind the wheel to and from the shipyard on

Friday! It seemed to go all right, but I would have gotten completely lost if your mother wasn't helping with navigation. We plan to take turns as much as possible from now on.

Wednesday, June 23

As you can see, I'm going to continue this letter for a little while. It helps me to write to you often this way, especially in the evenings after work and I'm missing you so much.

It's especially strange to be here in your room. In a way, it makes me feel closer to you. Seeing your pictures on the wall, your clothes hanging in the back of your closet... Even the slight scent of you is here. But on the other hand, it makes me miss you more.

It would be easier if you were on a trip somewhere and we could cross off the days on a calendar until we could see each other again. But we can't—and that's what makes it so difficult. I hope and pray our day comes sooner, rather than later.

As Kara read this over, she pondered the truth of it. Even though she knew how long the war would last, she had no idea when Jerry would come home. An injury could send him home at any time, or he could be one of the men whose duties would linger afterward. And there were more unknowns, too terrible to voice. The uncertainty of it all was horrible and yet, in a very strange way, it helped to make Kara feel somewhat normal. It reminded her that she was mortal and finite, in spite of being aware of how some of the world's history would unfold.

Thursday, June 24

Today the weather was much cooler and they say rain is in the forecast. That makes it a little easier for those of us inside the shipyard, but it doesn't quite eliminate the heat emitted from the machinery or from the many workers within a tight space. I'm not actually complaining, though. I just hope for no more emergencies. And I really hope for more shifts outdoors. I don't think I'd even mind working on the top deck in the rain!

How is the weather where you are? I know that sounds trivial, as if we don't have better things to talk about. But I wonder what you're seeing and feeling. In fact, I wonder so much about what is happening to you. Every day I hope to get a letter but I'm trying so hard to be patient and not worry.

Your parents are doing well. Their health is good and they try to keep busy. Your mother's days are now completely filled up and we all take turns making dinner. Even your dad, who has turned out to be quite the chef!

(Did you ever taste your dad's cooking before? He makes a mean pot of chili!)

I'm going to turn in now, Sweetheart. I'll add some more soon.

Kara touched pen to paper and took a deep breath, adding her final thoughts:

Saturday, June 26
Dearest Sweetheart,

It feels so nice to call you Sweetheart! It's the end of another work week and I'm a bit tired—but not too tired to write to you.

I'm not sure of everything that Betty and your parents write, so I'll try not to repeat too much. As you might already know, Betty is going to be volunteering with her friend, helping roll bandages on Saturdays here in town. The Red Cross just opened a place downtown in one of the storerooms and Betty was thrilled to know she was old enough to volunteer. Today was their first day and she said it felt so good to contribute in this way. They'll be spending two hours every Saturday morning rolling bandages. Your mother and I may be volunteering occasionally there soon, as well.

Most weekends just have me listening to the radio or reading. And missing you. I imagine it's the same for your parents since they rarely go out, either. Sometimes Betty goes to the soda fountain with friends or to a movie, but tonight everyone is staying home and we're all going to play canasta. It was your mother's idea. Would you believe we haven't played it since that last time when you were here? It won't be nearly the same without you, but I think it will do us all good.

Well, Darling, I need to close this soon since your dad is heading out to mail the letters in just a few minutes. There's so much more I'd like to write. About myself and my childhood...things I think about. Some of this will have to happen in person when I see you again. If you have specific questions for me, though, ask away and I'll do my best.

In the meantime, know that I love you very much. I look forward to that day when we can be together again.

Yours Always,
Kara

She folded up the letter and then headed downstairs to look for Mr. Jeffers. Walking through the living room, she found Betty finishing sweeping in the kitchen but no one else around.

"I have this letter for your dad to mail. Do you know where he is?"

"He and Mama both left on a little walk together."

"Any place in particular? It's kind of rainy outside."

"I think they just wanted to get some exercise and talk together. They used to do that a lot and just haven't for a while. I did notice they took an umbrella," she told her as she placed the broom back in the closet.

"Well, hopefully, they're not walking to post his letter without this one."

"I don't think so. I watched them leave and he didn't have a letter with him." She sighed and plopped down on a kitchen chair. "I mailed my second one yesterday." Then she added, "When do you think we'll hear from Jerry again?"

"I don't know...he said it might take a while." When Betty didn't answer, she added, gently, "Sometimes, they don't have a chance to write for days—even weeks. Other times, mail can't go out right away or it all gets jammed up. You know that."

"I know. But I...." Betty swallowed. She seemed to be working hard to keep her emotions in check.

"But what?"

"It's just that...I know a girl from school. She lost her brother last year in the Pacific."

Forcing her own fears down, Kara stepped over and slid her arm around Betty.

"I know...I worry sometimes, too. But we can't focus on the fears—we just can't." Kara worked to keep her voice steady. "We have to keep hopeful."

Betty nodded. "I guess I'll feel so much better when we finally get some word from him."

They heard the door open then and Kara went around the corner, still clutching her letter. Mr. Jeffers was leaning the dripping umbrella by the door.

"I have a letter for Jerry all ready, Mr. Jeffers."

"Good. I'll be heading downtown to mail them in a few minutes. I have to stop at the hardware store anyway."

He then headed upstairs while Mrs. Jeffers hung up her jacket. "Well, that was invigorating, I must say! It's been a while since I walked so briskly on a drizzly day!"

"Did you want some lemonade? I just made it," Betty asked, peeking out from the kitchen entry.

"Perfect, thank you, dear." She plunked down into the armchair with a smile.

"Has the mail already come today?" Kara asked, sitting down across from her. "I've been upstairs writing, so I wasn't sure..."

"I'm afraid it has. There wasn't anything," she sighed.

A minute later, Mr. Jeffers returned and Kara handed him the envelope.

"I'll take the car—be back in a little while." Then, he hurried back out the front door just as Betty came back, carrying the glass of lemonade.

"Bye, Daddy!" She handed her mother the glass. "I think I'll go work on my sewing now."

"Very well, dear. Let me know if you need any help."

"All right, thanks, Mama." She bounded up the staircase.

After a minute or so, Kara peered over at Mrs. Jeffers. "So...you had a nice walk, then?"

"Oh...yes." She took a long sip of her lemonade, her expression hard to read.

"Betty mentioned you used to go on walks, often."

"Yes, it's been a while. I'm not sure why." She seemed to be gazing at nothing in particular. Then, she glanced over at Kara. "Mr. Jeffers...he's always been such an easy-going person." Kara nodded, not sure where she was going with this. "But ever since Jerry left overseas, there's been a change in him. Of course, it's been a difficult time for all of us—including you. But, well...you know he was in the first war, didn't you?"

"Yes, Jerry told me."

"He never was able to tell me everything he went through back then. It was before I met him. He had been just a few years older than Jerry when he enlisted. I always got the feeling it was terrible, though. Seeing his own son head off to fight the way he had to...well, it has stirred up old memories. And worries. He knows firsthand what it's like over there."

Her voice sounded calm and steady, but Kara saw the tears forming. She handed her a handkerchief, wondering what she could possibly say. It was such a personal disclosure, and on top of that, it nudged at her own fears.

"Of course, I'm not going to break any confidences…only, I don't mind telling you, it's a little hard to see him like this. He's tried not to show it, but it's been more difficult than he's let on. He's even had a few nightmares…nightmares about the war. He told me he hasn't had any of those since before we were married." She reached for her hankie, blotting her eyes. "Forgive me, Kara. I was just feeling a little overwhelmed and it kind of spilled out. The walk was actually a good thing for us, though! Really! The exercise…the conversation. I think he was holding everything in for too long."

"Please don't apologize," Kara answered, finding her voice. "It's all so understandable. I just wish they didn't both have to go through this."

"Ray would do it again in a heartbeat if it meant defending his country. War is horrible, Kara, but sometimes the only alternative is to let evil take over. We can't do that. But yes, it's sad that this world has to keep warring with itself…over and over again."

***

It was about three hours later that they all began to worry. Kara had finished helping Mrs. Jeffers and

Betty prepare dinner and they were trying to keep it warm.

"I think maybe I should go walk downtown and look for him." Mrs. Jeffers was slipping on her white gloves as she spoke.

"No, please let me. You've had your walk today and I haven't," Kara offered.

"Well, all right, but Betty, you go with her, dear." As she removed her gloves, her brows furrowed. "Where can he possibly be? It's just not like him. He's never gone this long without at least telephoning…"

The rain had stopped and it was still very light out, despite the clouds. Still, both girls grabbed their sweaters and Kara snatched up the umbrella as they hurried out the door, just in case.

Kara tried to stifle her worry. He had become like a father to her—even more than her own, if she was honest. She didn't want to further upset Betty, but as they hurried down the street towards town, all kinds of fearful possibilities circled her mind.

CHAPTER TWENTY

They strode quickly through the neighborhood. Kara kept hoping they might pass Mr. Jeffers on his way back home but they never did. They did pass near the home of the Morrisons, however. As they rounded the corner, Kara glanced down the street, catching a glimpse of the front porch where her great-grandmother had stood. No one from the family was in view now and besides, there was something more pressing to focus on.

Neither one of them said anything until they reached Main Street. "I'll check the hardware store around the corner and you stop into the post office. We'll meet back here after we've asked around," Kara said.

Reaching the hardware store, she was disheartened to see it had closed at five o'clock, just twenty minutes earlier. In fact, most of the shops were now closed and very few people were around. She realized the post office would also probably be closed by now, too. Turning the corner, looked back down on Main Street. *At least the soda fountain was open.* Sprinting in that direction, Kara's eye caught sight of the barber, locking up his shop.

"Excuse me, sir. Have you seen Mr. Jeffers?"

"Why yes, Ray Jeffers was just in getting a haircut a little while ago. In fact, he was talking to Pete for some time in here. I think they went off to discuss war and insurance business or something."

Relief washed over her; he was probably fine. "Oh, thank you!" She paused. "War and insurance business? Do you know where they went?"

"No... I can't say as I do. Wait, they may have gone to the little diner at the end of the street for coffee. Seems I heard something said about that as they were leaving."

Kara had forgotten all about that diner. "I think I know where that is. Thank you!"

She had heard about the little diner, though it had been long gone in Kara's time. She had heard it was mainly a place for locals to eat when they were out of options. Most people dined in the next town over. When they wanted a real night on the town, they headed all the way to the bright lights of Portland.

At the very end of the street, she found the unassuming little diner with a crooked "open" sign on the door and let herself in. Kara's eyes tried to adjust to the dim light...and there he was. He sat alone in a booth toward the back, sipping coffee and staring out the window. She glanced around and saw only one other booth in the place was occupied—an older couple on the other side of the diner.

Mr. Jeffers looked up, a little startled, as she hesitantly came over.

"Kara! What are you doing here?" He half stood politely as she approached his booth and she slid in across from him. "So what brings you...Oh..."

He checked his watch as if it had never occurred to him to do so before.

"Everyone was getting worried. When you didn't come back, I mean." She felt so awkward—as if she was bringing back a wayward child. She began wishing she had left this errand to Mrs. Jeffers, after all.

"I had no idea how late it was. I'm going to ask to use the phone, excuse me..."

Kara watched as he was allowed back to use the diner's telephone. He returned to the booth within minutes.

"All right, everything's fine. I'm just going to take a few more sips of coffee and we can head back. Or would you care for a cup?"

"Oh, no, thank you. Betty's here, looking for you, too. Should I go find her and meet you back here?"

"I don't think that's necessary; it looks like she's here now."

Betty ventured through the door and spotted them, so he motioned her over.

"Daddy, there you are!" She nearly ran across the diner to him. "What happened? We were so worried! You're never late for supper and you knew we were going to play games tonight!" Her voice was a mixture of accusation and relief.

He stood up and gave her a quick hug. "I'm sorry, munchkin. Here, sit down. I'll try to explain." He slid over to the wall and she scooted in next to him.

Kara frankly wished they could all just simply go on home. The last thing she wanted was for him to think he had to answer to her or give out explanations. She waited uncomfortably as he took another sip of coffee and then set it down.

"I really didn't mean to get everyone upset. I guess I completely lost track of time." He lowered his voice. "You see, I stopped in to chat for a moment at the barbershop and as it turned out, Pete Bradfield has connections with the AWS and...Well, to make a long story short, I'll be volunteering."

Was he joining up again, too? Kara hated to appear ignorant, but there were times she just couldn't seem to avoid it.

"The AWS?"

"You must have heard about the Aircraft Warning Service."

"So, you'll be watching for enemy planes?" Betty's voice was also nearly a whisper, but it held excitement.

He nodded. "I'll be getting trained and then assigned a post." His eyes held a renewed twinkle as he paused to take another sip. "It couldn't have come at a better time. There's a real need for it and, well...with Jerry over there fighting, I couldn't sit around doing nothing. Mr. Bradfield and I finished talking just a while ago, but I guess I got a little lost in my thoughts. Anyway, that's what happened. I'm sorry I worried everyone."

Betty hugged his shoulder. "I'm proud of you, Daddy. But...oh, wait, Mama is home waiting to hear..."

"Never mind, I just phoned her."

"I think it's great—what you'll be doing. I heard you...you served in the last war, too."

Kara wondered if she should have brought such a thing up, after what Mrs. Jeffers had confided, but he had already done so much for his country.

"Yes. I was one of millions. It was supposed to be the war to end all wars. That's what it was called." His expression clouded. "It wasn't supposed to be so that we'd get older, have sons and send them off to repeat it all over again."

He stared at no one. Kara had never heard that tone in his voice before, or the look in his eye. After a moment, he seemed to recover and took a long, deep breath.

"But...here we are again. And nothing can change that. There's just a lot of evil in this world. We have to do our part to combat it, that's all. I'm just grateful that I still can."

Tuesday, June 29

Dear Jerry,

Well, the weekend has come and gone, and now it's already almost the middle of another work week. My job went well today—I just had to make it through the day with a headache. The weather has turned warm again and inside the building, the heat and lack of fresh air seemed so stifling. I'm starting to feel better now that I'm sitting here by the open window, writing to you. It's after seven and there's a cool breeze just beginning.

Saturday was a bit of an interesting day. Everything's fine now, so don't worry. Your dad went to mail our letters and stop at the hardware store, but suppertime came and went and he hadn't come home. Your mother was worried—we all were—so Betty and I went looking for him. We found him in the diner and all was well. But he does have some news—I'm not sure how much we're supposed to tell and what will get censored, but I will say that he'll be doing his part for the war effort.

I'll confide that he hadn't been quite himself lately, but now that he will be doing something to contribute to the war effort, it's made a world of difference already. I think you have such a great father, Jerry. And I suspect you take after him in a lot of ways.

His business has slowed a bit lately but money isn't a worry for your parents. He's still working—and now, of course, your mother is working, too. I honestly can't believe how much they pay at the shipyard compared to other jobs. As for me, it feels wonderful to be able to pay toward food and utilities with my paycheck.

I think I mentioned in my last letter that we were planning to play canasta Saturday night. Well, in spite of all of us eating supper a little late that night, we still played and it was a lot of fun. Your dad was in a much better mood by that evening, and everyone had a great time. I guess the game night was just what the doctor ordered.

Next Sunday is the Fourth of July and we're all going to the town picnic after church. There's also a parade on Saturday where they'll be selling war bonds. It all sounds fun—but I sure wish you were here with me.

Sweetheart, it's excruciating to have to wait for your second letter. I hadn't planned to write again so soon but I was aching to "talk" to you this evening. It helps to write like this whenever I'm especially missing you. I know you have no control over the mail system or even when you're able to write, but it will put all of our minds at ease when we finally do hear from you again and know you're all right.

Perhaps when you get this letter, you'll have already written and our letters are crossing one another on different planes over the sea.

I suppose I should say goodnight now. The mornings start early and I do much better when I get a good night's sleep. But I'll be dreaming of you and how it will be to see you again.

With all my love and prayers,
~Kara

***

The rest of the week crept by. Every day, Kara came home from work hoping that a letter would be waiting, but the weekend arrived and still, there was no word from Jerry. She had been so certain she would have heard from him by now. Without any more letters, it was harder to feel like entering into all the celebrations she had been so looking forward to. Mrs. Jeffers said that this kind of thing happened all the time, so Kara tried to push her worries aside as they headed into town.

The simple parade went down Main Street and Kara loved the old-fashioned charm of the small-town festivities. More than that, she could feel the surging patriotism that was unique to these war years. They were celebrating American freedom while at the same time, fighting to keep it. Kara was acutely aware of this as she drank in all the sights and sounds, the warm noonday sun overhead.

When it had ended, the family started shuffling through the small crowd. Festivities were over for the morning and everyone was dispersing. As they passed through the jumble of people, Kara nearly bumped into someone. She started, realizing in a flash that it was Beth Morrison.

"Excuse me...oh, hello," Beth said, smiling shyly.

Kara attempted a smile in return and then in a glance, caught sight of the middle-aged couple next to her. *Beth's parents.* There was the jostle of folks all around but for just a second, she locked eyes with the mother. She felt a strange recognition and wondered if the woman had sensed it, too.

The whole interaction lasted only a matter of seconds, but as Kara continued alongside the Jeffers family, it was hard for her to shake it away. She looked back, trying to spot them but they were lost in the crowd. Her great-grandparents—whom she'd never had a chance to meet—had just passed her without a word and were now walking away.

CHAPTER 21

It was the following Thursday when the letters arrived.

No one else was home when Kara and Mrs. Jeffers returned from work late that afternoon. Kara carefully pulled the car into the driveway. She was now almost feeling like an expert behind the wheel of the '38 Chevy.

The day had been exhausting and she couldn't wait to finally relax and put her feet up. Betty would be out this evening but it had been her turn to prepare supper beforehand. All Kara and Mrs. Jeffers would need to do now is re-heat it. As they entered the front door, Kara noticed the mail that had been pushed through the slot and she routinely bent to pick it up. A name caught her eye.

"From Jerry!" she squealed.

She fumbled through the rest of the mail, finding a total of three letters. There a separate letter for Jerry's family and two envelopes addressed just to her. Within seconds, Mrs. Jeffers had retrieved the letter opener but for a moment, all they could do was sit there on the divan, gleefully admiring the long-awaited letters.

"I guess we should actually open them," Mrs. Jeffers laughed.

"I'll go upstairs and read mine, if you don't mind. I've waited so long...and it's where I usually write to him."

She hurried upstairs, forgetting how fatigued she had felt only moments ago. When she reached her room, she kicked off her shoes and nearly scampered across the floor to the other side. Finding the envelope with the earliest postmark, she sat at the little desk by the window and carefully slid the opener across the top. Her hands were shaking with excitement as she pulled out the contents.

June 29, 1943

Dear Kara,

Wow, I received your letter a few days ago. I wish I could describe the joy and relief I felt when I read it. Even in the midst of all this! I had spent the day eating K-rations out of old tin plates and sleeping on the hard ground in the middle of nowhere, but when I was able to read the words in your letter, I might as well have been in a palace. I can't wait until this war is over and we can start our life together.

I think it's great that you and Mom are both working at the shipyard now. Although she worked plenty hard around home when I was growing up, I never knew her to have a job. She tells me it's going very well and I'm proud of both of you!

The last few weeks have been tough—there's no getting around it. Tough in so many ways. Body, mind and soul. But getting letters from all of you back home has been like medicine. Especially yours...with the wonderful word, YES. I feel ready to take on anything tomorrow brings. And tomorrow—that will hopefully be one day closer to you.

You asked about the weather. At first, it was unbearably hot but now that we're in another location, it's so bad. Right now, I'm sitting here, thankful for a time to rest and write to you, but off in the distance, we can hear artillery. After a month, we've grown so accustomed to it that it actually seems to make all of us uneasy whenever it stops.

I have a pocket New Testament and Psalms I carry with me. It really helps to read it and be reminded that I'm not alone out here. That I actually have someone I can turn to in the worst moments. Keep praying for me. I'm praying for you and the family, too.

Well, Darling, I'd better close for now. Keep writing whenever you can and don't worry if you think it sounds mundane. I like hearing about your days and life back home. I want to keep hearing that everyday life and simple pleasures go on because it's sometimes hard to imagine out here.

Did I mention that I love you? If not, let me mention it a couple hundred more times...because I do. ~Jerry

Kara set the paper down. She wanted to soak in his words before opening his last letter.

It was such an incredible relief to know he was all right. And yet, on another level, some of his words unknowingly instilled more worry. He didn't describe much detail, but it was almost worse trying to read between the lines.

She finally opened the second letter.

July 3, 1943

Dear Kara,

Things have eased up a bit out here the last few days. It's given the men in our unit a bit of down time and some much-needed reprieve. And then, mail call today and another letter from you! My unit has moved several times since the day I first arrived, and I'm thankful your letters keep finding me.

I've read your wonderful, long letter so many times (and the first one, too). I think I must have them memorized now. They're better than a good book any day, and they make me feel as if you were right here, next to me. As if I wasn't thousands of miles away from home after all.

Before I forget, I have a request. Please send a picture of yourself in your next letter. A small one that I can carry around with me. I haven't forgotten what you look like, but boy, it would be so wonderful to be able to gaze at you out here.

I'm glad that things are going well at work, but please promise me you'll be careful. I've written Mom the same thing. You two are the most important women in my life and I want you to be safe and sound when I come back. I guess I never stopped to think about all the hazards you both would face. Still, I don't want you to think you have to keep anything from me because I might worry.

As for me, I wish I didn't have to keep things from you, but you know I have to. Not just because of security but because there are some things that you would not want to read about. As I said, things have quieted down for the time being. But there were several nightmarish days recently, moments that will be hard to shake...times I wasn't sure how I'd get through. But somehow I did. Maybe someday I will tell you a little about it. But only a little, I think.

I set this letter aside for a couple hours and now I'm back. I'll try to lighten the mood a little if I can. Let's see...I sure wish I could have had some of that strawberry shortcake you mentioned. I heard something about a special menu tomorrow for Independence Day, so we'll see. We have plenty of our own fireworks here, and not the fun kind. But for now, things are relatively quiet. A few of us were even able to get in a couple of games of cards yesterday. Which reminds me, I hope everyone had a good time playing that game of canasta you mentioned. Who ended up winning? Dad, I bet.

Sweetheart, remember, there may be times again when I can't write. Or mail is slowed down. I know it isn't easy, but please try not to worry whenever you don't hear from me for a while.

I suppose it's only fair, then, if I say I'll try not to worry about you at the shipyard, either. Because as I said, I'm so proud of you. But take care of yourself for me, Darling.

Love Always,

~Jerry

She impulsively put the letter to her lips. Perhaps she could survive the next few weeks on these two letters, but she hoped she didn't have to.

Even though he had admonished her not to keep these things from him, she regretted now having gone on about heat strokes and heavy, swinging steel plates in her last letter. The last thing he needed to do was worry about her when he was the one trying to survive.

She skimmed the letter again.

"But there were several nightmarish days recently, moments that will be hard to shake..."

How close had he already come to death? His own and those around him? It was agonizing to think of what he must be going through. How would he endure more months—or even years?

"I have a pocket New Testament and Psalms I carry with me. It really helps to read it and helps me to remember that I have someone I can turn to in the bleakest moments"

Kara had always believed in God, but she wished she had Jerry's strong personal faith. Maybe one day, she would. For whatever reason, it seemed God had placed her here. Perhaps it was only to find Jerry—she wasn't sure. Everything was still such a mystery. For now, at least, she was going to pray for him. That much she could do.

***

Kara stood on the small step stool in the back yard, plucking cherries from the higher branches. The direct rays from the summer sun were a bit intense. Thankfully, they were tempered with a delicious breeze, and for the most part, she was shaded in a canopy of leaves. Her basket was just about full now, and Betty had already retreated into the house with hers.

There were times when Kara had memories trickle in from her original life. At this moment, as she gazed around the yard, she was thinking of how there had never been any cherry tree when she lived here alone. There *had* been, however, a pear tree on the other side of the yard. She glanced that way as if expecting it to appear, but the area was completely bare. Only a patch of grass filled the space.

It occurred to her that this yard bore little resemblance to the one she had known. When she first became a home owner, her spare hours were given over to fixing up and decorating the house, a little at a time. She hadn't had a chance to do much with the yard, so seeing it like this was a delight to her eyes. With the victory garden, flowers, and lovely lawn chairs and umbrella, Kara thought it held so much charm.

She plopped a few more ripe cherries into the basket and carefully climbed off the stool. Another week had gone by since receiving Jerry's letters. Nine days, to be exact. She had already written and mailed off another long letter and planned to write again this weekend.

"Ready to make the cobbler?" Betty asked when Kara entered the kitchen.

"You certainly have more energy than I do today. You've already worked at the Red Cross, picked cherries and now still raring to go! Just let me get a drink of water, first, if you don't mind," she laughed. "Is your mother joining us?"

"No, she walked downtown to do some shopping."

"That's something I need to do soon, too. I really need to add a few things to my wardrobe now that I have another paycheck."

"How I wish I could work there with both of you!" Betty got down the mixing bowl and placed it on the counter. "I need money desperately. Besides, it must be simply wonderful, helping to build Liberty ships. I'm almost old enough to work there so it doesn't seem fair that I'm stuck here at home while you and Mama go off every day..."

Betty suddenly halted her little speech and put her hand over her mouth.

"I'm sorry, Kara. It's not your fault. I honestly don't mean to complain." Her hair was pulled back into two French pigtails, which Kara thought looked very sweet, but made her look much younger than she probably wanted to at this moment.

"It's okay, I understand," Kara answered, gently. She couldn't help but wonder if Betty might be slightly jealous of all the time she got to spend with her mother. "I really wish you could work there with us, too. It would be so fun if we all could ride together every day." At this, Betty seemed slightly appeased. "Are there other ways you can make money this summer?" Kara asked.

"Well, I *am* babysitting tonight. But it's not every week and I never know when I might be needed. Too many of my friends are also babysitting. Plus, too many families with older sisters," she sighed.

Kara nodded, as she helped to gather ingredients. "I see…they've got built-in babysitters in those families. So no other job prospects?"

"Not at the moment. I guess I'll have to be content with occasional movies and soda money. Mama promised to help me make a few new outfits and we get to buy a couple things before school starts again, though," she said, brightening.

"That's nice! I certainly wish I could sew."

"I'm surprised you never learned! Perhaps Mama could teach you? There are some dreamy patterns I have my eye on." Betty was mixing the ingredients as she spoke. "I think this is ready to pour into the baking dish now."

The two worked together to finish up and soon the cobbler was in the oven.

"I think I'm going to go write another letter to Jerry while this is baking," Betty announced, hanging up her apron.

"What kinds of things do you write to him about?"

"Oh, I don't know. There's not a lot to tell. But I write about the movies I've seen or the latest book I'm reading. It's all probably pretty boring. And how much I miss him, of course."

"That's exactly the kinds of things your brother wants to hear about. He told me so, himself."

As they left the kitchen, Betty paused and turned, looking straight at Kara. Her expression appeared clouded.

"Sometimes I wonder what he's going through. You see, I've known him all my life and I can't imagine him having to shoot at the enemy. He's always been so kind...so soft-hearted. But I know he's brave, too. Yet, sometimes...late at night...I lie awake and worry about how much danger he's in," she confided, her voice breaking.

Kara reached over and put her arms around her. Once again, she tried to swallow her own fears down as she searched for the right words to say. But no words seemed to come.

Later that evening, Kara was upstairs sitting at the desk, trying to compose a new letter but not knowing where to begin. She was missing Jerry desperately but couldn't seem to express all she was feeling. Her page remained virtually empty and she felt so restless.

A song drifted up from the radio downstairs. She slowly got up and headed toward her open doorway so she could hear it more clearly. She recognized Frank Sinatra's voice and the tune seemed vaguely familiar. The words and melody were hauntingly beautiful and she strained to listen..."There are Such Things". She stood, leaning against the doorway and as the song played on, she felt momentarily transported into Jerry's arms again.

***

More letters finally arrived a few days later, easing the tension in the air.

On Tuesday, a letter came for his family and the following day, one addressed to Kara. This letter was actually more of a note, hastily written when Jerry hadn't had much time. Still, she was grateful for any word at all.

The weeks afterward seemed to drag on. A heat wave descended on the area, making working conditions almost intolerable. Water and salt tablets were dispersed throughout the stations but, for Kara, nothing seemed to help very much. There were reports of several more workers succumbing to heat exhaustion and even heat stroke. Everyone seemed to be struggling as the searing days continued.

One particular day, Kara was the one who fell victim. It had been late on a Thursday afternoon, toward the end of July. She had been working particularly hard on a project and the air had felt stifling. Soon, she began to feel light headed; then, nausea crept in slowly, forcing her to pause from her task. Before she could even start to remove the welder's mask, she had felt her balance teetering. A fellow worker had helped to break her fall before she hit the ground.

Kara was helped to the first aid station and then had been told to go on home, but with two more hours to go, she had to wait for Mrs. Jeffers to finish her shift. She had ended up waiting it out in the shadiest spot she could find. She couldn't check the time from outside but Mrs. Jeffers had found her sitting on an out-of-the-way dock, her shoes off and feet dangling in the water.

"That's probably not the cleanest water around," Mrs. Jeffers had observed, startling Kara. Her voice seemed a mixture of concern and amusement. "Are you all right, dear? I got the message just as I was clocking out that you had taken ill."

Bringing her feet out, she tried to shake off the water. "I'm much better—just a little light-headed, I guess. How did you know I was here?"

"Someone saw you come out this way. Here, let me help you..."

Kara noticed she still felt wobbly as Mrs. Jeffers helped her into the car.

The following morning, she still was a bit unsteady. The temperatures were supposed to soar to 103 degrees, so Mrs. Jeffers advised her to stay home and fully recover. All that day, Kara had lounged around with cool washcloths, sipping water and lemonade. She couldn't help but feel a little spoiled—especially while Betty went around doing all the chores, preparing supper and even bringing her all of her meals.

Yet, Kara couldn't remember the last time she had relaxed all day. Besides napping, she spent most of her day writing part of a letter to Jerry, reading magazines and listening to various daytime radio shows. It was still warm in the house, but it was a hundred times better than what she would have faced at work. A little metal electric fan in the living room had been aimed directly on her as she lay on the divan; Kara didn't think there was anything more heavenly.

Throughout the day, though, Kara kept worrying over Mrs. Jeffers battling the heat, and hoped she would be all right. To her relief, she had returned home, safe and sound, at the end of the workday—though looking pretty worn and disheveled. After checking on Kara, she had gone directly upstairs to soak in a cool bath, muttering how glad she was that at least the work week was through.

The hot, uncomfortable weeks had been difficult for other reasons, too. No more letters had come, and the waiting seemed to hang heavily over all of them.

But none of them could guess how the afternoon of August 7th would change everything.

CHAPTER 22

"I still wish you'd come with us!"

Betty was bounding down the stairs, her loose hair tied back with a blue ribbon that matched her checkered blouse.

"Maybe some other time. I know you'll have a great time, though—the weather's perfect today."

"Exactly why I think you should come along! There's no reason for you to stay home all day, Kara. Mama, you make her come with us!"

"Leave her be, Betty. She doesn't have to give you reasons if she doesn't want to go." Betty's mother sat in front of the sewing machine at the dining room table, concentrating on finishing a seam. For the last few hours, she had been helping Betty make a dress while Kara observed, trying to learn what she could.

"I'd rather just do a few things at home today. Besides, your friends don't even know me."

The truth was, the thought of going to the creek without Jerry felt depressing to Kara today, but she didn't want to try and explain all of this to Betty.

"My friends wouldn't mind in the least if you came along!"

"I'm flattered you want me to go but…just not this time, okay?"

Betty's expression turned to resignation. "Okay. But you're really missing out!" She breezed past them into the kitchen. "Oh, thanks for getting the picnic basket down for me, Mama," she called behind her as she began to gather food to take along.

"How long to do you think Mr. Jeffers will be at his post today?" Kara asked.

"He wasn't sure. He should be home soon, though." Mrs. Jeffers finished the seam and pulled the dress from the machine, holding it out for examination. "There! Betty, you'll need to try this on again this evening," she said, her voice rising so her daughter could hear from the kitchen. Turning back to Kara, she added,

"I was thinking, perhaps you might want to walk to Main Street and do a little shopping with me. Since we already have gotten a few things done already, we could finish the rest of the chores when we get back. What do you think?"

The idea sounded appealing, but she hesitated. She didn't want to jilt Betty further by jumping at another offer today.

"Well…I do need to buy a couple things. When are you leaving?"

"I thought right after lunch. In about an hour or so? I'd love for you to join me, but of course, if you'd rather stay home, I do understand."

"Can I let you know in a little while?"

"Of course." Mrs. Jeffers had been in the process of gathering up her materials, and now lifted the sewing machine effortlessly. As she headed upstairs, Betty emerged with her filled picnic basket.

"Well, I guess I'm ready. We're all meeting over at Janie's house and then walking over from there together."

"All right, have a great time!"

"Thank you, but like I said, you're going to be missing out! Millie Anderson is bringing her new camera and she's going to take a group picture of all of us by the creek."

"Oh, that reminds me! This weekend, will you take another picture of me for Jerry? I want to send him one wearing my new blue dress."

"Sure, I'd be happy to!" She scurried to the front door. "Mama?" she called out. "I'm leaving now!" She vanished out the door in a cheerful puff.

***

A half an hour later, Kara was in the kitchen slathering mayonnaise on sliced bread. She was making cheese sandwiches and decided to put together an extra one for Mr. Jeffers, in case he was home in time for lunch. Her mind seemed to wander in a hundred different directions as she went about the simple task.

Thoughts drifted to Betty and her friends, traipsing off to the creek. The whole idea of their excursion sounded so fun and she found herself feeling a bit wistful. Not that she'd changed her mind about going—it still had no appeal to her at the moment. But she was happy for them. Kara supposed it was good to find pieces of normalcy—to have moments free from worry and longing and simply savor life, even when the world around was falling apart. After all, she thought, that's what Jerry and all the others across both oceans were fighting to keep.

However, Kara wouldn't have enjoyed being social in her present mood today—and she definitely wouldn't have been very good company.

What was Jerry doing right now? She seemed to wonder this about a thousand times a day.

"How are the sandwiches coming along?" Mrs. Jeffers asked as she wandered into the kitchen.

"They're all ready now. I have some apples sliced, too."

"Good! Why don't we eat outside? It's so lovely out right now."

They brought out the plates and sandwiches to the back patio and sat under the shade of the umbrella. The weather truly felt nearly perfect, Kara observed. Especially after enduring the long, unbearable heat wave.

She gazed up at the two puffy white clouds lazily drifting along. They reminded her of a couple sailboats adrift in a sea of blue. Mrs. Jeffers was making small talk and Kara was doing her best to join in, but she barely heard anything she was saying. She missed Jerry like crazy. *And everyone and everything...*

She rarely pined for her original life, but as she sat here now, she felt almost homesick. She wasn't sure why—perhaps because Jerry wasn't here and she had no idea when she'd ever see him again. She longed to be with him now with every fiber of her being...to hear his voice, feel his hand in hers...know he was as real as she remembered.

She suspected this wasn't unique to her and her situation. She imagined most of those separated by war needed to be reminded now and then that their loved ones were solid and true—not just handwriting on a page or a picture in a frame.

Still, she ached to go write to him again—right this very minute. Mrs. Jeffers continued to talk about various subjects and Kara tried to nod at all the right places. She normally loved the times when she and Jerry's mother had time for long conversations, but it seemed impossible for her now. She resolved to simply stay home and write him a long letter after all.

The faint sound of the doorbell, barely audible, drifted out to them and Mrs. Jeffers excused herself to answer it. "Don't tell me my husband locked himself out," she muttered with a smile.

Kara took her last bite of apple and followed her inside. They had forgotten to bring out a beverage and there was leftover lemonade in the refrigerator. As she came through the patio door, she felt an eerie silence. Instead of heading to the kitchen, she eased toward the front door to see who was there. Mrs. Jeffers just stood numbly in the entryway, a small paper in her hand.

"What is it? What's wrong?" Kara hurried over to her but there was no sound, no movement. Kara gently took the paper from her hand and scanned it.

"We regret to inform you…Missing in Action"

The words blurred and made no sense, no matter how long she stared at them. NO, NO, NO. *He couldn't be… he was still there—right there with his unit—writing letters to me. They were just late, that's all. Didn't they know they were simply late?*

Her irrational thoughts tumbled over shock waves while the two of them could only seem to stand there, frozen and silent.

Slowly, the sounds of pent up sobs could be heard. Mrs. Jeffers couldn't keep them from escaping.

However, Kara refused. *NO!* It was simply not possible—none of it!

A moment later, the front door opened and Mr. Jeffers appeared, stopping short and the color draining from his face. "What is it?"

Kara handed him the telegram but shook her head in defiance.

It wasn't true, any of it. He was still out there somewhere, probably writing letters from his bunk at this very minute.

***

Kara spent the rest of the afternoon in a dark haze of unbelief. Jerry's parents had each other and that was good, but she wanted to be alone.

She had immediately gone upstairs and began writing a letter to Jerry—just as she planned. Ferociously writing—spilling out her anger and fear and telling him to hurry and dispel this ridiculous myth that he was somehow lost. *Or worse...*

When she had finally written everything down onto paper, the stubborn denial gave way as the truth sank in. *He was missing.*

Kara knew the stories. She knew exactly what this meant. It meant that there was a very good chance that he had been killed, but they simply couldn't confirm it. Oh, she supposed it could also mean that he had been taken prisoner. The first possibility gave her no hope at all. The second, with its small inkling of hope, only caused more fear for what he could be going through.

And then, some received this kind of telegram and never, ever had any closure.

The bleakness and despair seemed to smother her like a cloud of poisonous gas. She collapsed onto her bed and let the tears fall as the hours ticked away.

***

When Kara finally opened her eyes, it took her a moment to let everything sink in. She had fallen into a strange half-sleep, worn from crying, and now she felt ragged inside. Rubbing her groggy eyes, she stood...slowly...feeling the weight of gravity like never before. She headed for the bathroom and took her time washing her face with fresh, cool water. It helped a little. She still felt as though she had suddenly fallen from a cliff onto the cold hard ground, dazed and uncertain about what to do next. She also knew she wasn't the only one probably feeling this way.

Heading downstairs, she found the living room empty. She peered into the kitchen and found Mrs. Jeffers intently scrubbing the kitchen floor. She was on her hands and knees, facing away from the doorway, vigorously pushing the scrub brush around as if her life depended on it.

Kara opened her mouth to speak, but she wasn't sure what to say. She quietly backed away and looked outside to see Betty and her father, sitting at the umbrella table, deep in somber conversation. Kara wondered what time Betty had returned from the picnic...how she had handled the news. Swallowing the constant lump in her throat, Kara returned to the kitchen entryway.

"Is there anything I can do to help?" she asked softly.

With her back still to her, Mrs. Jeffers stopped scrubbing and slowly sat up from her stooped position. A long audible sigh escaped her and she wiped at her forehead with the back of her hand.

"Kara," she simply said, but she didn't turn around.

Kara softly walked to the other side so that she was facing her.

"Mrs. Jeffers...are you all right?"

Her eyes lifted to meet Kara's. They held a dead, defeated expression—something Kara had never witnessed in her before and it was startling.

"I don't know," she answered candidly. Then her expression softened slightly. "I guess I should ask the same thing of you. You were in your room for so long. I didn't disturb you since I thought you needed to be alone."

Kara nodded, not thinking she needed to answer. She wasn't fine, either. None of them were.

After plopping the brush into the bucket beside her, Mrs. Jeffers slowly got up from the floor. She brushed herself off and then walked over to the sink to rinse her hands.

"You don't need to do anything today if you don't feel like it. As for me, it helps to keep busy." Mrs. Jeffers wiped her hands on a dishtowel and turned around. Her resolute face seemed to weaken and Kara witnessed the tears begin to suddenly form in her eyes. "I just.....I don't know what to do. The not knowing—it's so hard."

Kara reached over and put her arms around Jerry's mother as the woman's tears spilled over. She let her own tears fall alongside them. Perhaps it was something that should have happened at the very beginning, but somehow Kara couldn't face it then. She didn't want to face it now, either, but there wasn't any choice. She realized they might as well try to walk through this together.

***

She hadn't been exactly sure just how, but somehow she and Mrs. Jeffers managed to wake up on Monday morning, just as they always did every weekday. Somehow the two of them drove to work. Just as if the world was still turning and life still went on.

They had had all weekend to try to process the news, and Kara knew that staying home would probably only give them more time to think. Besides, as Mrs. Jeffers had pointed out, by going to the shipyard, they would be doing their small part to help fight back.

Neither one had spoken very much as Kara took her turn behind the wheel. Once they arrived, Kara had gone about the day, methodically performing her tasks and duties. It required just enough brainpower so that she didn't have to think too hard about anything else. Her worry and distress simply clung like fog to the back of her mind and heart.

The weather had clouded over a bit as Kara pulled the car into the driveway late that afternoon The sunshine was fading into gray shadows—and for that, she was actually thankful. All weekend it hadn't felt right that the sun could continue cheerfully shining, as if it hadn't heard the news.

Betty would be getting supper ready. She did so most weekdays now that she was home for the summer and the only one who didn't work full time. She had even been doing some of the grocery shopping, using their rations. Kara could now smell something nice wafting out as they opened the front door. It reminded her that she had barely eaten anything in the last twenty-four hours.

Betty appeared in the entryway as they came in. A scene, strangely familiar and yet so eerily different, played out before them then.

"Two letters came today," she said, flatly. Her eyes were lifeless.

CHAPTER 23

Kara held the envelope, her usual anticipation missing. In its place was a sense of dread that mingled and swirled with grief. Another part of her longed more than ever to read his words, so she sat on top of the bed and slowly took out the letter.

July 26, 1943

Dear Kara,

I received your last two wonderful letters both at once yesterday. They came just when I needed them most. I loved reading everything—well, except about what happened to you at work. I'm glad you're all right now, Sweetheart.

We haven't had a major heat wave like that here, but yesterday, it probably reached close to ninety degrees. Lugging our equipment around wasn't much fun, I can tell you. It seems things are changing out here constantly. We move from set-backs to gaining ground in a matter of hours sometimes. Things got a little intense again this week. I don't want you to worry and there's not much I can say in a letter, anyway. But when I look back at some of those recent moments, all I can say is that a guardian angel must have been looking out for me. So keep praying.

I'm staring at your picture right now as I write. Since it came a few weeks ago, I have probably brought it out a million times. You're so beautiful, sweetheart. Looking at you makes me feel we're not actually thousands of miles apart.

There's this one guy in my unit I've gotten to know pretty well. He is always talking to me about how wonderful his wife is. She found out she was expecting a baby right after he got out here. He'll be a father in just a few months and he's beside himself with excitement. And longing, too, I suspect. He's not sure when he's going to see her again or meet his baby. He's going crazy, wanting to be with her right now.

Anyway, I can't wait until we can start our life together. And hopefully a family, too, of our very own.

The words on the page began to blur and Kara had to wipe her eyes to continue reading. Her throat burned and her hands were trembling as she picked up the letter again to read the end.

Well, I guess it's time I say goodnight. It's beginning to get dark and there isn't much light to write by anymore. Hopefully, this letter will leave here tomorrow and get to you soon. I was hoping to find a place to get you a little gift, but in all the time I've been here, I've never been able to do anything like that. I remember you said your birthday is Sept. 30. How I'd love to be able to send you something by then! I keep hearing about those lucky fellows who have had time off to stroll through foreign cities, buying trinkets. But so far, there's been no sightseeing or much time to relax at all. Two months... It feels more as though I've been here for two years.

Anyway, as I keep telling myself time and time again—each day that goes by is one day closer to coming home.

Although I can't send you anything yet, I still hope to. In the meantime, I'm hoping you're wearing the watch I gave you. That promise of our future.

Take care of yourself, sweetheart. (No more fainting in the heat, now!)

I wrote my folks and Betty, but just in case, give my love to them. And know that I love you with all my heart.

Yours Always,
Jerry

Kara gripped the letter and held it close, the tears giving way to sobs that convulsed her whole body. She couldn't run to pen and paper to write him back as she had always done. There was no way for it to reach him.

He could be dead. She shook the thought from her brain. *He was alive...he had to be!* There was no way to write to him, though...the War Department didn't know where he was.

Missing. Kara thought the word held such hopelessness. There was nothing she could do but sit here, clutching his letter to her heart, and cry.

And pray. Jerry had asked her to pray. She didn't grow up praying very much. She had probably prayed more in these past few months than she ever had in her whole life. Through her tears now, she begged God that if he was still alive, He would keep him safe. To bring him back to her.

After a few minutes passed, she could hear the sound of the front door opening and closing downstairs, the muffled sound of voices. She knew it was Mr. Jeffers arriving home. She realized she shouldn't stay up here forever the way she did when the news first came. She should go be with them, but again, she first had to somehow get herself together, wash her face...

She looked down at Jerry's letter still in her hand.

No, not yet. Even though she might never be able to mail it, she knew she had to answer him.

Dear Jerry,

You have to be all right. Don't you see? I came all this way to meet you. It had to be for a reason.

Because we were meant to be together, even though time and space made it otherwise impossible to meet.

I think I loved you from the first moment I saw you. I never believed in love at first sight, but when I first looked into your eyes, it was as if I had known you forever. I can't imagine my life without you.

I'm sorry I haven't been wearing the watch you gave me. If only you could understand why...only, it's too unbelievable to understand—even for me. But I hope to someday explain it all. If only I can see you again.

Jerry, you have to come back to me. I want to be with you... to live my whole life with you. I love you more than words can say.

Forever Yours,

Kara

Folding up the letter, she put it in an envelope and wrote his name on the front without an address. Then she placed it, along with his most recent letter, in the little box with all the others. After changing her clothes and washing up, she quietly went downstairs.

***

That night, Kara tossed restlessly, sleep refusing to come. Thoughts of Jerry and worries over his fate troubled her mind and kept her awake and fitful.

When she had first gone downstairs to check on Jerry's family that evening, the mood was melancholy, yet it seemed to be tempered with a kind of stubborn hope. Mr. Jeffers had said that these things happened all the time...that they shouldn't give up but keep praying for his safety. It felt just a little easier not to despair when Kara had been with them.

But now, alone in the dark room, her worst possible fears seemed all too real. She finally bolted out of bed and turned on the light. It was already past eleven and she and Mrs. Jeffers were supposed to rise early in the morning and try to make it through another day at the Kaiser Shipyard. If she couldn't fall sleep soon, she wasn't sure how that would happen. Never mind her emotional state—lack of sleep would make her even more of a safety hazard.

She pulled out the box of letters and leaned back in bed, reading them over, one by one. As she did, the tense worries gave way to a sense of mourning—a mourning of what might never come to pass. Inside her, everything began to crumble.

"If you only knew everything...how I found my way to you. And how much I need you now..." she whispered out loud.

Before she knew it, she was heading through the house and up the attic stairs, his last letter gripped in her hand. She flicked on the light and padded across the attic, the wooden floorboards creaking beneath her bare feet.

It felt strange to her, being up here again. She peeked behind the partition and then moved slowly towards the trunk. There, on top, sat the box...and the watch he lovingly gave to her the last time she saw him. The one he had wanted her to wear until he returned.

She couldn't stop thinking about how much he wanted to send her a gift but couldn't. Because, instead, he'd been most likely sleeping in ditches and seeing death all around him.

And had he already now seen death himself?

She gazed at the watch. It broke her heart to think he'd been so troubled by not sending her anything. *But he had given her this...*

Without thinking, she reached out and picked it up. Tears clouded her vision.

"Although I can't send you anything yet, I still hope to. In the meantime, I'm hoping you're wearing the watch I gave you."

It was what he had wanted so much—for her to wear the watch he gave her when they parted at the train station. When he last kissed her good-bye. It was his promise to her...

His words in the letter echoed over and over in her brain while tears spilled down her cheeks. All the loyalty and love she felt for him suddenly coursing through her, she slipped it onto her wrist, hoping that if he was alive, he could somehow feel her heart wherever he was at that moment.

And then it began.

It started before she could even grasp what was happening. Violent streams of blinding light sparked outward. Just as before, she instinctively tried to throw off the watch but it was all happening too fast. Her vision, her balance—everything spun frantically out of control and she grasped at the trunk as if it could somehow steady her. But it couldn't.

CHAPTER 24

It didn't take her more than a few seconds to know what had happened to her. More than a few seconds to speed through nearly eighty years, just as she had done before…

NO! With one unthinking gesture, she had hurled herself away from the one person she loved the most. Panic seized her as she struggled to sit up, to think…

Find the watch…that was what she needed to do. She had thrown it off, hadn't she? It was no longer on her wrist. She frantically looked around her, feeling around the floorboards as her breaths came out fast and jagged.

Where was it? Had it simply disappeared?

If other things could change when soaring through time, she knew the location of the watch could, too. But without it there might be no way back. Her body crushed under the thought. She slowly tried to stand, her knees buckling slightly as she fought to regain her equilibrium. Outside the attic window, the night sky was dark, just as it had been. But still, *she knew*…

She dreaded going downstairs to see how everything would be different now. When all of this first happened months ago, she only wanted to return to her original time. Now that she was actually here, her stomach churned and a sense of loneliness began to overpower her. She would be all alone. The family she had grown to love as her own would not be waiting for her downstairs.

She wasn't sure how she forced her body to move, but she finally edged her way to the attic stairs and carefully began the descent. She peered down at what she wore in the faint light. It was the same nightgown and robe she had worn only minutes before when she couldn't sleep and made her way up here. *Maybe nothing had really change, after all...* She took a deep breath and opened the door.

The kitchen... The sight hit her with such force she was unable to withstand it. The Jeffers' kitchen was gone— and with it, so were they. She fell to the floor, a guttural cry of anguish escaping her lungs. All she could do was lie there and weep uncontrollably. In her worry and grief over Jerry missing, her brief lapse in thinking had taken her forever away. The torture of this regret was more than she could comprehend. She had let it all slip through her fingers in a matter of seconds.

She remained on the cold floor for most of the night, half crying and half sleeping. It was only when dawn crept through the windows that she roused herself enough to get up. She still couldn't bear to examine the rest of the house yet so she stumbled over to the sofa—

her old sofa—and collapsed. It wasn't until hours later, bright sun illuminating her living room, that she opened her eyes. And with a crushing blow, she remembered everything.

***

Kara sat at her little dining table, sipping a glass of water. It was the only thing she could seem to get down. She had already wandered through the entire house and it had been torture. Everything was neatly in place, yet as far as Kara was concerned, it had felt as if she had been walking through her home after some horrible natural disaster.

Gradually, she gazed outside to the backyard where she had spent so many wonderful moments this summer. *This summer.* Working in the garden...the party, when she danced with Jerry...

She had no more tears at the moment. Only complete numbness, as if she were in some strange coma. She had loved and worried over Jerry...now there was suddenly no one to worry about—or love. It was too much to wrap her mind or her heart around so she continued to sit silently, staring out the patio doors.

She supposed if she were someone else, she might assume now that she had simply been rendered unconscious at the very start. Instead of traveling through time, perhaps she had been more like the character,

Dorothy—and 1943 had been her Land of Oz. The idea actually made more practical sense than time travel, after all.

Still, she didn't truly believe that. Everything of the past few months had been all too real. From the smallest, most mundane details to her most blissful and heartbreaking emotions.

Now that she was back, why wasn't she hurrying to find those she left behind here? *Shannon*...she did miss Shannon. The only one she really had here besides her best friend, though, was her father—and she doubted he truly cared. She had some acquaintance-type friends and a few relatives, like Aunt Carol. But no one else. The deepest part of her had been left behind.

What happened when she left 1943, she wondered now? Was it as if they never knew her or would they wake to find her missing?

And right this minute...right this minute in time, they were all gone! Jerry's wonderful parents who took her in. Even Betty, so full of life, was probably gone. *And Jerry*...All of them gone. It was nearly eighty years ago.

Oh, Sweetheart...no. I want to come back to you. To wait for you!

Kara had assumed her tears were all used up, but she'd been wrong. They brimmed over and trickled down her cheeks, only quietly now. Although she experienced longing and grief when Jerry had gone to war and then later, had been declared missing, she knew now that she had only tasted it then.

A knock on the door caused her to jolt. She sat frozen, not sure what she should do. How could she face anyone now? Especially anyone from this time—a time that seemed more foreign to her now than anything from 1943.

The knock was persistent. Slowly, she got up and walked to the front door. Still, she hesitated. The stubborn rapping on the door continued so Kara finally reached for the handle and opened it.

To her shock, Shannon stood on her doorstep. Her expression seemed to move from worry to extreme relief within a flash.

"Oh, Kara!"

She rushed over and put her arms around her and Kara mechanically hugged her back. It *was* good to see her again, but she couldn't seem to shake off the numbness. Shannon broke away and let herself in.

"You had me beside myself! Why didn't you answer my calls? My texts?"

Kara stared at her blankly as the worried look crept back across her friend's face.

"Kara, are you all right? We just flew in from our trip late last night. I would have come over then but it was two in the morning when we got home. I woke up early and had to come see if you were okay." Shannon paused and seemed to be examining her. "So, *are* you?

It's been four days since I last heard from you. You look...have you been sick all this time?"

Four days? Kara tried to make sense of this. Had she been indeed lying up there for four days in some kind of coma?

"I'm okay," she muttered.

Obviously, Shannon wasn't buying it. "You *have* been sick, I can tell. Do you need me to take you to a doctor?"

At the question, the memory of kindly Dr. Barris flashed through her mind.

"No, I don't think I need a doctor..."

Shannon's hand felt Kara's forehead in a motherly fashion. "What have you eaten lately?"

Kara shrugged.

"Well, you don't feel warm now, but it's obvious you've been sick and out of it for days. I'm going to hang around here for a little while today and take care of you, missy."

"What day is it?" Kara dared to ask.

"Hmm. Are you sure I shouldn't take you in? What's your regular doctor's name?"

"No, please...not right now. I'm fine, really."

"It's Tuesday. Can I fix you something? Some toast, maybe?"

Kara nodded, not because she was hungry, but because it might ease Shannon's worry.

Four days. Only four days...

A few moments later, Shannon returned with a small plate and a glass of orange juice. Kara couldn't help but notice that her friend's long, curly blonde hair still looked a little unruly this morning. She remembered it had always taken Shannon a few products and a good hour to tame her wayward curls.

"The bread was looking a little stale, but it's still good for toast," she informed her as she handed her the plate.

Kara saw she had slathered lots of jam on it. Shannon sat down next to her, staring as if still taking inventory of her health.

"You look so pale. But maybe it's because you've been too sick to eat and just need a little nourishment. By the way, where did you get this sweet nightgown and robe? I've been through your closet and dresser a hundred times and don't remember seeing them. So vintage looking."

My nightgown and robe! She stared down at them and a sudden delight shot through her in the middle of all her turbulent feelings. *It was all true, I know it! It all actually happened!*

"What? What is the smile for?" When there was no reply, her voice became more intent. "Kara, what in the world has been going on with you?"

Kara fingered the sleeve of her robe. "Oh, Shannon...you would be surprised."

***

True to her word, Shannon had stayed until late afternoon. Finally, she left sometime after three o'clock, explaining she should unpack from her trip and do laundry. Before she left, Kara had to faithfully promise her she would at least open one of the cans of soup in the cupboard and have it for dinner.

"I'll call you this evening," she had told Kara as she had headed out the door. "And whatever you do, please pick up this time!"

When Kara was finally left alone again, her thoughts first drifted to what an incredible friend Shannon was. It was obvious she had been frantically worried about her and had stayed all day, despite getting in late the night before from her trip. Though Kara's world felt completely turned upside down, Shannon's friendship was the one consolation in coming back here.

Had she not returned, what would have happened? She supposed she would have just gone missing. It bothered her to think about the pain and confusion that would have caused her dearest friend.

Again, Kara's mind couldn't help but contemplate what transpired through her strange leaps through time. She took a sip of coffee from the mug Shannon had made for her before she left, pondering how this whole thing worked in a way she couldn't comprehend. Her time in the past took place over several months. Yet, she was apparently gone for only four days here.

What did it mean for Jerry's family now that she was gone? What if he came back...and I wasn't there? Or if his parents had to write him, telling him I'd left... He would have had to live his whole life always wondering... It was crushing to think she might have simply disappeared from their lives, and just like with Shannon, they were now frantic. From either time, it seemed someone would be left to worry or feel pain.

In her thoughts, it was as if the Jeffers were currently in two different dimensions. She wondered what they were all doing right this minute without her...yet in this present year, none of them were probably alive. It left a sickening feeling in her heart.

The thought suddenly came that she could easily research the Jeffers family history. It would be so easy to do by simply a search on the internet. She might even find out what became of Jerry...if he came home. *If he married...*

She wanted desperately to know if he had lived a full life, but at the same time, to see another woman's name beside his would be so painful. It would be even worse if she found out anything tragic. No...she really didn't want to find out what had happened to him. At least not for a very long time.

It felt strange sleeping in her own bed again. Her room—the master bedroom that belonged to the Jeffers—was now hers with all her own things around her again. Earlier in the day, she somehow had the presence of mind to call the preschool director and apologize for not coming to work the past two days. She explained she had been too indisposed to have called in sick and she would need at least one more day to recover. Psychologically, this was true; she knew she wasn't yet ready. There was too much to come to terms with.

Shannon had called to check up on her that evening and they had chatted for a while. Afterward, Kara had sat up in bed with her laptop, catching up with things from the last four days. At first, it felt novel to be able to have internet again because, really, it had been much longer than four days since she had experienced it. But after a while, even this lost its charm and she had set her laptop aside.

Finally, she had fallen asleep listening to relaxing music drifting from her cell phone. Still, her dreams had been fitful. Scenes of dancing with Jerry invaded her sleep...followed by horrifying images of him in the trenches, grenades exploding nearby. More than once, she had awakened, calling to him—only to find herself sitting up in bed, frightened and drenched in perspiration.

When morning finally came, she woke with a start, thinking that she had to leave for the shipyard. It took her a few moments to orient herself and remember. Tears blurred her sleep-filled eyes.

Jerry... I'm so sorry.

CHAPTER 25

She just knew she had to get out of the house for a little while. She felt compelled to see the world again just as it looked now—in her original time. Maybe by doing so, it would somehow settle her mind. At least that's what she hoped. Perhaps, the familiarity of it all would force her to accept what she lost.

She managed to eat a bowl of cereal, noticing the milk was just beginning to turn. Then she showered and dressed, throwing on the jeans and a t-shirt she always used to wear, and headed out the door. She wasn't even sure where she would be going—she only knew she had to see for herself that the world had really changed.

The rising sun was unseasonably warm on the back of her neck as she turned onto the sidewalk. *Was it still springtime here?* The scent and sight of May blooms everywhere answered her question. The season was just how it had appeared when she first met Jerry.

She took in her surroundings…the new construction, the modern vehicles passing and parked everywhere, a fast-food and coffee drive-thru on the corner, a high-tech business building that sprawled outward in the distance, surrounded by a giant parking lot. So many of the old houses were gone now and only a few remained. In their places, newer homes, condos, and apartments had sprouted up. She had never thought anything about it before she left here—it had all seemed natural. Now everything seemed strange and intrusive.

She suddenly wanted to see the place where her grandfather's house had stood. She knew that humble home with the front porch had been torn down ages ago and track homes and condos would now line the street. Rounding a corner, she paused when she was fairly sure she had found the spot. Everything faded in her imagination as she remembered her great-grandmother leaning on the porch, waiting for Beth and her friend to come home. *And waiting for her son, Grandpa George, to return from the war.*

Kara reluctantly moved on, deciding to head downtown. She knew that very little had changed in the structure of the old town area, but as she approached Main Street, she noticed that the area indeed was more different than she remembered. Besides many shops having changed hands, there were other unexplainable things.

She slowed down as she came closer to the Amberton Bijou and glanced up at the marque. It advertised a current title she had no desire to see, but the memory of seeing the movie here with Jerry caused a smile to form on her lips.

A part of her didn't even want to view where the old soda fountain used to be. It wasn't there anymore and she had forgotten what had taken its place. But she kept walking and when she knew she must be in the right spot, she looked to see that the space was currently vacant and in the middle of changing business hands. She thought she remembered an old bookstore near here that she had wandered through once, but it hadn't stuck around long. It was hard to imagine this space had once been the wonderful, lively soda fountain. She peered into the dark window and swallowed the lump forming in her throat before slowly moving on.

As she wandered aimlessly around the streets, Kara felt a sense of heaviness. Back before everything happened, she used to like to come here now and again. Now, nothing seemed right. It wasn't as if she didn't like some of the newer shops, but somehow, everything felt glaringly out of place.

The cars were all wrong, too. There were no 1938 sedans parked along the street. The pedestrians wearing summer flip flops and shorts while staring down at cell phones, the occasional purple hair...they all seemed so foreign to her now.

Of course, she knew people were still people underneath what they wore, but she missed the simple elegance she used to see strolling down Main Street. Men in suits and hats, women wearing gloves...but something even more intangible than that. The charm was missing now. But then, nothing was the same without Jerry. She was sure she could feel at home almost anywhere—any place in time—if only Jerry could be with her.

But that chance was now gone.

After returning to the house, Kara scoured the kitchen for something for lunch. She discovered a small container of yogurt in the back of her fridge. She knew she had to go grocery shopping soon.

Still feeling restless, she meandered through her living room with the yogurt and spoon in hand, observing all her books neatly in rows on her bookshelf. Her DVD collection underneath her small flat-screen TV, her candles and a couple antiques she had collected—everything that was her own. Everything that used to make her feel at home was now around her once again. Yet, all she felt while looking at her cozy belongings was hollow inside.

She heard her phone go off then as it sat on a shelf, charging. She was still so unaccustomed to the sound. Picking it up, she saw it was Shannon's number.

"How are you feeling now?" Shannon immediately asked.

"A little better, I think. I took today off, though."

"Good. I think you really need the rest. Do you have enough food in the house?"

"Well, no. I'm thinking of going to the store in a little while."

"I don't know. You looked so pale yesterday. Why don't I bring you over some pizza?"

Kara had to admit, the thought of that sounded wonderful. She could use the company to keep her from thinking too much. Besides, it felt like ages since she had relaxed with a pizza. She hesitated, though—Shannon had such a giving nature and she didn't want to take advantage.

"You've done so much already—you're still resting up from California, after all."

"Oh, don't worry. I slept in this morning and am pretty much caught up with everything. I didn't have to work today, either. I'm officially still on vacation and don't go back to the office until tomorrow. Anyway, there are still more pictures on my phone that I didn't show you from the trip. Let me bring over a pizza and maybe we can watch a movie or something."

It felt like forever since Kara had relaxed at home with a movie and pizza—and her best friend. She used to reminisce over their times together when she thought she'd never see Shannon again. Now was her chance.

"If you're sure…that would be great."

"Good! I'll see you in about an hour."

After they hung up, Kara noticed her mood had picked up a little. Maybe this was just what she needed.

Almost exactly an hour later, Shannon arrived with the steaming pizza in her hands.

"Sausage and mushroom?" Kara asked as she let her in at the door.

"Sausage and mushroom, just for you."

"Aw, I don't deserve you. You're the best." Kara took the box and set it on the coffee table. Soon they were comfortable on the sofa, eating and chatting about nothing in particular.

"What movie did you want to watch?"

"Oh, I don't know," Shannon said between bites. "But don't forget to have me show you those other pictures in a little while." She took a long sip from her water bottle before glancing over at Kara. "And by the way...what did you mean by what you said yesterday?"

Kara looked her way. "What did I say?"

"When I asked you what's been going on with you and you said I'd be surprised. At the time, I assumed you were just kidding around since we both knew you had been sick all week. But I was just thinking about it now. What was that about?"

Kara's mouth went dry. There had been so many times she thought about what it would be like to face the truth with Jerry. But Shannon? The idea of ever telling her had only been a fleeting thought. How could she possibly make her believe such a thing? She set her plate onto the coffee table, her half-eaten slice of pizza no longer quite as appetizing.

"What is it?" Shannon persisted when she didn't reply.

334

Kara shook her head. "I was just...talking. You said it yourself."

There was a long pause before Shannon said, "Listen, Kara, I've known you a long time. I know you're not quite yourself right now, but I also know when you're hiding something. Come on, you know you can tell me anything."

Could she? At the worst, Shannon could try to have her committed. But in this day and age, it would have to be for a lot more than just telling a story. Besides, she would never do that to her. Shannon *would*, however, probably be even more worried about her than she already was. Still, a part of her was longing to tell her everything and not have to keep it inside anymore.

As if sensing her indecision, Shannon went on, her voice a bit gentler. "I don't want to badger you or anything. If you feel you can't tell me what's going on, I'll understand. I just want to help, though."

Kara looked back over at her best friend—this close friend she'd known for years—waiting with an expression full of concern.

"All right," she said, quietly. "But I give you fair warning. You probably won't believe a single word of it."

CHAPTER 26

The only sounds that could be heard as she paused in her story were the ticking of the clock and the distant hum of a neighbor's lawnmower. Kara had been avoiding eye contact as she spoke, but now she carefully peered over at Shannon to try to read her expression. She found no skepticism there, but her eyes were wide and she seemed rather frozen. Kara assumed she was either trying to absorb the story—or terrified for Kara's well-being.

"Please…say something, Shannon."

Kara had just finished recalling the good-bye at the train station. There was so much more to tell, but she knew she couldn't continue without first hearing Shannon's reaction.

"I…" Now it was Shannon who had no words. After a few seconds, she seemed to try again. "So, you're saying you…you actually went back in time?"

"Yes, that's what I'm saying." Silence fell between them again. Kara wanted to describe all the many details she experienced while there, but she wasn't sure it would make any difference at the moment.

After a little while, Shannon asked, quietly, "Have you thought about the possibility that you could have been so sick that you were delirious? Or maybe struck unconscious, somehow?"

Kara nodded. "Of course. When it first happened, I wondered about that, too. In fact, when I was suddenly brought back here, I asked myself that same question all over again. But everything was all too real." She paused, and then added, "And...I came back wearing that nightgown and robe, remember? I had bought them there—in 1943."

Shannon's already stunned expression grew more incredulous.

"You see, it was the watch that started it all," Kara added.

"Where...where is the watch now?"

"I don't know." Kara realized this fact didn't help her credibility. "As I mentioned, Jerry gave me the watch at the train station when he said good-bye. I was so afraid to wear it since it was what had started everything in motion to begin with. By that time, I was...I knew I loved him. I didn't want to leave anymore."

"But...then what happened? How did you come back?"

Was Shannon beginning to believe her or just humoring her, she wondered?

"Before I get to that, I guess I need to backtrack a bit." Kara went on to tell her how she then began working at the Kaiser Shipyard and had learned to weld...how she drove back and forth to Portland with Mrs. Jeffers in the beautiful 1938 Chevy...and how the first letter from Jerry came, asking her to marry him.

"I wrote him back, telling him yes. And...well..." Her calm, cool voice she had been trying to maintain began to falter. "You see, at first, I had been consumed with how I might return to my old time...back here. Or at least I had been torn. After a while, I knew that I only wanted Jerry. I never wanted to leave him...or his family."

Shannon listened in stunned silence.

"His letters...they were so wonderful. They would either come all at once or not at all," Kara went on. "And then, one day...we received a telegram. He was missing in action." It was harder to keep her voice steady. "It was all so horrible...wondering if he was all right...if he was even still alive. And now...now it doesn't even matter because it's...decades and decades later...I'll never see him again..."

The despair overwhelmed her again and a sob escaped her throat. It had been the first time she ever verbalized everything out loud. Shannon moved closer, putting her arms around her. "Shh, it's okay," she whispered.

But it wasn't okay! It couldn't be when she had lost Jerry forever.

As Shannon tried to comfort her, Kara wondered what her friend could be thinking. She wouldn't really blame her if she assumed she had completely lost it. Everything sounded so unbelievable.

Shannon grabbed a tissue from the box on the end table and handed it to her. "But...how did you leave that time and come back here?" she asked Kara again after a few moments.

Kara drew another deep breath.

"It was the watch. I had kept it on the trunk in the attic. I had first found it inside there, remember? So when Jerry gave it to me at the train station, I was in shock. It had been the first time I had seen it since everything first happened. I was so afraid...afraid of what it could do. So I just kept it there, away from my view...on top of the trunk."

Kara wiped at her eyes before continuing, not wanting to relive what happened next.

"Several letters came after the telegram. In one of them, Jerry said how he hoped I was wearing the watch he gave me and...that night, I couldn't sleep so I went up to the attic. I don't know...I guess I was beside myself with worry over him. Without thinking, I put it on my wrist...just like I did when it all first happened. How could I have been so stupid, Shannon? It only took a split second..."

She began to cry again as her friend hugged her shoulder. Finally, after several minutes, Kara sat up and dabbed her eyes.

"It's okay—if you don't believe me, I mean. I won't blame you if you don't, honestly. I know how crazy it all sounds."

Shannon took a long, deep breath. "To be honest, I...I don't know what to think. I mean...forgive me, Kara, but it's no secret that you love antiques and things from the past. It could have entered your subconscious when you were out of it from something..."

"But Shannon, I spent four months there!"

"But you didn't, really. Perhaps it only seemed that way. Only four days passed and in that time you could have been unconscious. Besides, if you...if you actually went back in time, then why have only four days passed instead of four months?"

"I really don't know...perhaps a different time continuity or something," Kara muttered. She felt a growing desperation; she had to somehow make her understand! "Shannon...I *really* was there. I know it. It was four months of living, breathing, sleeping, eating...Of conversations, of tears...of actually falling in love." She paused to catch her breath and think, and then suddenly added, "How do you explain the nightgown, Shannon? I was wearing the same nightgown and robe I wore there the night it happened. I bought it there—right there, in that time. You said it yourself—you've rummaged through my wardrobe and know I never owned that before."

Shannon's expression faltered. "I have to admit, that... this whole thing... Could someone possibly even go back in time?"

"I wouldn't have thought so before, but I guess I've gotten past that strangeness. And now...the hardest part for me is that...while I was there, I found real love. Maybe the reason I was able to go back in time was that he was the only one I could ever truly love that way. It was the only way the two of us could be together. But in a moment of stupidity, I threw it all away."

Kara let the tears fall quietly and they sat in silence for several more minutes. Finally, Shannon broke the silence, asking gently, "You said it all happened with the watch?"

Kara nodded.

"Why can't you find it now? Where did it go?"

"I'm not sure." Kara crumpled up her Kleenex, blotting the stray tears.

"Can you show me where it happened?"

A few moments later, Kara led the way up the attic stairs. The two reached the top, the boards creaking as they slowly walked across to the other side of the partition.

"So this is the trunk you were rummaging through." Shannon walked closer to get a better look. "Isn't there a light we can turn on or something?"

Kara reached over to pull the chain on the ceiling, but as usual, it did little to illuminate the rest of the attic.

"The watch must have flown off around here somewhere when....wait a minute. If it had flown off my wrist in 1943, it probably wouldn't be here now—in this time. It could be anywhere."

A vague sense of despair swept over her. The watch had always seemed to be the key. And without it, she'd never be able to return.

"I think I understand what you're saying. But if that's true, why were you still wearing the nightgown you wore then?"

Kara thought for a moment. "I suppose because of the fact that I was actually wearing them. The watch must have flown off before I changed times."

Shannon bent near the right side of the trunk, in the dark corner by the wall, and picked up what looked like a loose paper. "What's this?"

Kara took it and they stepped over by the light. As her eyes focused, she felt the blood rush to her head like a torrent.

"Shannon. It's Jerry's letter..."

CHAPTER 27

Kara's hands were shaking. *His beautiful letter.* She would still have this part of him—a small part of his heart to hold onto forever.

"Kara? Are you telling me this is the letter he wrote you when you were back in time?" Shannon's face looked pale as she leaned in close to read the first few words.

July 26, 1943
Dear Kara,
I received your last two letters both at once yesterday. They came just when I needed them most....

Her friend stared up at her, shaking her head over and over. Her overwhelming shock was plain to see. "Kara...."

Then, unexpectedly, she dropped down to sit on the floor. Shannon was simply sitting there, stunned, in the middle of the attic floor so Kara slowly sat down next to her.

"If I never see him again, at least I'll always have this letter," she whispered, mostly to herself.

The two of them remained there as many minutes ticked by.

"May I see it?" Shannon finally asked, quietly. "Is it all right if I read it?"

Kara hesitated for a second before relinquishing it over. She waited as Shannon read the entire letter in silence. When she was through, she looked up at Kara with tears in her eyes.

"I don't know what to say."

Kara knew there was not much to deny anymore. The letter was an authentic V-mail letter, addressed to her. Shannon handed it back to her and pulled her close into a hug.

After a few more minutes, they finally headed downstairs. Kara carried Jerry's letter tenderly. Though she had lost all his other letters, she had come away with this one. She'd put it in her jewelry box—the one she inherited from her mom—and keep Jerry with her forever.

***

That night, sleep evaded her once again. It was getting to be habit—her brain always seemed to be turning things over every time she'd lie down.

Shannon had stayed a little while longer that evening when they returned from the attic, and they spent the next hour quietly talking. During that time, Kara had told her more bits and pieces of her story while her best friend listened intently. She told Shannon all about her work at the shipyard, Jerry's parents and sister, and some of the simple details of her daily life. She tried to describe how different things were there—the fashions, music, and even the manners. How it all seemed to possess a class and charm she couldn't quite define.

"There seemed to be a kind of bravery I've never seen before, too," she had told her.

Kara now believed brave people existed within every generation, but the bravery of World War II seemed to her more widespread and unified. She saw it in those who served overseas but also in those left behind. And she had actually become one of them.

"I'll be forever grateful that I got to be a part of it all, even if it was for just a little while."

"And Jerry...you two honestly fell in love, didn't you? I mean...it was very real."

"Yes...we knew each other such a short time, but yes. It was real love. More real than anything."

Shannon had nodded. "I could feel that in his letter."

"More real than I'll ever experience again. I still love him, Shannon. I guess I always will."

Later, they had agreed that neither one of them would tell anyone else because there wouldn't be any sense in it. It was simply too incredible.

Shannon hadn't stayed late to watch a movie. Neither of them seemed in the frame of mind. So she had given Kara a hug, and as she left, turned and looked her in the eye.

"I know it happened, Kara. I'm not sure how, but I know it did. Your secret will always be safe with me. And whenever you need to talk, I'll be here."

Hours later, Kara lay alone in the dark. She tossed off part of her blanket and tried to get comfortable, but it was no use. The May evening felt humid and her thoughts tumbled over one another. She was wearing her cotton nightshirt—one she used to wear in this time on very warm nights. It was roomy and went down to her knees, and had come with little slippers when she had bought it.

With a sigh, she threw off her blanket and sat up. She tucked her feet into the slippers next to the bed, grabbed her robe and her cell phone from her nightstand, and headed downstairs. It seemed a lost cause to just lie there any longer. Making her way to the kitchen, she poured herself a glass of water from the filtered pitcher in the fridge. Then she leaned back, sipping it, still feeling the stifling heat.

As she stood there, she thought about everything that had happened lately, especially finding the letter and her conversations with Shannon. She still had an ache inside that wouldn't let up, but she was grateful that at least Shannon truly believed her.

Kara realized she had usually been able to count on Shannon as long as she had known her. Her friend wasn't perfect, of course, and neither was she. There had even had a few squabbles now and then over the years, but Shannon was a true friend in every definition of the word.

She took another long sip of water, hoping it would cool her, and then glanced at the clock. *11:30.* Tomorrow morning, bright and early, she was supposed to go back to work. It had seemed like forever since she had worked at the preschool. She did miss the children, of course. The thought of returning, though—just as if nothing had ever happened—seemed so strange at the moment. It was a bit far-reaching to think about being a responsible teacher when her world was still reeling.

Her life didn't even feel like it belonged here anymore. She supposed she would get used to it in time…She'd go back to work and eventually things—and this world—would begin to feel familiar again. She knew, though, that she would never be the same.

I really should go back to bed—at least try to sleep. However, as she lingered there, her mind kept turning over and over. Soon, those thoughts returned to the attic where everything began.

Strange, how the watch flew away, but I managed to hold onto Jerry's letter. Had the watch truly disappeared into a different time?

After a while, she set her glass down on the counter and purposely headed up the dark, narrow attic stairs. Once reaching the top, she switched on the light, feeling the wave of heat greet her as she padded across the floor. As she turned past the partition, a realization hit her.

What on earth has been wrong with me? Why haven't I searched inside the trunk?

The only excuse Kara could think of in that second was that she had been in a perpetual state of shock. Not just recently, but really from the moment everything first changed. How could she expect herself to always be able to think clearly?

Anyway, it didn't matter, she told herself. Whatever reasons behind her skewed reasoning, she hoped she might be on the right track now.

Of course, the watch might not even be in the trunk at all, but still lying on the floor in 1943. She knew she couldn't rest easy, though, until she checked every last square inch. She had to least see…

She stepped closer and using her phone as a light, she quickly unlatched and lifted the top of the trunk. *It has to be here…* Her hand brushed the stacks of papers, lifting them and moving other items around gently. *It has to be here…*

Over and over, she spoke these words in her head, as if willing them to be true. She lifted the blanket out, setting it on the floor next to her and then kept carefully rummaging through the trunk. As the seconds ticked by, she could already feel some of her sudden hopes fading. It all seemed too reminiscent. She had searched in vain like this before, only to come up empty—except then, it had been for completely different reasons.

Then, her fingertips touched the smoothness of a wooden box. Kara lifted it out and her heart skipped a beat. It was the cedar box—the same box Jerry had given to her! She wished her heart wasn't pounding so hard inside her chest. She forced her shaking hands to open the small lid. And then, her mouth dropped open—and with it, her heart.

The watch wasn't there.

Kara stared at the empty box with unbelieving eyes. She didn't understand…

For a moment she sat back on her heels, feeling defeated and hopeless. Then she suddenly dropped the box in frustration and began digging through the trunk, callously tossing a fragile stack of papers aside. Tears stung the back of her eyes. She went on this way for a full minute when her hand felt something again that caused her to suddenly stop. Reaching down to grasp it, she began sobbing.

She stared at the precious watch in her hand, hardly believing it was true.

But what if it can't send me back this time?

The question assaulted her mind out of nowhere. There had been so many disappointments already, one after another. Nothing held any guarantees.

"Where are you in this, God?" she heard herself say out loud. She was sitting on the attic floor now, her legs crossed under her and items from the trunk scattered carelessly around. "Where do you want me to be?"

She may not have felt very close to God all these years, yet she believed He heard her. Though she didn't have an audible answer to her question, a realization began to take shape. If He controlled the universe, and if what she had once heard was true—that He cared about each person in it—then maybe she could just leave the decision with Him.

When this thought came, Kara began to feel a little calmer. It dawned on her that perhaps she didn't have to writhe and strain for this to happen—or worry if it didn't. She also realized she'd been beating herself up over the impulsive gesture that sent her plummeting back here. Now even this burden began to ease, too, ever so slightly. Perhaps some things were completely out of her hands.

She set the watch on the floor in front of her, gazing at it.

Do I honestly want to go back...forever? Do I want to leave my dearest friend and never see her again? I can't even be sure I'll actually see Jerry again...really get to marry him...perhaps he won't even make it...

For a split second, she faltered. If only she didn't have to choose between two worlds! It seemed this choice kept being put to her over and over again.

But deep down, she knew. If she went back and something happened to Jerry, she could learn to live there. After all, she didn't have him here, either. It was a chance she had to take. The love she had for him was worth everything.

Yet, it wasn't completely her choice to make.

"All right, I'm leaving it up to you." She whispered the prayer as her hand reached for the watch. Then she stopped, her hand in mid-air. Letting her hand drop, she took a deep breath.

Not quite yet.

She rose to her feet and hurried down the attic stairs, taking only her phone. Once in the kitchen, she threw open one of the drawers, pulling out a pen and piece of paper from the large notepad and then found a seat at the dining room table.

All the warm memories and love for her dearest friend rose to the surface as she began her note. She had never gotten the chance to say good-bye last time. She couldn't take that chance again.

Dear Shannon,

I want to tell you how very much your friendship means to me. No one could ever ask for a better friend than you. You have stuck by me through everything and I wish I had words to express how grateful I am. Especially for your believing in me.

I want you to know, I found the watch. If nothing comes of it, I'll be telling you all this in person. But just in case I never get a chance to see you again, you will know not to worry. If this happens, I'm sorry to leave you to deal with any loose ends here. Most of all, I'm sorry to leave you and our friendship. I'll treasure it forever.

Just know that if this takes me back, it's where I need to be. And I'll be happy. Even if he doesn't make it, I think in time, I can truly be happy there.

I wish you so much happiness in life, too, Shannon. I wish, more than anything, I could take you with me. But know that wherever I am, you can be sure that it doesn't take away my memory of you. It never did before—so please know I'll be thinking of you and you'll always be in my heart.

Love,
Your Friend,
Always and Forever,
Kara

She set the pen down, fighting back her sudden tears. If only she actually could take Shannon back with her! She knew, though, that even if that were possible, it would be unfair to ask her to leave her own family and the life she knew. *But our friendship won't ever end...not really.*

She had to leave the letter somewhere obvious for Shannon to find it... *On top of the trunk!* Still, she had to be sure she'd know to look there right away. Reaching for her phone, she stopped for a second to think. Then she sent her a quick text: *If you don't hear back from me for a while, don't worry, I'm fine. And I have something for you up in the attic. Please let yourself in. Love you!*

She knew she could never tell her anything in a text. It had to be an actual letter, for so many reasons. At least now, she was confident Shannon would eventually understand.

Kara always left the key under the planter for her whenever she needed to let herself into the house, so she retrieved the spare from the kitchen drawer. Hurrying over to open the front door, she slipped it under the planter in the pale moonlight.

On impulse, she ran up the main staircase and picked up her mother's jewelry box. Her eyes lingered on the contents—Jerry's letter, her mother's simple costume jewelry, as well as several cards she'd given her over the years. She stood there for a moment before gently closing the lid. Then, clutching both the jewelry box and her letter to Shannon, Kara hurried back down the main stairs.

She threw one last glance around her living room with all her belongings as she passed through. She couldn't help but wonder if it would be the last time she'd ever see it all like this again.

CHAPTER 28

She knew it might not happen. She had tried to prepare herself—tried to tell herself that she would let God decide all of this for her.

She had slipped the watch back onto her wrist with her heart beating like crazy. Now she was lying on the attic floor, the watch still clasped around her wrist. There had been no crazy sparks…no violent spinning. Nothing had seemed to change.

She lay scrunched up in a fetal position, feeling as if she were in mire and unable to move. It had been so easy to say that she trusted God for the outcome when she could still cling to her hope of seeing Jerry again. Now the pain of having that last hope gone was more than she could imagine. She clutched the jewelry box now, as a child would to a stuffed animal. *Her hope was gone.*

She wasn't sure how long she lay there crying, but finally, she slowly sat up. She peered down at the watch, still dangling from her wrist. She didn't understand…any of it!

Yet, this watch… Jerry had given it to her. She didn't know why it hadn't brought her back to him but at least she could wear it now. It would be her way of remembering him always, just as he had intended it. Her fingers touched its delicate face, almost as if it were Jerry's face instead.

She felt chilled and pulled her robe tightly around her, in spite of the earlier heat. There was no use in staying up here any longer. She had nothing left to do now but simply go back to bed. Her grief was turning into a strange numbness—she didn't seem to have anything left to feel.

As she trudged down the attic stairs, she realized that the highs and lows of all her emotions and dashed hopes had taken their toll. She felt drained to her very core. She would have to call in sick, yet again—there was simply no way she could possibly go back to work tomorrow.

Stepping down into the dark kitchen, her slipper-clad feet shuffled across the floor. She nearly bumped into something and then stopped short. *Hadn't she left the light on?* Finding her way to the switch, her fingers fumbled to flip it on. Then she stared, frozen in wonder. She had been through so much; she almost didn't dare believe it. But the longer she stood there, the more she realized it was true…*She was actually back!*

***

Adrenaline pushed through her veins. She ran to the dining room...then quickly peeked into the living room. The soft light of dawn was beginning to sift through the curtains, allowing all the rooms to slowly come into view. The Jeffers' furniture—all their belongings—were here again!

Kara's eyes were glistening with pure joy. She hurried around, touching everything to make sure that they were real—the dining room table...the sofa...the bookcase...She picked up Jerry's photograph from the shelf and held it close.

"I'm back again, sweetheart," she whispered, a tear cascading down her cheek. "Now you have to come back to me, too."

Outside, birds tentatively began singing their first early morning notes. Glancing at the clock, she saw that it was nearly five o'clock.

Five o'clock already? That didn't seem quite right. Then she remembered that this strange time continuity wasn't anything she could count on. Months had equaled days...perhaps days equaled hours. Maybe the Jeffers' hadn't even had time to miss her, she thought, hopefully!

Kara realized the family would probably be getting up soon. She was so excited; she knew she couldn't possibly go back to bed now. It was amazing to think she had been too depressed to move only minutes ago and now she was brimming over with joy!

She didn't think she could sleep a wink until she saw everyone, but she couldn't wake them now, of course. Carefully, she placed the picture back and tiptoed upstairs. She was still carrying her mother's jewelry box and glanced down at it, smiling, glad for the presence of mind to bring it with her.

As she quietly entered Jerry's old room, she turned on the light and placed the box on top of the dresser. She decided to slip off the watch for now and place it inside.

Immediately afterward, a panicked thought seized her. She quickly looked around and held her breath. After a while, she was able to breathe again. Nothing happened—she was still here. Taking off the watch hadn't sent her plummeting away again; however, it had sent a wave of fear and she knew she could never take the chance of wearing the watch ever again. She would have to figure out what to do with it a little later, though. Right now, too much had happened for her to think.

Kara gently closed the lid and suddenly glanced at her robe. How would she explain her new robe and slippers from the twenty-first century? Not feeling like dressing yet, she quickly changed into her one other nightgown, pushing her modern sleepwear to the back of the drawer. Then, she went to lie down for just a while.

Without realizing, Kara dozed off, in spite of her excitement. The sound of her alarm woke her and after instinctively turning it off, she rolled back over. Within seconds, her eyes burst open, remembering. She sat up and was relieved to see she was still in Jerry's room.

It had actually happened. I'm back!

She smiled, feeling just like a child on Christmas morning. She could now hear the wonderful sounds of the family stirring. How she had missed them! Remembering to whisper a thank you for the miracle, she hurried out to the hall.

Mrs. Jeffers stepped out of her room at about the same moment. She was already dressed, but not wearing her usual shipyard attire. Kara had thought she might never see her again and she longed to rush over to greet her with a hug but knew she wouldn't quite understand.

When Mrs. Jeffers suddenly caught sight of Kara, she froze where she stood.

"Kara?" She looked pale, all color drained from her face. It was reminiscent of the moment they had first received the telegram. She wondered if Mrs. Jeffers might be ill and quickly ran over to steady her.

"What is it? What's wrong?"

"What's wrong?" she repeated, slowly and quietly. Kara was beginning to be truly worried now.

Mr. Jeffers emerged from the bedroom now. "Kara! Where were you?"

"What do you mean...?"

Oh no.

It was Mrs. Jeffers who threw her arms around Kara now. "We were so worried!" She pulled away to look at her. "Where were you? What happened?"

"I..." If only she knew how long she had appeared missing, she might be able to answer somewhat coherently. "I'm so sorry I worried you."

"Kara!" Betty came bursting upstairs and threw her arms around her. "What happened? "

"Kara, we had the police searching for you. When you were nowhere to be found all day yesterday, we were all beginning to get frantic," Mr. Jeffers was saying.

A horrible guilt engulfed her for making all of them worry so much—this family who obviously cared about her well-being. Although she knew the situation had been mostly beyond her control, it didn't stop her from feeling crushed as she looked around at their faces.

It also felt as if she were being chased to the edge of a cliff. She had no possible excuse which could account for her having been missing an entire day. She stammered, and the lump in her throat threatened to give way to yet another bout of sobbing if she wasn't careful.

"I...I'm truly sorry. I didn't..." She swallowed, trying to gain control, but her eyes filled, blurring her vision. "I never meant to worry any of you. I can't offer any excuses. Only that..." She uttered the only truth she possibly could. "I was so upset. I missed Jerry so much and I was so worried."

All their eyes remained on her, waiting for more of an explanation.

"I don't think I understand. Where did you go?" Mr. Jeffers finally asked.

"Just... *away*. Farther away than I ever wanted to. I didn't plan any of it, really!" she added quickly. "Please believe me, I never meant to hurt you. Any of you. I can't explain it all now...but I hope in time, you all will forgive me for worrying everybody like this."

Mrs. Jeffers slid her arm around Kara. "It's just that we've grown to love you," she said, softly. "Please...if you ever feel the need to leave again, just tell us. You're a free person and can come and go as you please. It's just that...we were so worried that something terrible might have happened when you just disappeared like that."

Kara's heart wrenched as she looked from face to face. "I'm so, so sorry."

Did they all actually love her, she wondered? She had hoped they were fond of her but to hear that they loved her was almost too good to be true.

"I'll go make a phone call and let them know you've come back safe," Mr. Jeffers said, softly patting Kara's shoulder as he passed them. She felt the simple gesture was his way of saying he was forgiving her, too.

"Betty, why don't you and I go make breakfast."

Betty nodded and headed downstairs. Mrs. Jeffers paused, looking back at Kara. "But...when did you actually get back? When we all went to bed last night, you hadn't come home yet."

"It was very late."

"And you left before we all got up yesterday morning..." She paused, looking even more closely at Kara, as if trying to read her thoughts. "Are you all right now? Really all right? You must have been so upset to leave like that. You know, if you ever need someone to talk to, I'm always here to listen."

"Thank you." Her voice came out sounding strange. She cleared her throat and blinked hard against the tears. "I think I'm okay. Just very tired. And a little emotional, I guess. I am mostly so sorry for the worry I caused all of you. You have to believe me—I never planned to leave and be gone so long! It just sort of happened. I got back here just as soon as I could."

Mrs. Jeffers smiled gently. "Well, I think you'd better rest today. You see, I actually hadn't planned on going into work myself. Not with...you...Anyway, I think we both should take the day off, don't you?"

Kara nodded and hugged her. "I'll be down in a little while."

***

The shower felt warm and cleansing, and Kara lingered there a little longer than usual. Her emotions and mind still felt so precarious.

Too many changes too quickly, she thought. She kept telling herself that at least she was back—and now she knew beyond a shadow of a doubt .that she never wanted to leave again. Her heart still ached for Jerry but the Jeffers were the closest thing to family she'd ever have. It felt so comforting to be back with them again.

A half an hour later, Kara headed downstairs, feeling somewhat refreshed. She was thankful, though, she didn't have to face a full day at the shipyard quite yet.

Betty was the first to greet her as she stepped into the kitchen.

"We're having blueberry pancakes," she informed her, smiling brightly. "Mrs. Peterson, next door, has blueberry bushes in her backyard and she brought us over some yesterday." She handed Kara the wooden spoon. "Here, you can mix the batter I just made."

"Blueberry pancakes sound wonderful."

Betty leaned in and gave her a quick hug. "I'm so glad you're okay." Her voice lowered into almost a whisper. "I was so worried, Kara. Worried that something had happened to you…or that maybe you just decided to leave us without saying goodbye."

Kara wanted to blurt out that she would never do such a terrible thing…but then, she had found she never seemed to have very many guarantees where these things were concerned.

"I'm so sorry, Betty. You and your family mean so much to me. In fact, I feel like you *are* my family. I...I would never intentionally leave like that."

After breakfast, Kara insisted on doing all of the dishes herself. When she was finally through, she wandered into the living room. Mr. Jeffers had already gone to work but Mrs. Jeffers was sitting in the comfortable chair, hemming one of her pairs of work pants.

"Thank you for doing the dishes—have a seat and relax now, dear," she told Kara. "This second pair of pants is way too long. I think I need to take off a whole inch."

Kara found a seat on the sofa. "What's Betty up to?"

"She's upstairs getting ready. One of the neighbors hired her to watch her two children while she goes to the dentist this morning."

Kara picked up a random magazine from the coffee table and they sat in comfortable silence for a moment until Mrs. Jeffers gently cleared her throat.

"Dear, I wanted to ask you something."

Kara had been thumbing through the pages, pausing when she saw an interesting article. It was all about movie stars volunteering at the Hollywood canteen.

"Hmm?" She was thankful for the chance to relax like this after everything. To not even think.

"I was just wondering...I know I'm probably prying. But where *did* you go when you were gone all day yesterday? Was it, by chance, to see your family?"

Kara looked up sharply.

"I'm sorry; I don't mean to upset you. It's just that I know so little about your background and I've often wondered where you came from...what your home life was like. I know it sounds like I'm just being nosy, but honestly, I only want to help. You're like a daughter to me—in fact, you *will* be my daughter when...when Jerry comes home and you two marry. So, I want you to always know you can feel safe to confide in me."

Kara swallowed. "Thank you. But...no, I...I wasn't seeing my family." She knew Mrs. Jeffers was waiting to hear more. "I know I haven't talked much about them," she said, quietly. "I think I told you that my mother is gone now. My father remarried and moved away and we just sort of lost touch."

"I see. I just couldn't help but wonder. Especially when you said you had traveled pretty far yesterday and that you were so upset. There's not anything else you'd care to tell me?"

"Something else?"

"Oh, I don't know. No one else from your past?"

Kara tried to think what she could mean. She hoped she wasn't worried she had secret boyfriends or husbands hiding away somewhere.

"No, there's no one from my past." Kara fingered the page of the magazine in her lap.

"Well, forget I even asked, then. The most important thing is that you're back with us, safe and sound. Just remember, if you ever want to talk, I'm here to listen."

"Thank you, Mrs. Jeffers. That means a lot to me."

Then Kara was sent a scolding half-smile. "You mean, Marjorie, don't you?"

Kara laughed, the tension easing away. "It just slipped out. I meant, *Marjorie*."

"Anyway, it's just as well I'm taking the day off." She had gone back to her hemming as she spoke. "I'm so behind in all my sewing. Now that you're safe and my mind's at rest, maybe I can tackle a few other projects today, too. Mr. Jeffers has a couple pairs of socks that need darning and I promised to help Betty with a few finishing touches on her dress."

Kara nodded, gazing back down at her article just as the doorbell rang.

"I'll get it! I'm on my way out, anyway," Betty announced, bounding down the staircase.

Kara watched from the sofa as Betty threw open the door…then saw her body become rigid. A young boy wearing a Western Union uniform stood solemnly on the front step.

Within seconds, Mrs. Jeffers was out of her seat, running to the door. Somehow, Kara wasn't able to move.

CHAPTER 29

She seemed to watch everything in slow motion. Hadn't she gone through all of this already? Had she returned now, just to face something even worse? Kara knew she should be there, standing with Mrs. Jeffers and Betty as they were handed the telegram…as they opened it. *Why couldn't she move?*

She finally forced her muscles to obey and propel her towards them. As she reached the doorway, Mrs. Jeffers thanked the delivery boy and closed the front door slowly. She held the telegram and her hands trembled uncontrollably while Betty's eyes welled with tears.

"Do you…want me to read it for you?" Kara managed to ask.

"No," she answered quietly. "I'll be all right."

"Maybe we should all go sit down," Kara suggested, putting her arm around Mrs. Jeffers. She nodded in reply and they all found their way to the divan. Mrs. Jeffers proceeded to study the telegram first, while Kara and Betty each clung to her on either side. Then, a sob escaped the woman's throat. Kara began crying instinctively as she leaned over, trying to read it.

"He's all right! Jerry's all right!" Mrs. Jeffers shouted before Kara could even comprehend the words on the paper. All of them began hugging and crying a sort of joyous wail.

Jerry...oh, sweetheart, you're still alive!

Tears were streaming down Kara's face and she realized she was shaking with relief. After several minutes, she asked to see the telegram. Mrs. Jeffers handed it to her and she strained to read it through the tearful blur in her eyes.

```
    I am very pleased to inform you
that your son, Private Gerald R.
Jeffers, who was previously reported
missing in action, has been found
safe. He is currently in transit to an
Army Hospital in Algeria where he will
be recovering from wounds and illness
related to dehydration.
    At this time, he is expected to
make a full recovery and to return to
the United States as soon as he is
deemed well enough to travel. We will
be updating you with more details to
follow.
```

Kara finally set the telegram down. She was filled with incredible joy and relief, but there was still so much they didn't know. What was the extent of his injuries and illness...and what had happened to him while he was missing?

One thing seemed certain and surpassed all else, though: *He was coming home!*

Mrs. Jeffers phoned her husband minutes later. Kara tried not to eavesdrop, but she couldn't help but hear. She wished she could see the look in his eyes as he heard the good news, but instead, she tried to imagine it.

"Things are slow at the office," Mrs. Jeffers simply said when she hung up the phone. "He's coming home early." She was practically beaming, her cheeks still wet with tears.

Betty bounded past them. "I'm just so excited...I wish there was a way for us to be able to talk to him right this minute!" she said, heading toward the front door. "How do we know where to write him?"

Betty had seemed to speak Kara's thoughts and she turned toward Mrs. Jeffers. "How long do you think it will be before we have more news?"

"I'm sure they'll let us know as soon as possible. I've heard they're very good about this sort of thing. It's the waiting that's the hardest. But now, the waiting will be so much better, won't it? At least we know he's safe." Mrs. Jeffers glanced at the clock. "Betty, don't you need to be leaving now?"

"Yes, I was just going. Boy, how I wish I still didn't have to babysit now! Just when we have this wonderful news! I suppose I can't let Mrs. Parker down, though. She *is* waiting to see the dentist...It's just that I feel like I'm going to burst!"

"I know, dear," her mother laughed. "But we have lots of time to celebrate, so you go run along now!"

"I know exactly how she feels," Kara said after Betty had scurried out the door. "I'm just so excited that I'm not sure what to do with myself!" She could feel her own giddiness rising again.

"I know, I'm having a hard time containing myself, too!" Mrs. Jeffers smiled. "Mr. Jeffers should be home in about an hour or so. Do you want some coffee?"

Kara nodded and followed her into the kitchen. Then, for the next hour, the two of them sat at the dinette table, sipping coffee and talking. Kara loved conversing with her like good friends on the heels of such wonderful news. While they chatted, Mrs. Jeffers shared more tidbits of Jerry's childhood and then the conversation drifted toward wedding plans.

Wedding plans! Kara had often imagined life with Jerry, but for some reason, she had never actually envisioned the wedding. The idea wound around her head like a charming wreath of flowers—fragrant and lovely. Of course, she knew they couldn't actually plan anything yet. Not when there were still too many unknowns.

"So, what kind of wedding would you like?" Mrs. Jeffers had asked.

"Well, I don't really have any family. And my friends…they're too far away so I couldn't have a big wedding, even if I wanted to. A small, intimate ceremony with just a few of Jerry's family and friends—that's all I think I would want." As she had said the words out loud, she knew it sounded just about perfect.

Mrs. Jeffers had smiled warmly. "That sounds lovely, Kara. And I would help you as much as you wanted me to."

Kara had thanked her, before dreamily taking another sip of her coffee. As she set down her cup, she asked,

"Do you think Betty would be my maid of honor?"

"Oh, I know she would be thrilled!"

Kara had smiled…but then a soft, quiet sadness followed. How much she would have loved for her best friend to be beside her in all of this.

Oh, Shannon, are you doing all right? Did you find my letter? I'm always going to miss you…

Later that evening, Kara was upstairs, composing a letter to Jerry. She knew they weren't sure where to send anything quite yet, but she was too filled with relief and happiness not to let it all spill out onto paper.

Her hair was once again pulled up in a style appropriate to the times, and she brushed a stray strand from her forehead. There wasn't much of a breeze and the summer evening felt humid as she sat at the desk by the window, hoping for some cooler air to drift in.

She could hear the strains of a beautiful song drifting from the radio downstairs…"You'll Never Know". Frank Sinatra had just recorded it earlier that year, and the lyrics only further fueled her need to write. *If only you knew how much I missed you, too,* she whispered, as her mind echoed the lyrics. She picked up her pen and began pouring out her thoughts to him.

August 11, 1943

Dearest Sweetheart,

I wish I could describe the incredible joy I'm feeling right now. Just today, we received word that you're safe. Oh, Jerry…it's been so terrible, not knowing what happened to you and worrying if we'd even have the chance to see you again. Someday, I hope to explain just how harrowing it's been for me personally since receiving that first telegram. But right now, all any of us can do is shed tears of relief and gratitude!

I keep wondering what you must have had to go through, though. As I write this, we still know very little. Only that you have been wounded and suffered dehydration—and that you'll be spending some time in the hospital.

I'm praying for you, though. I'm praying for your recovery and for healing. Not just for your bod, but for any memories, as well. Lately, I've been learning that God is always listening. And He's answering, too. Sometimes, it doesn't look the way we would expect—but other times, it's even more wonderful. There's still so much I don't know about everything, but I'm starting to believe that He's always looking out for us. I admit, I never thought a lot about this before. God seemed so distant. I remember learning the song, "Jesus Loves Me", as a child when I was visiting Sunday school. I used to go to church with a friend for a while when I was little. To think—the song is really true and that He really does love us.

I also discovered that there is no other place I'd rather be right now than here—waiting for you to return. I can't wait to start our life together!

She paused and wondered if she should mention the conversation about wedding plans. Would it make him feel stress as he was recovering? Or give him even more incentive to get well? Thinking she knew him fairly well, she plunged ahead…

Your mother asked me for the first time today, what kind of wedding I wanted. I know most girls probably think about these things a lot—right down to the color of their bridesmaids' dresses—but I honestly never had. Yet I have to admit, talking about it all with your mother made me just a little bit excited.

The details are still so unimportant to me, though—I think I'd marry you almost anywhere! I don't really have anyone I can invite. I only want a small wedding with a few of your friends and family. I hope that's all right with you.

The most important thing right now, though, is for you to get well. We were told that it looked like you'd be coming home soon and my heart can't even contain the thrill of this!

And something else I want to say...although I'm praying for you to be healthy in every way, please know that you don't have to come home that way for me to love you.

Always Yours,
Kara

She folded the letter and tucked it into the drawer of the desk for now. Climbing under the sheets, she drifted off to sleep quickly.

That night, beautiful scenes danced through her dreams. She was wearing a long, white wedding dress and walking through the countryside with Jerry by her side...but all too soon, these scenes were interrupted with fearful images. He was suddenly lying in a hospital unit, bloodied and unconscious. And holding the watch he gave her.

***

The next morning, Kara returned to work at the shipyard. It felt good to be back and the routine was cathartic—almost like a welcoming friend.. She was still sailing on a silver cloud, knowing Jerry would soon be coming home. Throughout the day, she kept feeling herself beaming at the very thought.

When she returned to her room late that afternoon, however, the horrible memories of her dream assaulted her. She had thought she had forgotten them, but they flashed back now without warning. She tried reminding herself that he was safe now, but she couldn't help but wonder what he might have suffered before he had been found. If only she could simply pick up the telephone and call him—hear his voice from across the ocean and be assured he was truly all right.

She remembered how he was holding the watch in her fitful dreams…the image was so disturbing to her. She knew Jerry had given the watch to her out of love, yet in doing so, it had actually taken her away. She couldn't trust it now.

She realized he'd be expecting her to wear it when he came home. He might be hurt at first, but she knew wearing it was out of the question. In fact, she couldn't even rest easy as long as it remained anywhere near.

The only solution she could think of was to take the watch as far away as possible and dispose of it somehow. *How she wished she could just go throw it into the sea!* With a sigh, she remembered that the coast was about seventy miles away and gas rationing was in full force.

The creek? No, the creek was too shallow. And she couldn't simply give it away—Jerry might find out about that and be hurt. Besides, it had the potential to take someone else away from time and she could never take that responsibility.

Then it suddenly occurred to her. And it seemed the best possible plan.

The following morning as she got ready for work, she picked up the watch and tucked it into her purse before heading out the bedroom door.

The late morning sun was already beginning to beat down intensely by eleven-thirty. Kara walked along the pier, her lunch bag in one hand and her purse in the other. Her eyes scanned the horizon as she kept moving, distancing herself farther from the ships while a few seagulls called overheard. The clamoring of machinery and distant shouts of men could still be heard, but they began to grow a little fainter over time.

Finally, she stopped and glanced around. She was still technically in the shipyard, though far on the outskirts now. However, she knew she wasn't completely alone or safe from prying eyes. No one could walk this far unnoticed. Dangers of sabotage were always at the forefront in naval shipyards during wartime so she didn't want to bring attention to herself or cause unwarranted suspicion.

She set her lunch bag down and reached into her purse, retrieving the watch. It was certainly beautiful, glistening in the sunlight, and her gaze lingered on it just a little longer. There was no way she could part with it without thinking first about all the good it had done.

It had originally brought her here to Jerry. Yes, later, it had taken her away, but she couldn't deny that it had brought her right back again—full circle. Well, maybe the watch had just been a tool for everything, but nevertheless, she'd be forever grateful for its part.

She carefully gave another long glance all around her before resolutely tossing the watch into the dark, oily waters below. Waters that moved into the more pristine Willamette River...which merged with the Columbia...that ran swiftly into the vast, open sea.

***

The days continued but still, no more word arrived. Kara rose each morning and headed to work where she spent each day welding slabs of metal in the suffocating heat. At first, she had felt thrilled to be back at the shipyard. It meant she had truly returned—and knowing Jerry was safe now made everything all right.

As the days dragged on past a week, though, Kara had become restless and even a little anxious. She couldn't understand what was causing the delay; none of the family did.

She knew enough to realize that there were many different war departments—and each of these consisted of many, individual people. There were hundreds of thousands of enlisted and their families to keep track of on any given day. Snafus happened all the time.

But Kara had taken the War Department at their word—they had promised to follow through with more information and they hadn't. A sort of anger began to simmer inside. Why were they all being kept in the dark?

However, because they knew he was at a hospital near Algeria, his mother had done some checking and found an address where they could try sending their letters. Kara had immediately sent several she had already written.

As she sat now in front of the sewing machine, attempting to practice some simple stitches, she wondered if those letters would actually reach him.

Ten days had come and gone since receiving the wonderful news. It was Saturday afternoon and Kara now had the house to herself, something that rarely happened. Mr. Jeffers was at his post and Betty and her mother were off doing errands after helping at the Red Cross.

Kara re-positioned her material under the needle for what felt like the hundredth time. She had taken out so many wayward stitches already. Without Mrs. Jeffers here to help guide the process, it was becoming a lost cause. At least she was grateful the temperature had cooled down to a reasonable eighty degrees.

She leaned back slightly and peered around the corner at the kitchen calendar to double-check the date. *August 21.* The summer had been so sweltering but fall was right around the corner and Kara thought it couldn't come too soon. She longed for the cool, brisk air...she could just imagine strolling with Jerry through the crisp leaves and autumn colors.

She hunched over the sewing machine again in concentration. *How in the world could I learn to be adept at welding, yet still have so much trouble keeping a simple seam straight?* She pulled out her fabric and examined it. It was still not quite right, but her muscles were too tense at the moment to keep trying.

She stood and gave her neck and back a little stretch. After a moment, she decided to pour herself a glass of cold lemonade and head outside to the garden with a basket. She wanted to see if there were any new tomatoes to harvest.

A slight breeze greeted her as she walked across the patio. She set her glass on the umbrella table and continued over to the garden. It was lush and green now, and though they had already harvested most of the vegetables, there were parsnips, squash, and carrots still growing in rows. Tall stalks of corn waved in the breeze, but the cobs weren't ready for picking just yet.

As Kara bent toward the large bushes of tomato plants, their vibrant, spicy aroma tickled her nose. There were quite a few plump tomatoes hanging on the vines and she gathered up every last one she could find. The peas had been mostly picked over, but she found a few more ripe pods that had been hiding and plopped them into the basket, as well.

With a sigh, she paused to relax on the grass. She sat, her knees pulled up to her chin, admiring the lush growth of the garden and breathing in the fertile scents. The lazy sound of a bee's humming passed by her and then it flew nonchalantly on its way.

It felt so peaceful to sit here and not really think or worry for just a few minutes. As she drank in all the smells of the ripening garden, it seemed almost intoxicating.

She heard footsteps behind her and wondered which one of the family had arrived home first.

"Do you mind if I join you?"

At the sound of his voice, Kara whirled around from where she was sitting, and then stared in disbelief.

He had come home.

CHAPTER 30

For a few seconds, it was hard to wrap her mind around the fact that he was actually standing there in front of her. He had invaded her dreams too many times. She had traveled back and forth through time on the chance that she might see him again. And now, here he stood.

He looked slightly haggard, his face pale and gaunt, and he was leaning on a cane that was tucked under his left arm. But when she looked into his eyes, she saw nothing more beautiful in her life.

"Jerry…"

It was almost a whisper at first and then she shouted his name as she ran into his arms. She felt his right arm wrap around her back tightly and she clung to him, her tears giving way to sobs. He kissed her forehead, her damp cheeks, and then her lips before pausing to look into her eyes.

"I almost thought I'd never see you again." He reached up and gently wiped a stray tear and as he did, he looked ready to cry himself. "Mind if I just sort of hold you like this, forever?"

Kara couldn't seem to find her voice so she simply nodded. He pulled her close again and she felt as though she could very easily stay in his arms forever. Finally, she managed, through jagged breaths,

"Sweetheart...we hadn't heard anything for so long...how did you...we didn't know when you were coming home..." She pulled back to take a good look at him. "Jerry...what happened? Are you really here? Are you all right?"

"I'm all right. Especially now that I see you." He glanced down at his leg. "I...I had a little operation before being sent home. I'm supposed to be evaluated again here in the states. I guess the bad news is that the limp will probably last, they tell me. But the good news is I'll probably not be going back to the front lines."

Until that second, Kara hadn't even thought about the possibility of him having to return. It both startled and relieved her at the same time.

"I just can't believe you're here, sweetheart..." She wiped at her tears with the back of her hand. "But... it's all been so confusing. We first got a telegram saying you were missing in action...and then we received notice that you had been found. We were all so relieved and happy....we knew you were heading to a hospital in Algeria but we were supposed to wait for further word. None ever came." She paused to catch her breath. "Jerry...we were beginning to worry again...that something..." She stopped and stared up at him, her face suddenly relaxing. "Oh, but you're all right. You're here!"

She clung to him again and his hand reached up and stroked her hair. It felt too wonderful for words to be in his arms again. Slowly, she looked back up at him.

"Jerry, what *did* happen?" she asked, gently.

His face sobered. After a few seconds, he cleared his throat. "It's a long story. I promise to tell you all about it later."

She kissed him tenderly on the cheek. "It's all right. You don't have to talk about it right now. You're home—that's the most important thing."

He smiled then and nodded. "Yes, that's the most important thing."

He pulled her close once more, a peaceful blanket of silence settling over them. There had been so many times when she wasn't sure she'd ever be this close to him again.

After a while, Kara finally said, "Your family is going to be going crazy with happiness when they come back and find you here."

"Where is everybody, anyway?"

She explained each of their whereabouts as they slowly made their way across the yard towards the house, their arms wrapped around each other.

"They should be home any second now. Are you hungry? Do you want anything to drink?" she asked him as they came through the back door.

"Yes and yes."

She smiled. "What would you like, sir?"

"Oh, just a cup of coffee...a sirloin steak, baked potato and green beans, maybe some apple pie a la mode. But only if you have that handy," he teased.

"Hmm. Would you settle for a cheese sandwich and leftover Jell-O?" she laughed.

"If you're making it and then you'll come sit beside me, it will be the most perfect thing in the world."

As she quickly put a plate together and started the percolator going with fresh coffee grounds, she noticed her hands were shaking with excitement. All those days that she wasn't sure if she would see him again...now he was suddenly here and it was still so hard to fully grasp.

Just as she was setting the plate in front of him at the dining room table, the front door burst open. She could hear the murmur of their casual conversation as mother and daughter drew closer. Kara waited, her anticipation brimming, as they came around the corner and then both stopped short. Then Betty squealed and they both bounded towards him. His mother's tears ran down her cheeks as she reached to embrace him. Seeing their joyful reunion sent Kara crying again.

But she couldn't help but notice how Jerry had to struggle to pull himself up to a standing position in order to embrace them.

***

For the next twenty-four hours, Kara rarely had a chance to be with Jerry alone, but just having him home had been enough for the time being. Yet, there were still so many questions. And in the back of her mind, what began to pull at her most was the realization that she had things to tell him, too. She couldn't go forward toward their future together without first telling him everything. And that meant *risking* everything.

The first night of his homecoming had been filled with celebration. Before dinner, Jerry had taken a long nap. He had said he had gotten very little sleep with all the travel. While he rested upstairs, the family prepared as fancy a homecoming meal as their limited rations and short notice would allow—scrumptious fried chicken and fresh salad with the carrots and tomatoes from the garden. Mrs. Jeffers had looked relieved when Jerry managed to eat a generous plateful. It was obvious to everyone he had lost a good deal of weight and his cheeks lacked their usual color.

Right after dinner, Kara helped move her things into Betty's room. She had planned to sleep back in the attic, but Betty begged her to try rooming with her by putting the mattress on her bedroom floor. The mattress took up half the room, but she had reluctantly agreed to try it for a few nights.

Later that evening, the family had all relaxed together in the living room while Kara snuggled close to Jerry on the sofa.

"You still look kind of tired, son," Mr. Jeffers had remarked.

"Yeah, I think I'll turn in early. It's probably going to take a little while for me to catch up on my sleep."

"Take as long as you need," he told him.

"Yes, this is your time to recover and take it easy," his mother had added gently. So, everyone had said their good-nights early that first evening.

The following morning, Jerry had joined them for church and he had been greeted enthusiastically. Afterward, he had been asked several times about his injury, and Kara felt his discomfort as he had tried to dodge all the questions. Once they returned home, Jerry had excused himself to take another long nap. No one wanted to press him for answers he didn't seem ready to give.

Kara knew he needed to rest—to simply feel the peace of being home without having to relive anything that might have happened. Yet those unanswered questions seemed to hang over all of them like a heavy curtain.

It was finally late that afternoon, after Sunday dinner dishes had been done and everyone was resting once again in the living room, when Jerry began to finally tell what had happened.

"The day had been brutal. We had been pushing the Germans back a little at a time up till then, but that day, they seemed to come at us with full force." He paused for a few seconds, as if concentrating to keep his voice steady. "Two of us were together in one of the trenches when suddenly, a grenade flew in. A buddy of mine, Dan…he was gone instantly. It had hit him straight on."

He paused again, as if seeing images he didn't want to share. Kara held his arm tightly as he swallowed and took a breath. "I took some shrapnel in my leg and was bleeding a lot. But I couldn't stay there any longer—next to him—I just had to get away. I remember crawling out as things began to calm down a bit. I called out for a medic but there wasn't any answer. It was almost dark by this time and my leg…it felt like it was on fire. I somehow managed to take part of my shirt to wrap around it. After that, I guess I blacked out."

Kara instinctively slid her hand in his, as much for her sake as for his—to remind herself that he was actually now safe beside her.

"Did your company finally find you then?" Betty asked him quietly.

He shook his head. "No. I'm not sure how it happened. Usually, those who can help bring in all the wounded and they're taken to the nearby mobile unit. But somehow, wherever I had crawled to, it must have been a pretty good hiding place. Also, night had closed in pretty quickly. So...when I finally woke up, I was inside a house, lying on a bed.

"A house? You mean, a villager's home?" his mother asked.

He nodded. "A man had come by...he found me and saw that I was still alive. He seemed to be an older man, but still able-bodied and strong. Maybe in his sixties or even early seventies, I'd guess. He somehow got me to his house unseen during the night. I still don't know how he did that. He and his wife attended to my wounds the best they could for the next couple days."

"Why would they help you—weren't you the enemy?" Betty asked him..

"No, I wasn't their enemy. I don't think they wanted anything to do with the war. In fact, I'm quite sure they were Christians—at least, that was the feeling I had the whole time I was there. I just know they were risking their lives, having me there."

"Oh, son...this is a kind of miracle. God was using this couple..." His mother was speaking, her eyes filling with tears.

"Yes, there's no question in my mind. They were very good to me, too. Gave me food and drink, even if I wasn't able to eat much. Washed my wound and sterilized it, though the shrapnel was still there and there was nothing much they could give me for the pain. They didn't speak a word of English, but they had kindness in their eyes.

"The whole time I was there, I kept worrying that the enemy would discover me. I kept expecting them to burst through the door at any minute and either kill me or take me prisoner. And who knows what they'd do to the couple for aiding the enemy. But they never did…they never did find me."

He reached for his glass of water sitting on the coffee table and took a few sips before continuing.

"After a few days, I told them in my limited Italian that I was going to go back to try to find my unit. When the man finally understood what I was trying to say, he insisted I leave wearing some of his old clothes. I guess he figured I might not be picked up by the enemy so easily and I had to agree. So, I thanked both of them and then I set out.

"I carried my uniform along with the piece of bread and cheese the woman packed for me in a make-shift duffle bag. The man had even drawn a crude map to try to show where he had picked me up in relation to their house. I really didn't think I'd have any trouble getting back to my unit. But a whole day went by. I kept heading slowly in the general direction of where they were supposed to be and still, they were nowhere in sight. I eventually had to spend the night behind trees, trying to sleep a little and keep out of plain sight. I was definitely out in the country, only nothing looked familiar.

"By the next morning, I realized I must have taken a wrong turn. It could have easily taken me farther away from my unit and smack in enemy territory. I knew I had been heading west, which is what I seemed to need to do. But I think his well-meaning map was a bit off and maybe I was a little delirious, I don't know. Meanwhile, I had no water, no more food and my leg was starting to throb like crazy. When I tried to get my bearings and keep walking, I kept stumbling whenever I tried to put any weight on it. All I could do was pray, and keep moving—a little at a time."

Kara's chest had tightened. It was so painful to sit and listen to everything he had endured. She felt so helpless, but she kept reminding herself that he was here beside her now. And she knew she needed to hear his story—for his sake and for hers—everything he was able to tell.

"How did they finally find you?" Betty asked him.

"I finally started hearing the sounds of fighting off to the southwest that afternoon. I kept moving—only by now it was more of a crawl—until it became louder. So loud, it was deafening…but I still couldn't see much because the actual fighting was in the forest up ahead. I had to carefully stay out of sight of the enemy somehow…to stay out of the way of stray bullets and figure out which side was mine.

"Again, another miracle because by then, there wasn't much energy left—I couldn't even walk anymore. I probably wasn't thinking too straight by then, either. Somehow I figured out which direction to head for and moved parallel to the forest. I just kept crawling…

"Meanwhile, those grenades…they kept blasting to my right. I was trying to head behind the battle lines. When I thought I was far enough behind, I kept inching my way through the tall grass toward the trees. And then…someone was leaning over me. Someone had found me. It wasn't my own unit but close enough for me. That whole part is a blur since I think I was losing consciousness by then. A medic looked me over and from there, I was sent off to a hospital in Algeria."

He grabbed his glass and took another long swallow of water. He continued to hold his glass in both hands, tightly, as if it might slip from his grasp. After a moment, he added, quietly,

"My friend…the one who was blown up beside me…he and his wife had a baby on the way. It's all he would talk about. He had been so excited to get to meet that baby. You should have heard him talk…so excited…"

CHAPTER 31

Kara noticed that each day, Jerry seemed to grow a little stronger. He still had moments when she felt as though he was a million miles away; Kara thought that perhaps, in a way, he really was. But as time continued, he seemed to relax and become just a little more himself.

His limp, however, was still pronounced and he continued to lean heavily on his cane to get around. The latest of a series of letters from the War Department indicated that he was officially on leave for thirty days—with further service pending evaluation.

As much as she wanted Jerry to be healthy and whole for his sake, the thought of him being well enough to go back to the front lines terrified her. She felt guilty for selfishly wanting him to be declared unfit for duty, but he had already gone through so much. There was the gnawing fear that if he returned to battle, this time, he might not ever come back.

The days of recuperation were also days of their getting to know each other all over again. Or rather, as Kara realized, getting to know one another more. As the month went on, she and his mother continued to work at the shipyard every day, but each evening and weekend, Kara relished her time spent with Jerry. There were picnics and movies in these late summer days...moments of playful banter and hours to spend on long, uninterrupted talks. They spoke about so many things, but all the while, Kara was all too aware that there were important things yet to be said.

One evening, she was washing up the supper dishes when the phone rang. She could hear Mrs. Jeffers answer it, her voice muted and muffled. After a while, Kara thought she heard her hang up and then heard the soft voices of the family drifting from the living room. She couldn't hear their words, but their tones sounded strange...sad.

She rinsed the last of the glasses and set them on the rack to dry. Then she quickly wiped her hands on her apron and hurried out to where Jerry and his parents were sitting together on the divan. They were talking in hushed whispers. She paused when she first saw them, not wanting to intrude. Then she noticed Jerry suddenly lean forward and rest his head in his hands, and she rushed over, her heart beating rapidly.

"What is it? What's wrong?" She put her hand on his shoulder, but he didn't respond. She looked helplessly from one of his parents to the other.

Mrs. Jeffers gently pulled her aside. "We've just had some bad news, Kara," she answered, quietly.

"What? Please tell me!"

"Jerry's friend... his best friend. Jim Stevens—I think you knew him. We...we just found out he was killed in action."

Kara felt the blood drain from her face.

"Oh no..." She shook her head in disbelief. Her own eyes were welling with tears, but she had to try to comfort Jerry. She couldn't imagine what he was going through. The two of them had been best friends for so long. They had been through so much together...

Then, she suddenly realized that a part of her could identify with his pain after all. Though circumstances were vastly different, she knew what it meant to lose a best friend. She went to the divan and wrapped her arms tightly around him, feeling his shoulders convulse with his silent sobs.

***

It was over a week later, on a Saturday morning, when Kara drove him into Portland for his check up and evaluation. How could she have such two conflicting hopes, she wondered? On the drive, she had confessed them to Jerry and he had seemed to understand.

"You're only being human," he told her. "If I'm told to go back, I'll do it in a heartbeat, though. I know that's hard for you to completely understand, but a part of me wants to keep fighting as long as I'm able—as long as other guys are still risking their lives. Believe me, though…there's another part of me who wants nothing more than to stay right here with you. I saw so much over there that I'd just as soon never see again."

The appointment had taken more than two hours and when Jerry finally stepped back into the waiting room, he smiled at her with an expression that she couldn't quite interpret.

"Well, it looks like you won't be able to get rid of me so easy after all."

She stood and ran over to him. Tears of relief began to form, but she knew there was a price to pay.

"But...what does that mean, exactly? What did they say about your leg?"

"It's all a bit medical for me to try to explain very well. I guess the bottom line is that this cane isn't going anywhere for a while. He did say there's another operation I might be able to have later on—he thinks it might help alleviate the limp. For now, though, I hope you don't mind too much having me hobble along beside you."

She swallowed. "I would be honored."

Nearly another week had flown by, and on a slightly warm September evening, Kara was sitting next to Jerry by the creek. The water wasn't as deep now, but moved swiftly over the rocks, sparkling in the remaining sunlight.

The walk had been Jerry's idea. He told her that the doctor encouraged him to keep walking as much as he was able, in order to strengthen the muscles. They had set out, right after supper, and had taken it very slowly. Kara had time to soak in all the subtle changes as summer turned into fall, while the two of them talked leisurely the whole way.

"Remember how much I wanted to be able to buy you a present in Europe?" Jerry was asking, as they sat close together now on the edge of bank. "And now, your birthday is just around the corner. I guess the nice thing is that now I get to give you a gift in person. It may not be from Paris, but…"

"It's so much better this way, believe me. I'd much rather have you in person."

Kara quickly pushed away the memory of reading those lines in his letter…and how soon afterward, she had flown away from him.

That memory also brought her back to the secret she knew she couldn't hold onto any longer. For days now, it seemed to bore deeply into her more and more—this barrier which stood between them that he couldn't even see.

"I was thinking that maybe we should set the date," he was saying while they watched the creek amble by at their feet. "Did you want a June wedding? Because, frankly, I don't really want to wait that long."

They were huddled close together on a large, smooth boulder, just as they had been their first time together here. She pulled her sweater more tightly around her. She knew she couldn't put it off anymore, but at the thought, her heart began to pound incessantly.

"Jerry, I..."

He looked over at her. "You're not having second thoughts, are you?"

"Oh, no... It's just that...before we can get married, I need to tell you more about who I am and...and where I came from. And ...I'm just not sure you're going to believe me when I do..."

***

Kara pulled the knitted afghan up around her shoulders. It was now after midnight and everyone had gone to bed, but she sat alone on the sofa, unable to sleep. She had quietly come down from the attic and curled up under a blanket to think.

She had been using the attic again as her sleeping quarters for the past month, with the exception of a few very warm nights. At those times, she had made her bed on the downstairs divan. She had been too used having her own privacy and space, and besides—Betty had an unsettling habit of talking in her sleep.

Tonight, however, the air had turned cool and even the afghan couldn't seem to keep the chill away. As

Kara lay there, she kept replaying the whole scene by the creek a thousand times over in her mind. She wasn't sure how she had expected him to react, exactly. She had tried to plan out the worst-case scenarios and most of them revolved around Jerry thinking she was completely crazy. As wonderful a guy as he might be, she knew he'd have every right to question her sanity and eventually realize he just couldn't marry her.

Over the past month, she had also thought about that moment when she first told Shannon. Her best friend had actually believed her—though understandably, not at first. She had only hoped Jerry would eventually be able to do the same.

While she had sat there next to him, though, the risk she was about to take had suddenly seemed overwhelming. She kept thinking of how she had nearly lost him several times already. What if she had come this far, only to lose him in a completely different way? Still, there was no way around it. She would be miserable trying to pretend with him her whole life.

So, in the fading daylight, she had somehow gotten her story out—a little at a time. The fear has been overpowering, but she had forged ahead, handing him bits and pieces of what had happened in a jagged sort of way. While she spoke, she had been too afraid to even look his way—she was terrified of what might be showing in his eyes.

Jerry was strangely quiet the whole time. When she had finally paused and dared to look up at him, he wore a stunned expression. It was not unlike how Shannon had looked when she was just beginning to believe her. Only, Kara realized that maybe it wasn't actually belief, at all, but instead, a kind of shock and pity.

"Jerry...please say something." She had been trembling and she knew her voice was, too.

"I...I don't know what to say." He cleared his throat. "You're completely serious, aren't you?"

Kara had nodded.

"You're telling me that you came here...from another time..."

"I know, Jerry. I don't blame you for not believing me. But it's all true."

"And the watch...the watch I gave you sent you here?"

"Yes—before you gave it to me. I found it in the trunk in the attic. When it was my house..." She was hearing her own words and knowing how utterly ridiculous it all sounded.

Oh, how can he ever believe me? If it had been reversed, she doubted she'd be able to believe something so far-fetched.

The hopelessness of the situation had begun to overtake her then. Maybe she should have never tried to tell him a truth that was so impossible to grasp. Perhaps it would have been better, after all, to keep this secret from him for the rest of her life. But then, deep down, she knew she could never live that way.

His face had appeared pale as he had slowly looked away from her, back to the creek. After several minutes of silence, he finally told her,

"We'd better be getting back."

And that had been it. They had made their way back home in silence. In the growing twilight, the tears softly ran down her cheeks as she began to realize her worst fears were coming true. She had come this far to find him, only to lose him to the truth of what happened.

The walk back home had seemed like an eternity. Kara had the terrible feeling that this was the beginning of the end and a sense of loss and despair clouded around her. He didn't believe her...And the thing was, she didn't really blame him at all.

The horrible memory was hard to shake as Kara now huddled on the sofa. She wasn't even able to cry anymore. On top of the grief and rejection she felt, she wondered what lay in store for her now. She had told herself, time and time again, that if she had to lose him to the war, she would somehow make a life for herself here. But now, knowing Jerry was here but didn't want her...she wasn't prepared for that.

She shivered again and decided to force herself up and into the kitchen, hoping some hot tea might help to soothe her. She put the kettle on, being careful to stay nearby to lift it before it whistled and woke anyone up.

"You couldn't sleep either?"

Kara turned to see Jerry suddenly standing there, clad in his pajamas and robe, leaning on his cane in the kitchen entryway.

"No, not very well. I...I was just making some tea. Did you want some, too?"

She surprised herself how calm and cool her voice sounded. Inside, she was shaking and she knew she probably looked a wreck.

"Sure."

He went over and sat down at the dinette table as she got the teacups ready. She wasn't sure how to feel with him suddenly here with her...or what they could possibly say. She brought the two filled cups over to the table and tentatively sat down across from him.

"Thank you." He whirled his teabag around for a minute and then took a sip. "Kara?"

She looked up at him.

"I was remembering something. A story my grandmother told me before she died."

Kara took a sip of her own tea and waited for him to continue.

"It was just a story. A story a grandparent might tell to entertain their grandchild. Or so I thought." He paused to clear his throat. "I was a little boy, visiting her house one day. She showed me a watch she kept hidden away—the very same watch that I gave you. She told me a whimsical story about it, too. She said that once upon a time, there was a girl who lived very far away in the land of the future. She had no family and no one who loved her.

"One day, as her story went, she was walking and found a sparkling watch lying underneath a bush in the forest. She tried it on, when all at once the girl went sailing back into another time. There, she landed back in the 1880s, never to return again.

"At first, the little girl had been frightened, being in a strange place, but soon a nice family took her in and adopted her. Years later, she grew up and married a young man and had a family of her own—a family who loved her." He paused, then, and looked intently at Kara, before adding, "And she lived happily ever after."

Kara stared at him. She couldn't speak at all.

"So, you see…" he went on. "While I was lying in bed upstairs, I couldn't stop thinking about that strange childhood story. I also began thinking how everything you told me…it all seemed to suddenly make sense. The way my mother had mentioned that you didn't seem to fit in here at first….that you had just come down the attic stairs and...well, so many things. I guess what I'm trying to say is…this all seems impossible to believe, but…I do believe you."

Kara could only continue to stare at him, slowly shaking her head. Now, she was the one having trouble grasping it all.

"Are you all right?" he asked, gently.

She swallowed. "It happened...to your grandmother, too...?"

He nodded. "I don't understand it all...I don't know when or where she came from, but looking back and thinking over her life, I'm convinced, now, it did."

It was all too incredible to absorb. Kara felt light-headed...and at the same time, felt as though she was slowly coming back from the brink.

Jerry believed her...and she wasn't alone in this strange leap through time.

Still, she was unable to decipher what he was thinking or feeling now. His expression still appeared guarded.

"Where is the watch now?" he asked her.

"It's..." She swallowed. "Well, I hope you won't be upset..."

"Upset? Why?"

"You see, I was so afraid it would send me back—away from you. Because it actually did. While you were at war, it sent me back."

"What?"

"It did, and I thought I'd never see you again."

"It sent you back...?" he repeated the words, numbly.

"Yes... but then, it brought me back here again. It's a long story, but I couldn't take the risk anymore...so I...sort of... threw it into the sea."

"You threw it into the sea?"

"Well, into the river, anyway. I was afraid of leaving you forever and I...I just couldn't take that chance again."

She sat across from him, fingering her teacup handle and waiting for him to respond. She still felt so unsure of his feelings now in this strange, new light. When he didn't reply, she gathered her courage.

"Jerry...where does all of this leave us? I mean, with everything that has happened...with everything we know...?" Her heart thundered in her chest as she looked up at him.

As he sat gazing back at her across the table, a deep tenderness filled his eyes.

"Do you think my grandmother ever told my grandfather?"

"What? What do you mean?" His question made no sense, especially after she had just put her heart on the line.

"I mean, do you think she ever told my grandfather her secret—the way you told me today?" When she didn't answer, he went on. "Well, it doesn't really matter, does it? I guess we'll never probably know." His warm voice became nearly a whisper. "But I'd like to think she was as brave as you are." He reached out across the table and slowly took her hand in his, caressing it gently. "However, there are a few things I do know for sure. I love you—I've loved you from the first time I ever saw you. And I think God obviously wanted us to be together—so much so that it took this kind of miracle...a succession of miracles..." He paused, tears filling his eyes. "And...we can never take that for granted—not as long as we live."

EPILOGUE

Summer 1944

Kara fastened the last clothespin onto the line as the sheet she had hung billowed in the breeze. She paused and gave her back a little stretch before heading over to the garden. Picking up the spade, she pushed it deep into the earth, pulling it up around a weed that had grown between the cabbages.

Four months. Had it really been that long? But here it was, already the end of June.

She smiled as she smoothed out the dirt between the rows of little carrot tops which peeked out from the soil shyly. Four months ago, on the Saturday before Valentine's Day, she had walked down the aisle toward Jerry with a small gathering of family and friends surrounding them. It had been just as she had pictured it, with Betty as her bridesmaid.

One of the biggest surprises was that his parents had given them a five-day honeymoon trip to the coast. Staying at a hotel in Seaside, they danced to a real Big

Band and watched the winter waves crash onto the shore. *It had been perfect.*

She knew Jerry would be coming home from work any minute now. He was currently working at the insurance office alongside his dad. Later, it looked as though he might be getting his wish of college after all. The G. I. Bill had just been signed into law days ago and it would pay the tuition for returning soldiers. He wasn't positive yet what he wanted to pursue, but he had several ideas in mind. In the meantime, he had admitted that he was actually enjoying the insurance business for now. He said it felt satisfying to work alongside his father for the time being.

There was even more to this G. I. Bill, it seemed—it would also help secure low-interest mortgages. And to Kara, this meant that later this year, they would be getting a place of their own. It was interesting to think about how she had heard somewhere about the G. I. Bill as history once upon a time, but never would she have thought it would mean so much to her personally.

For now, she and Jerry shared the attic space and had fixed it up as their little apartment. It was cozy, with an actual bed instead of a mattress on the floor, a dresser, lamps, and a couple of little chairs. Jerry's family had long become her own in every way, so she was happy to stay there with them for the time being. At the same time, she was excited to find a first little place of their very own.

She sometimes thought about how strange it was that she was giving up this house that had been once gifted to her. However, she suspected that she and Jerry would someday inherit the house in the end. Still, none of that actually really mattered to her. She knew that what she had gained here in exchange for property was worth so much more.

As for work at the shipyard, Kara had continued on for a while after Jerry had come home so they could put a little money away. "For their nest egg", as his mother called it. It would go toward their future.

It hadn't been long, however, until Kara had noticed that the type of work she had to do was beginning to take its toll on her health. Heat exhaustion assaulted her more and more often and her hands had developed a constant ache, so they had eventually agreed that it was best for her to give her notice.

Jerry's mother was going to continue on there a little longer, but she said she would probably work her last shift before the summer heat set in again. Meanwhile, Kara did more than her share of housework and cooking for the family and continued to help alongside Betty at the Red Cross.

Of all the life-changing moments in Kara's life, one stood out to her most. Even more than the miracle of coming here to this time...even more than meeting Jerry.

It had been after a simple conversation with Marjorie back in January, just a month before the wedding, in which so many things came into clearer focus for her. She had realized that all through her life, she had always tried to figure everything out. She'd analyze them and make them more complex...even the idea of knowing God. But in a way she had never understood before, Marjorie explained that the beautiful irony was that God was indeed complex...but her relationship with Him didn't have to be. Jesus had given His life for her and all He ever wanted in return was her heart. So up in the attic on a crisp morning in January, she had given it to Him. Simply. And He had received it.

She set down the spade now and admired the little shoots of green sprouting so optimistically along the rows. It had rained in the night, giving them all a good dousing. Today the sun was out again and it felt pleasantly warm on Kara's skin.

"How is the gardening going, sweetheart?"

She turned to see Jerry approaching and she hurried over to greet him. He looked dashing in his civilian suit, hat, and tie, she thought, though she suddenly felt a little self-conscious with her hair tied back in a kerchief and a smudge of dirt on her cheek. These days, he still had to lean a little on his cane, but his limp was barely noticeable to her now.

They kissed and then she pulled away, wiping a stray hair from her face. "Oh, I'm a mess!"

"You look beautiful." The way he looked at her, she believed he truly meant it.

They walked arm-in-arm over to the umbrella table and sat down together.

"Do you want something cold to drink?" she asked him.

"Sure, that sounds wonderful."

"I'll get us both some lemonade then."

A minute later, Kara was back carrying two glasses and sat back down beside him.

"Mm, this is so good," he told her, after a long sip. "Did you make this batch yourself?"

"Jerry…." She waited until he looked over at her. He must have noticed the peculiar smile on her face and gave her a quizzical look.

"What is it, sweetheart?"

"I went to see Dr. Barris today. I had been so tired lately…"

His face turned to concern. "Is anything wrong, honey? Are you all right?"

Her beaming expression made it perfectly clear that she was indeed all right.

"Wait a minute…" His face went from worry to a sort of shaky disbelief.

Kara just nodded and continued to beam.

"Really?" Now, his expression was beginning to mirror hers. Only Kara thought she detected tears in his eyes.

"Really," she whispered. She swiped her own stray tear that had suddenly appeared, then laughed. "Really!"

He pulled her close to him while they sat under the shade of the umbrella. She leaned in and rested her head against him, his arm circling her tenderly.

"When will our baby be here?" he asked, nuzzling her hair.

"Sometime after Christmas. January, I think."

"January...We may be buying our first house just in time." He kissed the top of her head and she could feel him smiling. "A baby..."

Kara could hear the faint sounds of voices from inside the house and nearby, a blue jay called out, and then took flight. She knew his family would be overjoyed at the news, but just for this moment, it was theirs alone.

Across the world, the war raged on. A few weeks earlier, nearly a half a million troops bravely crossed the English Channel to Normandy. Thousands of ships and aircraft converged together onto those beaches and in those brave moments of chaos, thousands died, became wounded or went missing. But it had been a turning point and now the Allies were fighting their way across the dense landscape of the Normandy countryside.

It sometimes bothered Kara that she would know some of the course of history as it played out before her, but now it was no longer a secret she had to bear alone. Nor was she in charge of it.

And whatever happened, she knew that this was where she was supposed to be.

"Come on," she said, suddenly sitting up and taking his hand. When she looked into those eyes that still made her heart skip a beat, she saw her own joy mirrored there. "Let's go inside and tell your family the news!"

The End

Tammy Sinclair

ABOUT THE AUTHOR

Tammy Sinclair has loved writing stories from the time she was a small child. During her fifteen years homeschooling her children, she had a non-fiction article published in Homeschool Enrichment magazine. A history buff and romantic at heart, she can be found enjoying the outdoors, cozying up with a good book or watching classic movies in her spare time. She resides in Oregon with her incredible husband and two amazing, young-adult daughters.

Tammy Sinclair

Made in the USA
Monee, IL
26 March 2020